GHOSTS
FROM THE PAST

GHOSTS FROM THE PAST

Mission: Justice

Elizabeth A. Wilson

Ghosts from the Past

ISBN-13: 978-1-7332401-4-7 (paperback)
ISBN-13: 978-1-7332401-5-4 (eBook)

This is a work of fiction. Names, characters, businesses, places, events and incidents are either the product of the author's imagination or are used fictitiously.

Photo Credits - Cover:
Mansion: ID 53524418 © Alfred Wekelo | Dreamstime.com
Ghost: ID 143062655 © Jakub Krechowicz | Dreamstime.com
Lightning Sky: ID 120764608 © Ig0rzh | Dreamstime.com

Cover Design: Elizabeth A. Wilson

First Edition, 2019

Dedication

To Sis

About the Author

Elizabeth A. Wilson delivers action-packed crime novels, filled with suspense, unexpected twists and engaging characters. Her *Mission: Justice* series has been well-received by readers across the globe. Published in both non-fiction and fiction, she is happily retired from the world of business and now devotes her days to weaving danger and intrigue into the lives of her fictional characters. A lifelong resident of Lancaster County, Pennsylvania who shares her home with one very spoiled German Shepherd Dog, Elizabeth loves to hear from readers. Visit her author page at amazon.com/author/eawilson for updates on her other books.

Books by Elizabeth A. Wilson

Mission: Justice Series
Double Deception (Book I)
The Phantoms (Book II)
Ghosts from the Past (Book III)
Christmas Hostages (Book IV)
Trail of Death (Book V)

Acknowledgements

The late Edgar J. Hartung, FBI Supervisory Special Agent, Retired. His patience and willingness to answer my many questions concerning the Federal Bureau of Investigation and to share some of his experiences as an agent were invaluable in helping me weave fact with fiction. And his input gave me a whole new level of respect for agents in the field. While I have taken literary license with my lead characters, I've hopefully presented them in an honorable light that reflects the integrity of the Bureau and its agents. Any errors are solely my responsibility.

Phillip Wright, NRP, Susquehanna Valley EMS. Thank you very much for your explanations regarding the emergency medical procedure described in Chapter Two. Without your helpful suggestions and patience in answering my questions, the scene would never have achieved a fraction of the realism I've hopefully brought to life. Any errors are solely my responsibility.

Shirley Quevedo. Without your boundless help, advice and encouragement during every phase, this entire series would most likely still be tucked away in my computer. A *thank you* hardly seems adequate, but it is sincere.

My editors: Shirley Quevedo, Tamera Gehris, Susan Weaver and Dorothy Yohn. Thank you for encouraging me to keep the stories coming; your willingness to proofread and offer suggestions; and your ability to catch my typos. Any remaining goofs are my fault alone.

My creative design consultants: Beverly and Judith Beats, Tamera Gehris, Shirley Quevedo and my entire family. Thank you all for your help with the cover designs.

And lastly, but certainly not least, my family. You are the best. Thanks for being there through thick and thin.

Table of Contents

Prologue

J amie Kendrick fumed quietly, scowling at her office door as it clicked closed behind Andrew J. McDougal.

Patting her on the butt, not once, but twice had been bad enough, but the fact it had accompanied his latest proposition infuriated her.

All you have to do is be a little more agreeable and you'd make partner, honey.

Shaking her head in disgust, Jamie rubbed her hand across the seat of her pants trying to erase the sensation remaining from his touch.

Seriously. The old geezer was a United States Senator…and an attorney. Had he never heard of sexual harassment? His behavior was atrocious. And it had taken every ounce of her self-control to refrain from decking the pervert.

Too bad assaulting a member of Congress was a federal crime, not to mention professional suicide, considering the man was founder of McDougal and Associates, her employer.

Still, she'd been tempted. She didn't care if Andrew was seventy-five. The man had no redeeming qualities. None. Well, okay, he was good looking. But that was it. He had the morals of an alley cat, with an ego as vast as his list of extramarital affairs. On top of that, he was the worst kind of male chauvinist.

Jamie refused to classify him as a pig, though — no point in insulting an intelligent animal.

Oh, he was always cagey enough not to incriminate himself directly, but his meaning was clear. If Jamie wanted to advance within the firm, she would have to satisfy more than the firm's professional demands.

She flopped down in her office chair, heaved a disgusted sigh and reached for her coffee, taking a big gulp.

Yuk! It was cold.

She heaved another sigh and eyed the door warily again.

It was no wonder nothing was getting done in Washington. Andrew spent more time in Jacob's Valley than was good for the country or her. Every time he popped in, she was subjected to his unwanted attention.

And what was he even doing in the office. It was Saturday and a gorgeous summer day. Why wasn't he out on a golf course somewhere?

The only reason she was here was because she'd been in court the past two days and had some paperwork to clear off her desk. If she'd known the human octopus was going to be at the office too, she would have stayed home.

Propping her elbows on her desktop, Jamie dropped her head into her hands.

What the heck was she going to do? Certainly not sleep with him; that much she knew. No way. Hell would freeze over before she slept with Andrew or anyone else for the sake of a promotion.

Chapter One

"What do you make of this thing with McDougal?" FBI Special Agent Michael Devlin shifted in his seat to glance across the console at Special Agent Zachary Taylor and gave a humorless chuckle. "If he got a nasty letter, it's probably from the husband of one of his many conquests."

Zach took his eyes off the road long enough to glance at him. "A real Lothario, eh?"

"That's putting it politely," Mike replied. "You ever met the old man?"

Zach shook his head. "Never had the privilege."

Mike shot a dubious look his way and chuckled. "Privilege? That's debatable. But you're in for an experience, that's for sure. The family has been involved in politics since before the Civil War and built a fortune on various business ventures, including a couple questionable ones involving bootlegging. Andrew…the senator has an ego the size of Texas and more skeletons in his closet than a haunted house. But he's the only son of the family dynasty and he inherited more money than the treasury of some Middle Eastern oil emirates. And he's got the political power to keep those skeletons hidden."

The entire thing annoyed Mike. He'd lived most of his life in the town McDougal's practically owned. Although he didn't know any of them well, he'd read about their shenanigans and witnessed the cockiness of the senator's family members, most of whom thought they were above the law.

Whatever threats McDougal had received, Mike had no doubt the old man deserved them.

An elder statesman in the Senate, McDougal had the looks and charismatic personality to draw in voters and female admirers, but in Mike's opinion, he was about as slimy a politician as they came. In fact, given a choice, Mike would rather arrest the man than help him.

Babysitting McDougal on a beautiful summer day was the last thing Mike felt like doing with his Saturday. Especially since the senator's office was only a few miles from the 18th century fixer-up farmhouse Mike had purchased a year ago.

Nestled among stately pines and a winding stream, the sleepy valley town of Jacob's Valley where he'd grown up was located far enough from the hectic pace of Baltimore to be serene, but close enough for a manageable commute into Milford Mill for work. And although he'd grown up a couple blocks from the town center, Mike had always loved the surrounding countryside. So when he'd spotted a *For Sale* sign on a 1774 farmhouse that had barely been updated in the past two centuries, Mike hadn't been able to resist either the house or the price. He'd been living in the greystone while making massive renovations.

The wiring alone had looked like it might have been something Thomas Edison used to illuminate his first light bulb. The plumbing hadn't been much better, but the slate roof had been in amazingly good condition and the engineer he'd hired to inspect the place had declared it had *good bones*.

So Mike had snatched up the bargain.

While the updated electricity was no longer a fire hazard and most of the major renovations were completed, the house still needed finishing touches. And unfortunately, instead of working on his to-do list, it was his and Zach's weekend to work, so here he was on his way to visit the not-so-Honorable Andrew J. McDougal.

Two blocks past the park that marked Jacob's Valley town center, Mike spotted the expensive wrought-iron fence rimming an enormous three-story Georgian style mansion housing the offices of McDougal and Associates.

Dating to 1826, the original home was flanked on both sides by large single story additions which were only a few years younger than the main part of the house. Towering majestic oaks stood guard over the soft yellow concrete masonry home, with its stately white columns lining the front porch and black wooden shutters framing freshly painted white woodwork around large double-hung windows.

"Turn in there," Mike said, indicating the long driveway that culminated in a circle ringing an exquisite garden, the centerpiece of which was an ornate fountain.

Zach lifted his sunglasses to get a better look at the enormous mansion. "That's McDougal's law firm?" he asked with a healthy dose of awe.

"Yeah," Mike answered, absently studying the home.

The mansion had fallen into disrepair after the Great Depression and sat vacant until forty years ago when Andrew McDougal had purchased the neglected property for what was then his newly formed law firm. While Mike had no respect for the politician, he gave McDougal credit. The man had done a nice job fixing up the place.

The law firm's offices occupied the first floor. Rumor had it that the luxury apartment spanning the second floor of the central portion of the old home was McDougal's love nest, where he entertained his various mistresses.

Mike wasn't sure if the talk was true, but he wouldn't bet against it.

Pulling into a parking space in front of the mansion, Zach cut the engine and let out a soft appreciative whistle. Mike couldn't disagree. The home was an impressive piece of architecture, but he couldn't help wondering how much taxpayer money supported upkeep on the place, since the senator maintained his local political office inside the law firm.

Shaking away the thought, he led Zach up marble steps eroded by age and usage. He'd often wondered what famous Americans may have walked these same steps, visiting the original owner, a doctor well-known for discretely catering to the medical needs of Baltimore's elite citizenry.

Trying the handle, Mike was somewhat surprised when the ornately carved wooden front door swung open. Obviously, the senator anticipated their arrival, but it was the kind of place where one expected to be greeted by a butler. Instead, only a polite bell made a ding noise as they stepped over the threshold into an enormous lobby where four large white columns stretched from marble floors to twenty foot ceilings. Mike wasn't sure if the columns were structural or decorative. Whatever their purpose, they made an impressive statement.

Mike had been in the office several times and knew his way around, so with the large solid cherry reception desk sitting empty, he headed to his left.

They'd only taken a step when somewhere ahead, a fire door banged shut, the noise immediately capturing their attention. But it was an odor wafting into the lobby that stopped them in their tracks.

Adrenaline poured into every cell in Mike's body. He knew that metallic, coppery stench all too well.

"It's coming from in there," Zach whispered, motioning toward an office door that was slightly ajar.

In sync, they pulled their weapons and headed toward an odor that grew more pungent with each step. Just outside the door they stopped abruptly at the sound of movement coming from inside. Hair on the nape of Mike's neck snapped to attention.

He shot a questioning glance at Zach and when Taylor nodded readiness, Mike silently toed the door open. A graphic oath exploded in his head, but never left his mouth, as he took in a gruesome scene reminiscent of the movie *Psycho*.

Slumped against the front of his ornately carved mahogany desk, U.S. Senator Andrew McDougal sat in a pool of blood. The entire front of his pale blue polo shirt and the lap of his khaki slacks were stained red. A broken chair, scattered papers and blood splattered across the lavishly decorated office indicated a brutal fight had taken place. But the lifeless stare in McDougal's eyes told Mike all he needed to know.

The senator was dead.

To McDougal's left, were two more victims. A small auburn haired woman who appeared to be mostly nude was lying on her stomach, unmoving. Beside her a tall man wearing jeans and a red hoodie was sprawled face down on the floor just as still as the woman.

But it was something almost as shocking as the gory scene that held Mike's focus.

Mayor Edward McDougal was hovering over the shoulder of his brother, Sheriff Doug McDougal. In build and stature, the two men were a stark, almost comical contrast, but there was nothing humorous about the scene. And the fact neither man was helping any of the victims reinforced Mike's assessment they were dead.

What had started as a simple interview related to a threatening letter had suddenly morphed into a triple homicide investigation that was going to make national headlines.

Cursing under his breath, but keeping his gaze on the brothers, Mike pulled out his camera phone to briefly record video of Doug, who with latex gloved hands, was burrowing under the prone male victim, man-handling him with far more force than was necessary for someone who was as limp as a rag doll.

Questions pinged around Mike's brain while he videoed the two men. What were they doing? Had they stumbled onto the murder scene like he and Zach? Had someone else discovered the crime and called the sheriff? Or were they up to no good?

He shook away his curiosity. None of that mattered...at least not at the moment. The deceased was their father and they were contaminating a murder scene.

Ending his video, Mike silently slipped his phone into his pocket and turned to Zach. "Let's take it," he whispered.

With nods of agreement, they stepped into the office.

"Freeze...FBI," Mike called authoritatively.

Gape-mouthed, Ed turned and froze at the sight of guns aimed in his direction. The mayor's combative older brother wasn't so cooperative. Uttering a curse, Doug rose and spun around with his gun in hand.

"Don't do anything stupid, Doug," Mike hollered, keeping his weapon trained on the sheriff and praying the man didn't lift the barrel in their direction. Personally he couldn't stand Doug McDougal, but he doubted killing the town sheriff would score him any points in the Bureau.

"Go to hell, Devlin," Doug growled, his triple chin wobbling like gelatin as he tried to suck in his enormous beer gut to make himself look taller. To his credit, the weapon remained at his side. "I don't need or want any Feds interfering with this. So get out."

"We're not leaving gentlemen." Mike pointed at Andrew. "Your father was a U.S. Senator which makes his murder federal jurisdiction. We're taking charge of the crime scene. Now drop the gun."

Defiantly, Doug glared at him with his meaty hand still wrapped around the butt of his weapon.

"We're not telling you again, sheriff," Zach warned, weapon aimed and ready for any threatening moves. "Drop the damn gun...NOW!"

Clearly nervous over the exchange, Ed nudged his brother in the ribs. "Do what they say, Doug,"

Finally Doug relented, but he didn't drop the weapon; he merely holstered it.

Seething, Mike clenched his jaw. "I want you out of there, now," he said motioning the brothers to come to him.

In the hall, Mike kept his weapon on them while Zach frisked both men and confiscated the gun along with their shoes and gloves. Their activity had been suspicious at the very least. And even if the brothers weren't involved in the crime, their shoes were needed to match sole imprints to the bloody footprints marring the plush golden carpet as part of the process of elimination that would hopefully lead to a killer.

Doug's face, already reddened with anger, looked like he was ready to blow a gasket when Zach proceeded to handcuff both of them with Doug's supply of cuffs. "You can't do this. You have no grounds."

"Shut up and sit down," Zach retorted, pointing to a seat just outside the senator's office. "And you sit over there," he added to Ed, indicating a seat about twenty feet down the hallway.

"If you had any balls you'd give me my gun and let me take care of that guilty bastard in there," Doug spat.

Mike's heart slammed to a halt. Had he heard that right? "He's alive?"

"Yeah he's alive. So is she."

"Dammit, why didn't you say something sooner?" Zach snapped angrily.

Zach had taken the words right out of his mouth, but Mike kicked himself mentally. He and Zach should have checked the three victims rather than assuming anything. Still, what was wrong with Doug and Ed? Why wouldn't they have said something immediately?

"Did you call this in? Are ambulances on the way?" Mike asked.

"Hell no! He's guilty as sin. Who cares if he dies?"

Cursing, Zach unclipped his cell phone and disappeared into the lobby.

Mike didn't have to ask to know Taylor was calling for help and locking the front door.

"His prints will be all over the damn knife," Doug argued while Zach was on the phone. "There's no reason the Feds should be involved in this case. Just give me my gun and I'll save the taxpayers the money of a trial."

Mike shot a glance back into the room. He didn't see a knife anywhere, but that didn't mean Doug was lying. His attention flew back to the sheriff when he felt the man try to shoulder past him.

"Back off and sit down," Mike warned, blocking Doug's advance and pointing to the spot Zach had assigned to the sheriff.

Zach had separated the brothers to prevent them from talking. The FBI wanted independent statements from them, not a fabrication they concocted together. And on top of that, with Doug moving around it was impossible to concentrate on the crime scene while trying to ensure the brothers were behaving.

Doug stood firm, merely glaring at him.

"Ambulances and the state boys will be here in five and the Baltimore crime unit and medical examiner are on the way," Zach announced, before turning his hazel eyes on the sheriff. "I told you to sit down. Do it or I'll sit you down," he ordered with a look guaranteeing it was a promise, not a threat.

Begrudgingly, Doug complied.

Satisfied Zach had the brothers under control; Mike swiped a clean pair of latex gloves off the floor where Zach had dropped them after confiscating them from Doug's pockets. Snapping them on, he entered the senator's office.

The gory crime scene immediately snagged his full attention.

With three dead people, Mike would have photographed the entire room before disturbing anything. But that could wait. He had two unconscious people requiring whatever first aid he could render until the ambulances arrived.

First though, he had to secure the murder weapon. With a quick glance, Mike spotted a bloody letter opener lying inches from the prone man's fingertips. The last thing he needed was for the guy to wake up and start slashing people.

Shaking his head in dismay at Doug's carelessness in leaving the weapon so easily accessible, Mike quickly moved it out of reach atop the senator's desk.

Then, trying not to step in the pool of blood surrounding the senator, Mike squatted down next to the politician. His gaze immediately locked on a horrific wound on the senator's neck. Mike's breath hitched in his throat. Someone had cut the senator's throat from ear to ear.

While his stomach tried to hang onto his breakfast, Mike's investigative mind took over. The wound explained the amount of blood, but other gashes and slashes covered the front of the man's shirt and arms.

Since there was no carotid to check, Mike grabbed Andrew's bicep, feeling for his brachial artery.

McDougal was still warm to the touch and there was no sign of rigor. But in addition to a waxy appearance, his skin had a bluish-gray cast to it and his pupils were fixed and dilated. And considering all the blood lost, Mike wasn't surprised he couldn't detect a pulse or any evidence of breathing. He hadn't expected to find any.

He glanced at his watch. Twelve forty-five. The coroner would make the official ruling, but at least Mike had a frame of reference for time of death.

He side stepped around the corpse to where the woman lay.

"Who are these two?" he called over his shoulder as he squatted down on his haunches again to check her carotid for a pulse.

"I've never seen the guy before, but she's one of the firm's attorneys. Her name is Mary something. I don't recall her last name," Ed offered.

Mike considered the scant information. The woman shouldn't be too difficult to identify if she worked at the firm and hopefully they'd find some identification on the man. Until then, he mentally tagged them as Mary and John Doe.

"How is she?" Zach called from the door.

"She's got a strong pulse. But it looks like someone hit her on the back of the head. There's a nasty gash on her scalp."

Clad only in her bra and panties, Mike had no difficulty determining there were no other injuries on her back. So he carefully, rolled her over.

Short hair the color of a shiny new penny framed a pretty face. She looked to be about thirty, he thought quickly assessing her condition.

"I can't see any other injuries besides her head wound," he said. "She might need stitches, but it's not bleeding too badly."

"Better leave her for the paramedics then," Zach advised.

With a nod of agreement, Mike shifted around to examine the man.

The guy was literally lying face down in what appeared to be a puddle of bloody foam. His arms extended above his shoulders and a red hoodie obscured any view of the man's face and head, but all the blood caused an uneasy feeling to settle in the pit of Mike's stomach.

Focusing on the task at hand, Mike pulled back the hood. He reached over the man's shoulders to check his carotid artery while studying two nasty head wounds that had spilled deep red blood into the guy's neatly trimmed blond hair.

"This one's pulse is very weak and his breathing is labored," he called back to Zach as he gently turned the man over.

Shock nearly knocked Mike backward onto his butt.

Chapter Two

B ehind him, Mike heard Zach suck in a startled breath and was pretty sure he'd done the same. Mike blinked just in case he was imagining things, but he wasn't. There was no mistaking the face of the former All-American quarterback Mike constantly teased about being a chick magnet.

FBI Special Agent James Barrett.

Barrett was not only a good friend; he lived in the carriage house on Mike's property, helping Mike fix up the place.

He and Jimmy had struck a deal. No rent; just labor. Considering the fact Barrett's father had owned a construction company where Jim had worked through high school and college, providing him with experience in everything from plumbing to carpentry, Mike was sure he'd gotten the better end of the deal. But Jim insisted he loved the manual labor, which he claimed helped relieve stress from their job.

When Mike had left home this morning, Jim had been preparing to paint the kitchen. What was he doing in McDougal's office...covered in blood?

Before Mike even had a chance to consider any logical explanations, Jim sputtered a labored breath, spraying a mix of frothy foam and blood across the front of Mike's shirt and suit.

Shoving aside his shock and revulsion, Mike quickly turned Jim on his side to prevent him from aspirating the fluid.

Forcing himself to forget he was dealing with a fellow agent, Mike stared down at his friend, at the front of an old white tee shirt and blue jeans saturated with blood. The thought it might be Jim's sent his heart into overdrive. Although he didn't see any knife holes in the material, he yanked the shirt up to search for wounds.

Mike's brain had no sooner registered several deep puncture wounds when another of Jim's labored breaths forced more pinkish foam to bubble from a wound between two ribs. Mike wasn't a doctor, but he knew damn well the wound had to be deep, because that foam was oxygenated blood coming from a lung.

"Oh my God, Zach! He's been stabbed too!" Mike couldn't help the oath; he was too shocked to think coherently. But even shaken, he knew better than to reveal Barrett's identity aloud until he knew more about the situation.

Zach's cursed response was nearly drowned out by the front door rattling loudly.

"If that's the ambulance, get them in here fast," Mike hollered, hoping whoever was out there was someone who could help because he was definitely in over his head on this one. But he wasn't about to let his friend bleed to death without trying to help, so as Zach took off running for the door, Mike tried desperately to staunch Jim's bleeding with his hands.

What seemed an hour, but was likely seconds later, Zach reappeared with an ambulance crew. Urgently Mike waved them into the office. "He's gone," he said when they headed toward Andrew.

He motioned to Jim, "but this man needs help quickly. He's been stabbed."

"I'll take him; you get them," said the male, detouring over to Jim and waving his crewmate to check on McDougal and the woman. Dropping to his knees, the man whose name tag identified him as a senior paramedic, quickly took Jim's vitals.

"He's right; this one's gone," the female, an emergency medical technician called after checking Andrew and shifting away to examine Mary Doe.

Backing out of their way, Mike glanced down at himself and shook his head. What a revolting mess. His black suit masked some of the blood Jim had sprayed on him, but his white shirt and gray tie were beyond help.

"That's got to be the state boys," Zach called when the front door rattled again. "I'll let them in."

Mary Doe captured Mike's attention again and his gaze shifted from her to the weapon. Was it possible she was their killer? Could Jimmy have walked in on the murder and been stabbed by her before he could disarm her? Otherwise, what was she doing in Andrew's office? Had she and the old lecher been getting it on together?

That thought made him half nauseous just thinking about it. And it disturbed him even more that the idea upset him. Why should he care what she was doing? She was a potential suspect, not a prospective date. She could be married for all he knew. And why was he even thinking about her marital status?

A mental smack forced his brain back to work and he stared down at her again.

A tryst turned violent? Power and wealth could be a potent aphrodisiac to some people. And with the senator's proclivity for affairs it certainly wasn't outside the realm of possibility that the woman was involved with him.

All that aside, it didn't sit well with Mike seeing her lying there nearly naked the way she was. He had three sisters and several nieces and it grated him the wrong way to think of a parade of people seeing one of them in such a vulnerable state.

Mike walked over to the doorway, nearly tripping over something as he peeled off his soiled gloves. He glanced down to find the culprit sticking out from under a sofa.

A five iron? What was that doing there? Had McDougal been practicing a golf swing when he was attacked?

Something on the club caught his attention and Mike squatted down for a closer look. Without touching it, he studied a red substance on the club's head.

15

Was that blood? It sure looked like it. Leaning closer he noticed several short spikes of blond hair stuck into the red stain.

A sick feeling rolled through Mike's gut. Forensics would have to test the hair and blood to make certain, but he was betting it was Jimmy's.

Motion caught Mike's attention and he glanced up in time to see Zach escorting six state troopers down the hall toward them. He walked out to introduce himself to Sergeant Trinity Jackson, the thirty-something trooper in charge.

"I'd appreciate if your people could get these two out of here for us," Mike said, indicating Ed and Doug McDougal. "We're going to be tied up here and at the hospital for a couple hours, so if you can get official statements from them on why they were here and what exactly they were doing when we arrived, it would be a big help. And I want them kept separated until you have those statements signed." Mike thought a moment before adding. "And can you get your team to secure the building and search the offices for other victims or a perp in hiding?"

Jackson nodded. "Sure. Anything else?"

Until the crime unit got there, he and Zach had their hands full, so he certainly wasn't going to turn down an offer of help. "The woman is supposedly an employee here, but we don't have a name on her. If you can run the license plates for the cars out in the parking lots and see if you can find anything that seems to match her, it would be a big help."

Jackson nodded, quickly issuing orders to the troopers with her, two of whom corralled Ed and Doug.

"Is she stable?"

The paramedic's urgent question caught Mike's attention and he turned wondering why the fellow was inquiring about Mary Doe. Mike noticed an IV was already dripping into Mary's arm and oxygen was aiding her breathing.

"Yes," the EMT replied, putting the finishing touches on a bandage around Mary's head.

"Then I need you over here, stat," the paramedic snapped.

Mike's gaze shifted to see what was happening with Jim as the EMT scrambled over to help her crewmate. Jim's clothing, except for his underwear, had been cut off and tossed aside, exposing his body. The number of wounds Mike saw, sickened him. Stab and slash wounds peppered Jim's hands, arms and legs. Defensive wounds, Mike's mind told him. But the ones on his chest...man, they looked bad. Real bad.

Mike wanted to look away, but he couldn't. He was fascinated watching the rescue crew work.

A bandage taped on three sides covered the deep wound Mike had found between Jim's ribs.

"What do we have?" the EMT asked.

Grimacing at the sight of Barrett's grotesquely distended jugular vein, Mike waited for the paramedic to answer.

"He's crashing. The occlusive dressing didn't work; his lung collapsed and his BP is plummeting," the man responded urgently. "I'm going to do a needle decompression to get the air out of his chest, and I need you to intubate him for me."

The woman nodded and like a well-oiled machine, they went to work. Paper and plastic flew as the team ripped open sterile packets pulled from the large case they'd carried with them.

Mike stood mesmerized watching as the EMT tipped Jim's head back and pulled his jaw forward to suction froth from his throat. And then, she inserted a hard plastic breathing tube down his airway with the same ease Mike donned socks.

At the same time, the paramedic swabbed an area on Jim's upper chest staining the skin orange, then picked up the biggest needle Mike had ever seen, one easily four inches long and which was attached to some large tubing. Mike winced at the size of the thing and tried not to shudder when, with practiced efficiency, the fellow inserted it into Jim's chest several inches below his collar bone.

Apparently satisfied he'd hit the right area, the paramedic withdrew the needle and taped the inserted tube in place.

Immediately the plastic tubing fogged slightly.

Mike wasn't sure if it was his imagination, but it looked like Jim began to breathe easier. And even better, as if blown in on one of Jim's breaths of air, another ambulance crew suddenly appeared in the hallway.

"You take the woman," the paramedic ordered as soon as he saw the other crew. "This guy has lost a lot of blood and I want to stay with him until we get him to the ER."

For a moment after everyone left, Mike stared after them, trying to get a grip on his emotions. He wanted to go with them, to make sure Jim would be okay. But he couldn't. There was too much work to be done and that meant he couldn't afford to let his brain get bogged down in worry.

His gaze landed on the clothing medics had cut off Jim. Mike had seen Jimmy that morning; he'd been dressed to paint, but not in this clothing. When had he changed? And why?

For that matter, where were Barrett's wallet and cell phone? And his weapon. Where was that?

Mike never went anywhere without his weapon, even when he was off-duty. And he'd never known Jimmy to go without his either. So where was the weapon? And Jimmy's Bureau credentials. Where were they?

Mike glanced around the room while chewing on the puzzle. As his gaze landed on the spot where Jim had been laying, his mind went back to what he and Zach had witnessed when they'd first opened the door.

Could either Ed or Doug have taken Jim's things? Zach hadn't found them when he'd searched the brothers. So, if they'd taken them, where had they put them?

He glanced around at the disarray in the office. Blood, broken furniture and papers scattered everywhere. The place was a disaster area. Jim's belongings could be sitting under any of the debris. Best to let the CSI's find them, though. If he started digging for things he'd just disturb the crime scene more than it had already been disturbed. But Mike hoped Jim's things turned up. The last thing they needed was a federal agent's gun and badge missing from the scene of a murder.

Pulling out his camera phone again, Mike began the process of capturing a panoramic record of the crime scene. There was no telling what Doug and Ed may have touched or moved before he and Zach arrived, but at least he could capture a record of the scene as they found it. Graphic as it was, though, it wasn't something Mike was likely to forget.

In addition to all the blood and spatter near McDougal's body and where Jim had been lying, Mike found a trail of wet blood drops that led to a fire door in a small tiled foyer at the back corner of the senator's office. More blood was smeared on the door's panic bar.

Mike studied the blood evidence and the door carefully. Was this the door he and Zach heard bang closed as they'd entered the office building? His gut said *yes*. The direction was right for the sound they'd heard.

One thing was sure; someone who had been injured used the door. And while Ed and Doug both had blood on their gloved hands, neither of them had open wounds that could have left the blood drops. So who else was bleeding?

Mike filed the question away to be answered later. Finishing his panoramic tour, he turned his attention back to Andrew McDougal. He grimaced while studying the man's extensive injuries. This was no random crime. The sheer number of wounds indicated a crime of passion or vengeance. A blitz attack. And the use of a letter opener indicated a spontaneous crime.

Mike swallowed against the acid churning in his gut. He'd investigated a lot of crime scenes over the years, but never got used to the blood. Then again, maybe that was a good thing. He wasn't sure he'd want to know the person who could look at the annihilation of another human being and not be affected by it.

He snapped more photos of Andrew's body. Then he traded his camera phone for a note pad and pen he retrieved from an inside jacket pocket and began making extensive notes of everything.

"Looks like someone wanted the old man dead, real bad."

Without glancing up, Mike huffed a chuckle at Zach's dark humor. It was the only way to stay sane when dealing with death and violence on a regular basis.

"You think?" There was so much blood, it was hard to see all the wounds. Mike had lost count at fifty.

"The ambulance crew didn't find Jimmy's wallet," Zach stated. "So I gave the state police Jim's name and contact information."

Troopers were following the ambulances to the hospital to collect the victims' remaining clothing and have doctors run a rape kit on Mary Doe. Zach's quick thinking would help the hospital expedite Jim's care.

"I didn't mention he was FBI, though," Zach continued. "I think we need to sit on that for a while until we figure out what went down here."

"Good idea. Thanks," Mike replied.

Zach nodded, but studied him with a look of distaste. "Here." He handed Mike a striped tie atop a neatly folded and starched white shirt and khakis. "I'm embarrassed to be seen with you. Go get changed."

Agents...smart agents anyway...always had a 'go' bag with spare clothing and supplies stored in their car for when unexpected situations arose. Having Jim spew bloody foam all over his clothing definitely classified as an unexpected situation, but Mike's bag was in his car which was back in the Bureau's parking lot in Milford Mill.

Zach had apparently dug these items out of his own bag and because of their similarity in height and build, Mike had no doubt they would fit.

"I owe you one," Mike said, gratefully accepting the items.

"One? How about I add it to the list," Zach teased.

Mike chuckled at their long standing joke about which of them owed the other more favors, but his mind was on the work at hand. "While I change, see if you can spot Jimmy's gun and Bureau credentials. They weren't on him either and neither was his cell phone."

"Will do," Zach replied, his gaze already sweeping the area.

Eager to clean up and change, Mike went in search of a bathroom. He bypassed the private bathroom abutting the senator's office, knowing CSI's would want to check the drains for possible trace evidence. Just off the main lobby, he found a door marked Men's Room and pushing it open, he went inside.

A few minutes later, feeling much more human, Mike made his way back to McDougal's office, with his blood-stained suit and shirt stuffed into a clean plastic trash bag he'd found in the bathroom.

Zach looked around when he entered and with a gloved hand, held up a gun and cell phone. "They were under McDougal's desk."

Mike breathed a sigh of relief. Good. Especially the gun. That was one headache avoided. "What about his credentials?"

Zach shook his head. "Don't know why he'd do it, but maybe he left his creds in his car." He paused a moment. "Come to think of it, that car that was out front earlier looked like Jimmy's. But it was gone when I got the clothes for you."

Mike stared at him speechlessly for a heartbeat. "I saw a car, but didn't pay attention to it. But if it was Jimmy's and it's gone now, then who took it and why?"

Zach turned to look at the fire door. "Maybe whoever slammed that door?"

Mike considered the possibility and nodded hesitantly. The missing car was a minor issue to him at this point and his gaze dropped to the gun and cell phone Zach still held in his hand. "We need to have the phone dusted for prints."

Zach nodded absently while surveying the bloody scene silently. Shifting his gaze to the spot where Jim had been lying,

Taylor shook his head. "I'm sorry, but I refuse to believe Jimmy did this."

Mike agreed. On the surface, the case appeared to be an investigator's dream. Open and shut, nice and neat…with a dead body and a person covered in blood and a bloody letter opener within easy reach. And considering Mary Doe had been nearly naked, at a quick glance it appeared as if one of the senator's extramarital flings had finally backfired.

In Mike's mind that scenario had one major flaw. If they were to believe Jim stabbed the Senator; who stabbed Jim? Certainly he didn't stab himself.

"Something is not right here," Zach continued. "It's too pat."

Mike's gaze drifted to McDougal. Zach had hit the nail on the head. The scene looked as if someone had gift wrapped it for them. And he couldn't shake the feeling that Doug and Ed were their culprits. After all, what had they been doing leaning over Jimmy?

They certainly hadn't been helping him.

Noise in the hallway indicated the crime scene unit and coroner had arrived. Mike and Zach walked out to meet them.

Once the investigators began their work, Mike turned to Sergeant Jackson. "Did your people find anything during the building search?"

"No perps or other casualties," she answered. "But we ran the plates of two cars out in the employee lot. There was a black Honda that came back stolen. We'll have to check the surveillance videos to see if it's been out there for a while or if it has anything to do with the murder. But we also found a silver VW that's registered to a Mary J. Kendrick." Jackson pointed down the hallway. "One of the offices back there has a name plate for M.J. Kendrick. It looks cleaned out of personal belongings, though. So, I checked the auto registration against a license for that name and got a hit on one in this town for a thirty-three year old female, five foot two, red hair and green eyes. Sounds like your vic, so I contacted the hospital with her name."

Mike filed the name away and nodded. "That's great! Thanks."

"The third vehicle is a squad car belonging to the sheriff's office, so it's probably how the McDougal brothers got here."

The sergeant had been a huge help so far, but he wasn't ready to let her go. "We could use your help with several more things."

"Name them," she answered efficiently.

"Can you send someone out to notify the senator's family?" The press would be all over this murder. If Ed or Doug hadn't already notified their mother and siblings, it wouldn't do to have them learn about it on the news. "And we also need someone to put the deputies and staff at the sheriff's office on notice that they are not to discuss the murder with Doug or anyone in the McDougal family, until Doug and Ed are cleared."

Mike suddenly remembered an empty holster Zach had discovered on Doug's ankle. At a scene where two people had head wounds, that missing weapon became suspect.

"Oh, and we need Doug's backup weapon found and bagged for evidence. Doug claims it's in his desk drawer at the Sheriff's Department. And lastly, it would be a big help if your troopers located any surveillance cameras in the area that might have pertinent video of activity related to the crime."

Jackson nodded. "I already sent two of my troopers out to the senator's home to make notification. And we'll get on the other things right away."

"Thank you," Mike replied. "We really appreciate the help."

Her gaze swept the crime scene. "You've got your hands full with this one," she said, handing Mike a business card. "Call me if you need anything else." With that, she turned and left.

Another half hour passed before Mike headed to the hospital, leaving Zach to oversee the crime scene investigation. Mike doubted Jim had regained consciousness, but he was anxious to ask Mary Kendrick some questions and was hoping he'd find her awake. Anything she could tell him would provide ammunition to fact-check Ed and Doug McDougal's stories.

Chapter Three

An Emergency Room admitting clerk pointed Mike to a man in a white lab coat who was striding hastily toward the doors. "Doctor Wells is the neurosurgeon handling both cases. He can answer your questions."

With a quick *thank you*, Mike hurried after the doctor.

"If you want to talk to me, you'd better keep up, because I don't have time to chat," Dr. Bradley Wells commented, barely breaking his stride after Mike flashed his identification. "I'm headed up to surgery to meet with the family of a patient."

"What's the extent of Mary Kendrick's and James Barrett's injuries?" Mike asked as Wells charged up to a bank of elevators.

A ping announced the arrival of the car and when the door slid open, Wells motioned him inside. "Patient information is confidential. You should know that."

Mike wasn't in the mood for red tape. "Doctor, these two people are involved in a Bureau investigation. I can get a warrant if that's what you need, but it's only going to delay us finding a very dangerous perp. So can you cut me some slack and please just answer my questions."

Wells stared at him a moment then heaved a resigned sigh. "She sustained a bad concussion; he has multiple stab wounds and a depressed skull fracture."

Mike's mind immediately flashed back to the murder scene. Doug's empty ankle holster; the golf club.

"Do you have any idea what could have caused their head wounds?" he asked curiously, not wanting to lead the surgeon by mentioning his own suspicions. "Just your gut reaction. I won't hold you to anything."

Wells gazed at him with a wary expression, apparently not certain he wanted to commit to anything so soon. His internal battle ended with a shrug. "I have no idea what caused the man's head injuries. But the woman's wound…that one gave me a sense of déjà vu," the surgeon said.

Déjà vu? What did he mean by that?

Before Mike could ask, Wells, explained. "About a year ago I treated a guy with an almost identical injury. The guy was high on something and violently resisting arrest. Before the sheriff bashed him on the head to subdue him, the guy had already put one deputy in the hospital and badly injured two bystanders."

"When you say sheriff, you mean Doug McDougal?"

"Yeah. It wasn't the way I would have handled the situation, but McDougal stopped the guy from hurting anyone else."

No way had he misunderstood what Wells was saying, but still, Mike didn't want anyone to imply he'd jumped to conclusions hastily. "Just to clarify. You're saying Ms. Kendrick's wound was most likely caused by the butt of a gun?"

"Exactly," Wells replied without hesitation.

Mike took a moment to digest the implication of Well's comment. Now more than ever, he wanted McDougal's backup weapon. Maybe it was a wild goose chase, wishful thinking or just his general dislike for Doug McDougal at play, but Mike planned to have both of the sheriff's weapons checked for any traces of blood, skin and hair.

"How soon do you think I can talk to either of them?"

Wells shrugged. "Ms. Kendrick should come around anytime now. As I said, though, she's got a bad concussion and it's anyone's guess whether or not she'll remember what happened." He gave a shake of his head. "As for Mr. Barrett...at this point his injuries are too life-threatening to make a prognosis."

Even though Mike had seen Jim's injuries and logically knew Jim was badly hurt, the grim news still stunned him. For a moment, he didn't move when the elevator door slid open. But when he realized Wells was gone, Mike had to rush down the hallway to catch up to him.

At the entrance to the surgery wing, the doctor stopped to push a button on the wall and the electronic doors swung open.

"This way," Wells called over his shoulder, leading him inside.

Mike immediately recognized the imposingly tall, snowy haired man pacing impatiently in front of the registration desk.

FBI Supervisory Special Agent Gary Thornton.

Zach's adoptive father and as head of the Bureau's Criminal Investigation Division in Maryland, their boss, the man who'd dispatched them to McDougal's office.

Between the senator's murder and the fact Thornton had trained Barrett and worked as his partner for five years before being promoted to head the CID eight months ago; Mike wasn't surprised to see Gary.

PACING BACK AND forth in front of the nurses' station, Gary waited impatiently for the doctor to arrive. He wanted answers; he needed answers. But all he'd gotten so far was a royal runaround. No one would tell him anything.

He glanced down at the three piece navy suit he was wearing and shook his head. One minute he'd been sitting beside his wife inside a stately downtown cathedral, pretending to enjoy the wedding of her former co-worker, and the next his cell phone had vibrated on his hip. Gary hadn't recognized the number, but in his line of work he rarely ignored calls.

He'd left the sanctuary to take the call and discovered it was the hospital calling to tell him Jim Barrett had been hurt. Skipping the rest of the wedding hadn't bothered Gary in the least, but he wished it was for another reason.

Five years ago, shortly after Gary's longtime partner had retired, Barrett had graduated from Quantico. With more than twenty years as an agent, Gary had been assigned to show Jim the ropes. From the start he'd seen potential in the younger man and Barrett had proven himself to be a smart, astute field agent with natural instincts for investigations. Gary had never doubted Jimmy's ability to watch his back.

Over the years since, they'd not only worked well together, they'd become close friends. He and Katie considered Jimmy a member of their family; same with Mike and Lucas. But two years ago, when Jimmy's parents had died, Gary had agreed to be Barrett's legal and medical power of attorney.

He'd never expected to have to assume that responsibility so soon. But here he was.

And he just wished someone would tell him what was going on.

The doors to the surgery unit whooshed open, drawing Gary's attention and he looked around to see a man in a white lab coat charging into the unit, with another man close on his heels.

Gary did a double take recognizing Mike Devlin. What was he doing here? And where was Zach?

"Mr. Barrett's family?"

The man in the lab coat's voice snagged Gary's attention and he temporarily shoved aside his curiosity about Zach and Mike. His long strides quickly ate up the distance between them. After nothing more than a brief nod to Mike, Gary flipped open the leather case he'd fished from the inside breast pocket of his suit jacket.

"Supervisory Special Agent Gary Thornton, FBI" he said by way of greeting. "I'm here about James Barrett."

"Bradley Wells. I'm one of Mr. Barrett's doctors," the doctor replied, staring at the gold badge and Bureau credentials and immediately shaking his head. "But I'm sorry; I can't tell you anything more than I've told this gentleman," he said indicating Mike. "Patient information is confidential…"

Anticipating the doctor's response, Gary fished out the folded document he'd retrieved from the wall safe at home on his way to the hospital. "I'm Jimmy's medical Power of Attorney. Here's a copy of the POA for hospital files," he said handing the paper to Wells.

The doctor quickly scanned the document and then glanced up again. "Very good," he said with a nod. "What would you like to know?"

"They told me down in the ER to come up here and now I'm being told Jimmy is in surgery. What's going on? What happened to him? How is he?"

"Mr. Barrett was stabbed," Wells replied bluntly.

Gary stared at Wells incredulously for a heartbeat. "Stabbed?" he echoed in disbelief.

He'd assumed Jimmy had been hurt in an automobile or household accident. A violent crime had never crossed his mind because Jimmy had the weekend off. Gary knew that because he was the one who assigned work schedules for agents in his CID. That was also why he was concerned to see Mike, because he and Zach were on duty.

"Yes," Wells replied, dashing Gary's hope that he'd misunderstood. "His injuries are extensive."

A million questions flooded Gary's brain, chief among them, who had stabbed Jimmy? Why? And where? But as much as he wanted answers to those questions, they could wait. Right now he needed to know about Jim.

"Extensive?" Thornton asked. "What are we talking about?"

"His right lung collapsed and if the ambulance crew hadn't gotten it re-inflated and been able to stabilize him, Mr. Barrett never would have made it to the hospital. His liver and spleen have been lacerated and he's bleeding internally; he's lost a lot of blood. On top of all that, he has a skull fracture," Wells explained. "He's in extremely critical condition. But I assure you, Agent Thornton, our surgical teams are doing everything humanly possible to save him."

Gary could feel the color drain from his face.

Wells continued. "We're looking at hours of surgery and anesthesia, which can be hard on someone in Mr. Barrett's condition, but he's young and appears to be physically fit, so that's in his favor."

After more than thirty years in law enforcement, Gary wasn't easily rattled, but the grim picture the doctor painted managed to do just that. Pulling himself together with a deep breath, he handed Wells one of his business cards.

"Doctor, anything you need where Jimmy is concerned, just let me know and I'll make it happen."

Wells nodded, slipping the card into the pocket of his white coat. "I've got to run; my surgical team is waiting for me."

The doctor handed the POA back to Gary. "Give that to the nurse at the desk. She'll take care of entering it into the chart. And the hospital is going to need your signature on a ton of legal forms."

"Will do."

For a moment after Wells left, Gary merely stared after him. But then he turned to Mike.

This morning as he and Katie left home for the wedding, his secretary had called with orders from Washington that agents needed to go to Senator Andrew McDougal's Jacob's Valley office immediately to see the senator about a threatening letter. Gary had dispatched Zach and Mike to handle the call, since they were the agents on duty for the weekend. But Zach was nowhere to be seen now. Where was he?

Concern edged its way inside.

"Why are you here? Zach isn't hurt, is he?" God, he didn't even want to think about that possibility. Jimmy was bad enough. And Kate would be panicked if anything happened to Zach.

A hint of confusion clouded Devlin's blue eyes. "He's fine. I left him back at McDougal's office."

Okay...now Gary was confused. "Why are you here? Did you hear about Jimmy?"

A horrified look cleared the confusion from Mike's eyes. "You don't know...do you?"

"Know what?"

Mike glanced around and pointed at a small sitting room off the main waiting room. "Let's go in there where we can talk privately."

Impatient for answers, Gary followed him inside and lowered his six foot six frame into one of the sparsely padded chairs.

As soon as Mike sat adjacent to him, Gary repeated his question. "What's going on Dev? Why are you here?"

Mike Devlin sighed heavily. "McDougal was murdered."

Gary blinked. He had to have heard that wrong. Sure he had the weekend off, but he was in charge of Maryland's CID. He was on call 24-7 and if a U.S. Senator had been murdered in his jurisdiction, the Bureau would have notified him.

"McDougal? Murdered?"

Mike stared at him for a heartbeat before finding his voice. "Clark didn't tell you?"

"No, dammit" Gary answered tersely trying to contain the fury bubbling inside him. Breakdowns in communication had been known to happen, but this was no breakdown.

Chuck Clark, Special Agent-in-Charge of the Baltimore Field Office was a forty year old insecure moron. And ever since Gary had been promoted to head the CID, Clark had viewed him as a threat to his job and had been subverting him at every turn.

Mike cursed aloud. "I'm sorry, Thorny. We should have texted you directly. But we needed a crime scene unit immediately and Chuck told Zach he'd notify you."

Several choice cuss words rattled around Gary's brain. All of them directed at Clark. But he'd been in Mike's and Zach's shoes often enough to know with a fresh murder scene on their hands, they hadn't had time to make numerous phone calls. They'd made one to get what they needed and had relied on Clark to follow through.

But no way was Clark's silence an oversight. Gary would bet his pension it had been another deliberate attempt to undermine his authority.

Thornton heaved a disgusted sigh. He loved working for the Bureau, but he hated the damn politics involved in management. And if Director Everett hadn't personally asked him to assume the CID position, he would have been happy to retire as a Special Agent. He loved working investigations and he'd been damn good at it.

Gary hauled in a calming breath.

His beef was with Clark, not Mike.

"Don't worry about it, Dev. It's not your fault. Just tell me what happened."

Clearly still upset at being used as a pawn in Clark's agenda, Mike sighed. "When we got to McDougal's office, we walked into a fresh murder scene. The old man had been stabbed to death and was lying on the floor of his office; his body was still warm. A mostly nude woman, we've been told is an attorney at the law firm, was lying unconscious beside McDougal."

When Devlin diverted his gaze to the floor and drew in another breath, Gary knew whatever was coming next was something bad. He steeled his spine in preparation and waited until Mike's gaze lifted again.

"Jimmy was unconscious on the floor, too. His clothing was covered in blood and a bloody letter opener was right by his hand."

If someone had demanded an immediate response from him at that moment, Gary wouldn't have been able to comply. He was speechless again for the second time in only a few moments. It took him several heartbeats to refocus on Mike's explanation.

"…McDougal's two sons, who happen to be the sheriff and mayor, were both already on the scene when we arrived and they're claiming Jimmy killed the senator."

Gary stared at Mike incredulously. He had known Mike Devlin for most of the nineteen years Devlin had worked for the Bureau. In addition to the fact Dev had been Zach's partner, for the past eight years, Gary and Mike had worked together on several task forces. Devlin was a highly respected agent and Gary was among those who considered him one of the best. Dev wasn't given to exaggerations or jumping to conclusions. But the story he'd just related was too bizarre to believe.

Anger surged inside Gary, pulling him to his feet. "You can't possibly believe Jim Barrett murdered anyone," he stormed. "Let alone a United States Senator."

Mike reached over and put a hand on his arm. "Calm down, Thorny. I'm not accusing Jimmy of anything. In fact Zach and I believe he's being set up. But, you know the drill. Until Jimmy or the woman regain consciousness and can tell us their side of what happened, we've got to go with the evidence and witness statements."

Gary yanked his tie loose and popped open the button at his neck, while mulling over the implication. He dropped back into his seat, took a deep breath to clear his thoughts and listened with interest as Mike explained everything they'd found.

Later, while he scrolled through the photos Mike had taken; several things became crystal clear in Gary's mind.

Whatever Jimmy's reason for being at McDougal's office, if he was being set up, his fingerprints on the murder weapon would seal his guilt in the eyes of those clamoring for a quick arrest. And it wouldn't help that he was an FBI agent, especially for those who loved nothing better than to make members of law enforcement look bad. Unfortunately, that camp had been growing in recent years.

Gary frowned. "Do we have any idea why Jimmy was there?"

Mike shook his head. "No. There's nothing on the old man's calendar to indicate they had a meeting. And this morning, before I left home, Jim told me the only plans he had for the day were to finish painting the kitchen and start on the dining room."

"Check the call history on Jimmy's phone. See if there's anything linking him to McDougal or anyone else at the law office." A sick feeling settled in the pit of Gary's stomach. "And check for calls from Clark, too" he added.

With the games Clark had been playing, it would be just like him to go around Gary and send Jim to McDougal's office without telling anyone about it.

"I'll have Zach get on that right away," Mike agreed, pulling out his cell phone.

While Mike was busy, Gary mentally rehashed the details of the crime.

One thing was certain. If Jimmy was being framed...and Gary had no reason to question Mike's judgment on that issue...whoever was behind the charade had completely misjudged their plan. They hadn't counted on Jim being found by two men who knew him well and would recognize a frame. They also hadn't stopped to consider that it made absolutely no sense for an armed federal agent to defend himself by stabbing someone to death when he could have shot them instead.

The sound of his cell phone ringing diverted Gary's thoughts. He shot a quick glance at the caller display and groaned silently.

Director Everett. Before he even connected the call, Gary guessed the purpose of it.

If news had broken about McDougal's murder, pressure to solve the case quickly would come at the Director from all directions. And since the crime had occurred in Gary's CID jurisdiction, the Director would be all over him to relieve that pressure by finding the killer. But it spoke volumes about the Director's lack of faith in Clark, that he was calling Gary directly, instead of going through normal chain of command.

A few minutes later, Gary disconnected the call and shook his head.

He'd been right. And Everett's message had been very clear. Find the killer. Everyone from the President down to the lowliest Congressman on the totem pole wanted the case solved "yesterday."

No pressure there!

But seriously, Gary had expected that kind of reaction. The murder of a U.S. Senator was big news, shocking news and everyone wanted the murderer brought to justice quickly. He wanted the same thing, especially so he could clear Jimmy's name.

What he needed was an ace in the hole. And fortunately, Gary knew where he could find one.

Seeing Devlin had ended his call, Gary got right to the point. "I want guards assigned to Jimmy and the Kendrick woman, 24-7. But there's no point in continuing to shield the fact Jimmy is FBI. If the real killer has his shield and wallet, the information is bound to become public sooner or later. I don't want to give anyone a reason to claim cover-up."

Mike nodded. "I'll take care of it."

"And...we need to contact Lucas Shaw. He's got an inside track with McDougal's family."

Mike shot him a surprised glance. "Lucas? What's his connection to them?"

Not for the first time in his life, Gary was thankful for his photographic memory. He'd known and worked with Lucas for several years, so he was familiar with some of Shaw's personal history, but when he'd taken over the reins of the CID, Gary had made a point of learning all he could about the agents in his division, which is how he knew Shaw's background.

"He's got two connections. First, he and Edward McDougal roomed together at West Point and second, his kid sister is married to one of the senator's sons."

The comment snagged Mike's interest and he leaned forward. "That could be a stroke of luck for us."

Gary nodded. Friendships formed during four arduous years at a military academy were lifelong bonds. Zach was still close friends with Deputy U.S. Marshal Phil Watson who had been his roommate at Annapolis. And although it was his sister who had married into the McDougal family, Lucas would undoubtedly have some take on that family's dynamics.

"We can use all the help we can get," Mike said echoing the thoughts bouncing around Gary's mind.

Lifting his cell phone again, Gary scrolled through his contacts until he found Lucas' name. He pressed the number and when the phone started to ring, he put the call on speaker so Mike could hear.

Lucas answered on the second ring. "Shaw."

Considering it was the weekend and Shaw was off duty, Gary was half surprised he'd answered so quickly. "Lucas, it's Gary Thornton," Gary said in case caller ID hadn't identified him already. "We have a situation and need your help."

"If you're talking about Senator McDougal, the news just broke on television."

Good. That saved Gary from having to explain. "I know it's short notice but I need you at the crime scene as soon as you can get there."

"No problem. I'll be there in under an hour," Shaw replied, sounding pleased to be included in the investigation.

Gary ended the call and slipping his phone back in its holder, he glanced over at Mike. Normally his management style was to let his men run with their cases and to offer whatever logistic help they needed. Because of its high profile nature, this case was different. He had no choice but to get actively involved; the Director had ordered it.

"Dev, I know you are perfectly capable of heading this investigation and…"

A slight smile lifted the corners of Mike's mouth. "Thorny, if you're worried about hurting my feelings by taking over this case, don't be," he interrupted. "I know you're the one who is going to take all the heat from above. Plus that, Jim was your partner. I understand completely."

Relief flooded through Gary. Mike had always been a team player and his response was the one Gary had hoped for. "Thanks Dev. I'm going to need your help...Zach's and Lucas' too. So we'll work it together."

"Sounds like a plan." Another smile tugged at Mike's lips. "You know...if I was the killer, I'd be very worried right about now. Because there isn't anyone alive who has a more vested interest in solving this case than the four of us."

Gary chuckled softly. "You've got that right."

Chapter Four

An entire timpani section was trying to drum its way out of her skull. At least that's the way it felt. For several seconds Jamie debated the wisdom of opening her eyes, imagining what sunlight would do to the pounding in her brain.

But she couldn't very well keep her eyes closed forever. At some point she was going to have to open them and find out where she was and why her head felt like someone had split it open with an axe.

From the linens covering her and the soft pillow cradling her head, Jamie knew she was lying in a bed. But it didn't feel like hers and the strange antiseptic odor of the air definitely wasn't anything from her apartment.

Taking a deep breath for courage, Jamie slowly cracked open her eyelids. A quick glance around confirmed it wasn't her bedroom. The metal IV pole beside her bed and the machinery blinking behind her answered the question of where she was.

A hospital.

Thankfully someone had dimmed the lights and pulled the blinds in the room. Jamie and her pounding head were grateful for that.

But why was she here in the first place? What had happened to her?

Before she had time to search her brain for answers, the door to her room swung open giving her a glimpse of a uniformed policeman sitting outside her door. A state trooper if she'd identified his uniform properly. Jamie was still digesting that detail when the nurse who'd opened the door spoke.

"Well...you're awake. A lot of people will be glad to hear that, Mary," the nurse said absently, checking the readings for her vitals.

Mary? Really?

Jamie had hated that name since childhood and it had been fifteen years since anyone had dared call her Mary. The person had been her father, Major Harold Robert Kendrick.

The major. Just thinking about him caused a wave of sadness and regret. No matter how often Jamie had asked him not to call her Mary, he'd insisted on using the name...and had always made it sound like a curse.

Now, every time someone called her by that name, it came through her ears as his voice, in the same harsh, cold and demeaning tone he'd always used.

Jamie had never known her mother, who'd died giving birth to her. The major was the only parent she'd had and she'd tried so hard to please him, to make him love her. But she'd always failed. And he'd never made any secret of the fact she was the biggest disappointment of his life.

For years Jamie had thought it was all her fault. But the day she'd graduated from high school at the top of her class and the major had still found reasons to criticize her, she'd had an epiphany.

Nothing she ever did would be good enough for him. Not because of any shortcoming of her own, but because she could never be the one thing he wanted.

A son.

The realization had been liberating.

He was gone now; killed in an automobile accident that had nearly claimed her life a week after that high school graduation. Typical of the major, he'd been ranting at her about something instead of paying attention and had plowed into a tractor trailer that had stopped ahead of them. The major had been killed instantly. Jamie had been in a coma for several weeks and had spent even more time in physical therapy while recovering from broken bones, but she'd survived and had vowed to make the most out of her second chance at life.

While she had moments where she missed the major...or at least missed the idea of having a father...she rarely thought of him until someone called her Mary. Then it was like a scab being ripped open.

"I go by Jamie and I'd appreciate if you'd make sure people know that," she answered insistently.

The nurse barely glanced her way and Jamie wasn't at all certain the woman had heard her, even though she was less than two feet away. Annoyed at being ignored, Jamie pressed for information. "What's wrong with me?"

"You've got a concussion," the nurse answered bluntly. "The doctor will be in shortly to talk to you."

Jamie waited for more, but that was it. Frustrated, she heaved a sigh. "How did it happen? Was I in an accident?"

"The FBI has been waiting to talk to you. I'm sure they'll enlighten you," the nurse replied dodging her questions.

"The FBI? Why?"

Again, the nurse didn't acknowledge her question. "Press the call bell if you need something," she tossed over her shoulder as she left the room without looking back.

What the heck was going on? Why were they treating her like Typhoid Mary? And why did she know who Typhoid Mary was but not know what she'd had for breakfast or what had happened to her? Why couldn't she remember?

GOOD FOR HIS word, Special Agent Lucas Shaw walked into the McDougal and Associates office forty-five minutes later.

Mike had known and worked with the retired lieutenant colonel since Shaw had joined the Bureau eight years ago after a stellar career commanding an elite and highly classified Special Operations Force.

Mike waved Lucas into the senator's office where Gary was already studying the crime scene.

A man of few words, the tall, athletically built agent stepped into the room silently, his gray eyes assessing his surroundings before he greeted both of them with a friendly nod.

For several minutes after he'd listened to a recap of events at the murder scene, silence reigned, giving Lucas time to review Mike's crime scene photos and video. But after only a few pointed questions, he glanced between Mike and Gary.

"How can I help? What do you want to know?"

Not surprisingly, Lucas knew why they wanted him on the case. His connection to the McDougal family made him invaluable. So, there was no point in wasting time getting to the point.

Mike didn't. "Ed and Doug McDougal are claiming Jim Barrett murdered the senator."

Surprise widened Shaw's light gray eyes. "You're kidding. Jimmy?"

"I wish I was," Mike answered, holding Shaw's gaze. "You've been Jim's partner for over a year. Can you imagine him murdering anyone?"

Shaw shook his head silently.

No hesitation, no look of doubt in his eyes. Good.

"Well, this murder is definitely overkill, and smacks of a crime of passion," Mike continued. "And we all know those are usually committed by a family member or someone intimately involved with the victim. To your knowledge, does Jimmy have any connection to the senator or his family?"

The former special ops officer shook his head again. "Not that I'm aware of."

"So...before we tackle others who might have had a beef with the senator, we start with the family," Gary interjected, drawing Shaw's attention to him. "And you've got a unique perspective on the McDougal's. Mike and I would like to hear your take on them."

"Ed and I were roommates for three years at the academy," Shaw answered, matter-of-factly. "We're not as close as we were back then, though. Nowadays, we only get together a couple times a year usually to play golf."

Lucas gave his head a quick scratch before continuing. "Frank is my brother-in-law. He's been married to my kid sister, Carol for nearly twenty years. We live a couple blocks from each other and are close friends. He's a great guy and in my opinion he's the most normal one of the McDougal bunch."

Lucas gave a little chuckle. "But Frank calls himself the black sheep of the family."

Mike did a double take on that one. "Black Sheep?" he echoed.

"Yeah. He's the only one of Andrew's sons who didn't choose a career related to law or politics. He's a doctor...a surgeon...and the senator punished him for that choice by refusing to help pay for any of his schooling."

"Sounds like the old man was *Father of the Year* material," Gary quipped sarcastically.

Lucas nodded. "Yeah, Frank was upset for a while, but he's too successful in his own right now to care. And he's glad to be away from the drama that seems to swirl around his family. He and Carol only see his family about twice a year, usually around the holidays."

"What about the rest of the senator's family?" Mike asked. "Do you know them? How do they get along as a family?"

"I just saw the whole clan a couple months ago at a seventy-fifth birthday party for the senator." Lucas shrugged slightly. "I'm not sure why I was included, but a couple other classmates of Ed's and mine were there too, so my guess is it was a publicity stunt by Ed or the senator. Regardless, that family's dynamics are very interesting."

Lucas glanced between Gary and Mike. "The old man was a tyrant who ruled the roost with an iron hand. He was also the consummate politician; he could be shaking your hand and stabbing you in the back at the same time."

Shaw's gaze drifted to all the blood staining the carpet. "Okay, that was a poor analogy, but you get my drift. The man was vindictive. I know of at least two people he destroyed, career-wise, because they had the temerity to cross him. One was an attorney at the firm; I know her personally. She was fired from the firm after rebuffing Andrew's advances and when she threatened a lawsuit to fight her discharge, her license to practice law in the state was mysteriously revoked. She's now a school teacher."

Mike shot a glance at Gary, glad to see he wasn't the only one angered and appalled by Andrew's actions. He shifted his gaze back to Lucas. "You said you know of two instances. What's the other?"

Lucas nodded. "The other is Jacob's Valley's former sheriff, Gerry Shank, who is a good friend of Frank's; I've met him. When Doug was working as a deputy, Gerry got numerous complaints about him from town residents and people passing through Jacob's Valley. The complaints just kept piling up to the point where Gerry had to act, so he put Doug on notice. One more complaint and Doug would be fired. Within a week, the town council voted to fire Gerry for some trumped up charges of favoritism and Doug was appointed interim sheriff. I have no proof of it, but I'd be willing to bet Doug's subsequent election to sheriff was bought and paid for by Andrew. Fortunately Gerry was able to find other work in his field; he's been chief of police for a large suburb of DC for about ten years now."

Gary's face twisted in disgust. "Unbelievable." He shook his head as if still having trouble digesting Andrew's actions. "After that, I'm half afraid to ask...but what about the other family members?"

"Lauren McDougal, the senator's wife, is a piece of work, too. She is obsessed with money, status and power and she's fiercely protective of her boys. A couple years ago, one of our classmates tossed a joking insult at Ed. Ed laughed at the comment, but

Lauren took offense." Lucas chuckled humorlessly. "She banished Joe from the mansion and he's never been permitted to return. Don't mess with her kids. But she and the senator…they've been married for over fifty years and in all the time I've known them, I've never seen anything that even remotely resembles love between them."

When Lucas paused, Gary motioned with his hand for him to continue.

"Bob and Colin are both a little pompous and very intense, but they're both married and devoted family men. In my presence, they've often complained about Andrew's interference in day to day activity at the law firm and expressed anger and frustration over losing female employees because of Andrew's continued sexual harassment. But the old man never relinquished his controlling interest in the firm, so their hands were tied to do much about him."

"Doug. He's an arrogant jackass," Shaw said with a disgusted shake of his head. "…a born bully who thrives on his power as sheriff. He's been married and divorced twice. Both his ex-wives, Wendy and Nancy, have restraining orders against him and his three kids want nothing to do with him. For what it's worth, I don't trust him any further than I could throw him. And my sister Carol won't tell me why, but she's afraid of him; avoids him like the plague at family gatherings."

Lucas pulled in a deep breath. "Then there's Ed. He married shortly after we graduated from the academy and he and Sharon have two sons. From the time Ed entered the academy, the senator began grooming him to follow his footsteps into politics. And after Ed graduated from the academy, the senator got him an appointment to the Judge Advocate General's Corps where he spent five years working a cushy desk job at the Pentagon and getting a law degree. As soon as his required active service was up, Ed left the army and went to work as a full partner at McDougal and Associates. He was there until six years ago when the senator pushed him to run for mayor."

Mike's brows lifted. Interesting. In fact, everything Lucas had said was extremely interesting. But he still wanted to pick Lucas' brain a little more.

"Do you think Ed or any of the rest of the family is capable of murdering the senator?"

Lucas considered the question before answering. "Frank...definitely not. He doesn't have a violent bone in his body. But as for the others, I honestly don't know. I suppose anyone can commit murder under the right circumstance."

"Why do I get the feeling there is another *but* in there somewhere?" Gary asked.

Mike chuckled softly. Thornton could read people with such astounding accuracy it seemed at times as if he read minds.

Lucas met Gary's cobalt gaze. "Because there is one," he admitted. "While Ed might not be capable of murdering his father, I can see him covering up the murder if he thought it would protect his own aspirations. I don't know if it's learned or innate, but Ed's got his father's knack for politics and he's got some lofty ambitions in that respect." Shaw's eyes shifted between his fellow agents. "He's aiming for the presidency and to that end he was planning to announce a run for Governor next month. Now, though, in light of the senator's death, my bet is Ed bypasses the run for governor in favor of pressing for an appointment to the open senatorial seat."

"You have anything other than your gut to back up your statement that Ed's capable of covering up a murder?" Gary pressed.

Shaw nodded. "Our second year at the academy, something happened involving Ed that had all the brass in an uproar. Whatever it was, it was evidently bad. But then suddenly the chaos all disappeared and life returned to normal. When I asked what happened, Ed just bragged that he could do anything and get away with it because of his father's clout. In hindsight, I'm convinced some of the academy command staff let Ed's infractions slide because they didn't want to tangle with the senator."

Shaw shrugged. "None of the sons are particularly close to each other, but all of them, except Frank, will do anything they're told to do by either of their parents. And if someone in the senator's family is behind the murder, I wouldn't be at all surprised if Ed helped cover it up to protect the family name and his own ambitions."

Mike's thoughts went back to the scene he and Zach had seen when they first walked into the senator's office. The sight of Ed and Doug leaning over Jim's unconscious body, the gloves they'd been wearing and the way Doug had been manhandling Jim. They'd found the knife near where Doug had been squatting.

Was all that innocent or were they tampering with or planting evidence?

"Gut reaction, Lucas," Mike inquired. "What do you think Ed and Doug are doing in my video?"

Shaw looked Mike right in the eyes and didn't hesitate with his response. "I think they're staging the scene."

"You all ready for some interesting updates?"

Caught off guard by the newcomer's voice, Mike spun around in time to see Zach stroll into the senator's office. Taylor had remained at the crime scene while Mike had gone to the hospital. In addition to working closely with the CSI investigators, he'd been interviewing some employees of the firm, including senior partners Bob and Colin McDougal.

"What do you have?" Gary asked, apparently anxious to hear what his son had learned.

"First off, Doug and Ed have both lawyered up. They gave the state police their signed statements, but were released on condition they make themselves available to talk to us." Zach handed Gary the statements which state police had emailed to him.

"We've got an appointment to meet with Ed later this evening," he added. "And Doug agreed to a meeting at noon tomorrow."

Good. Mike was eager to learn if the brothers stumbled over any lies between their oral accounts and written accounts as to why they'd been at the crime scene.

"Unless someone has an objection, I'd rather stay behind the scenes for any family interviews," Lucas interjected.

"No problem," Gary acknowledged. "That would be too awkward and could potentially constitute a conflict of interest. Mike, Zach and I will handle the family interactions."

Mike glanced at Shaw and nodded agreement. "Since you know both Ed and Doug, I think we benefit the most if you observe the interviews and give us your take on their reactions to questions."

Lucas nodded agreeably. "Will do."

Mike shifted his gaze to Gary. "Thorny, I know you need to get back to the hospital soon, so Zach and I will take the interview with Ed, but I think you should handle Doug tomorrow. Lucas is right; he's an arrogant S.O.B. and you'll be a new face that might just keep him off-guard."

Gary gave a curt nod. "Works for me." Thornton turned back to Zach. "What else do you have?"

"The interviews with Bob and Colin McDougal were uneventful," Zach answered, pulling a small notepad from his suit coat pocket. "They were both visibly upset over their father's murder, but they were cooperative and answered all my questions, including admitting they had some major disagreements with Andrew over his involvement at the firm. But they both have solid alibis which I've already confirmed."

Zach glanced at his notes. "At the time of the murder, Bob was speaking at a luncheon on estate planning. Colin was coaching his son's soccer team at a tournament in Frederick."

Mentally, Mike crossed the two law firm partners off his suspect list...until and unless evidence brought them back into the scope of the investigation, but Zach's voice snagged his full attention again.

"They each admitted their father had garnered plenty of enemies during his years in the Senate, but the only person either of them could name who might have a motive to kill McDougal is a guy named ..." Zach glanced down at his notepad again. "...Joseph Kanell. Until a couple months ago, Kanell was a partner in the law firm, but he resigned right after his wife committed suicide. Kanell's wife and Andrew apparently had an affair and Andrew broke things off when he took up with a younger woman. The Kanell woman took it badly and overdosed on sleeping pills."

Mike cursed aloud. He'd known for years that the senator had trouble keeping his fly zipped, so he wasn't surprised about the affair. But nothing Zach had just told them had ever seen the light of day in the press because once again, the senator had used his power and money to keep a scandal under wraps.

"I also spoke to the youngest son, Frank, by phone," Zach continued. "He's willing to meet with us whenever we want to talk to him, but he's a heart surgeon over in Baltimore and was in the operating room when the murder occurred. I was able to confirm with two nurses on his scrub team that he never left the operating room."

"The senator's grandson, Kyle...who is a law clerk here, failed to show up for his interview" Zach continued. "Right after I told him I wanted to talk to him, he bolted out the door."

Mike shot a glance at both Gary and Lucas. From their expressions, they were thinking the same thing he was. That little stunt had not only been incredibly stupid, it had jumped the young man to the top of their suspect list.

"I told Bob and Colin that Kyle needs to contact us as soon as possible to reschedule, otherwise we would issue an APB for him," Zach added. "But I've been busy interviewing other employees and I don't know if he's called in yet. I'll check as soon as we're finished here."

Any other time, the Bureau might have dealt with the grandson using kid gloves in deference to the senator, but Mike knew this wasn't any ordinary incident; it was a murder investigation. If this Kyle kid was the murderer, he needed to be in custody, before he hurt someone else. If he was merely running scared for some reason, he needed to explain himself.

"The employees I spoke with are all support staffers. And in my opinion, none of them are viable suspects. Other than two sexual harassment complaints against Andrew, none of the women have a motive for killing him. And the two women who mentioned sexual harassment both have strong alibis."

Taylor pulled in a deep breath. "Interviews with all the other employees are lined up for this evening and tomorrow morning, but any meeting with Andrew's widow is on hold for now. She's apparently distraught and has been sedated by her physician. We're supposed to check tomorrow morning to see if she's up to talking to us."

Multi-tasking, Gary glanced up from the statements he was reading to respond. "Dev and I will handle the interview with Lauren whenever it takes place."

Zach nodded and briefly glanced at his notes again before continuing. "We also have some blood information."

Mike's interest stepped up a notch at the prospect of information that would narrow their suspect pool.

"Before troopers released them, Ed and Doug consented to give blood samples which the state boys sent to their lab to be typed. The results show Doug is A-Positive; Ed is A-Negative." Zach glanced down at his notepad again. "The CSI's typed the senator. He was A-Positive. And I just got off the phone with the hospital. The Kendrick woman is O-Positive. I don't have Jim's information yet because he's still in surgery and they couldn't get hold of his doctor."

"Jimmy is O-Positive," Gary interjected. He cocked a brow curiously. "But is there a point to all this?"

"Yes." Zach gave his father a pointed look and a grin tipped his lips, creasing dimples in his cheeks. "As a matter-of-fact, there is. The blood on the fire door panic bar and on the floor beneath it is AB-Negative."

"Yes!" Mike exclaimed enthusiastically.

Gary smiled. "Our killer cut himself."

Zach nodded confirmation. "But it gets even better. Preliminarily, the medical examiner thinks our killer is left handed. Most of the senator's chest wounds, including the one that is likely the fatal blow, appear to slant right to left. She'll know more when she gets McDougal on her table, but that's her eyeball assessment."

"For whatever it's worth, Ed is left-handed," Shaw interjected.

Mike shot a surprised look at him and filed the interesting nugget away for future reference. Jim Barrett was right handed; Mike was certain of that. So was Doug based on the fact his service weapon had been holstered on his right hip. But like the blood evidence, knowing they were looking for a lefty would help them narrow the field of suspects.

"Okay…next item," Zach continued. "I put an APB out on Jimmy's car. Mike and I suspect the killer stole it to make his getaway while we were busy inside here."

Mike nodded his agreement. The explanation was the only thing that made sense, since a stolen car had been discovered in the employee lot after the murder and Jim's SUV was gone.

"And lastly, Mike and I couldn't find anything on McDougal's calendar to indicate he was expecting Jimmy," Zach continued. "So I checked the call history on Jimmy's cell phone to see if there was anything that would show why he was here. I ran all the unidentified numbers and nothing comes back registered to anyone related to this firm."

Zach's gaze slid to Gary. "But he got a call from Chuck Clark's private line this morning."

Chapter Five

Gary cursed aloud, anger filling every cell in his body. Gut instinct had told him Clark was behind Jimmy being caught up in the senator's murder, but he'd hoped his personal dislike of the man had clouded his vision, that he'd misjudged Clark.

He hadn't misjudged anything.

Dammit! All the other shenanigans the SAC had pulled over the past year, paled in comparison to this one. This one could very well cost Jimmy his life.

Using every ounce of self-discipline he possessed, Gary shoved his anger into the recesses of his mind. He had a crime to solve and letting emotions side track him wouldn't help Jimmy or find the murderer. He had to keep his wits about him to stay focused…and that's just what he intended to do.

"What time did that call come in?" he asked.

"About forty minutes before you called Mike and me. I figure the killer was probably interrupted by Jimmy's arrival," Zach confirmed.

A ruckus suddenly erupted in the lobby, causing all four agents to turn that way to see what was happening.

From his vantage point just inside the senator's office door, Gary could see two state police officers physically restraining someone from entering the lobby.

"Let me in! This is a murder scene. It's my investigation. Get out of my way!"

Gary didn't need to see the intruder to identify who was raising holy hell. The hollered protest was perfectly clear from a hallway distance away. And he could think of only one person who would issue that kind of demand.

Sheriff Doug McDougal.

Gary mentally shook his head.

Some days he wished he was retired. This was rapidly turning into one of those days.

With his hands full of a gruesome murder to solve, the last thing he had time for was a battle of egos, but this battle was a no brainer. McDougal was a possible accomplice to the crime and Doug and his brother had already contaminated the crime scene enough. No way was the sheriff getting another crack at adding to the damage.

In the past two hours, Gary had gotten six phone calls. Six. All from the Bureau's Director and all reiterating that everyone from the President on down was expecting him...Gary...to solve the case quickly. And solving the case quickly is exactly what he intended to do.

No one...absolutely no one was going to stand in his way or interfere with his investigation.

Without waiting for the brewing battle to escalate, Gary hauled in a deep breath and headed out to the lobby. Mike, Zach and Lucas followed close on his heels.

Good. A show of force couldn't hurt, either.

When he got a look at the intruder, Gary knew he'd pegged the man's identity correctly. He recognized Sheriff Doug McDougal from Mike's video. Apparently being detained earlier hadn't been enough deterrent for him and Doug was trying for an encore.

If so, Gary was more than willing to oblige him.

He'd never met the sheriff, but anyone who tampered with a crime scene and pulled a gun on his agents already had two strikes against them in Gary's book. This display of arrogance by the sheriff was strike three.

Before speaking, Gary took a moment to study the lawman. McDougal's brown hair, worn in a short military style, topped a fleshy pockmarked face. Dark brown eyes and an even brow were marred by an arrogant expression that seemed to be permanently etched on the sheriff's face.

With an immense beer belly draped over what had once been the man's waist, McDougal was definitely not a prime specimen of law enforcement fitness.

Clearing his throat, Gary stepped forward and introduced himself. "I'm Supervisory Special Agent Thornton, FBI. May I help you with something, Sheriff?"

Instead of acknowledging the introduction, the sheriff glared at him angrily. "So, you're the one in charge, are you? Well, be warned. I'm considering suing you and the FBI for wrongful detainment of my brother and me."

For a heartbeat, Gary stared at him silently.

Sue him? Really?

If Doug thought intimidation would work on him, he was sorely deluded. Gary intended to relieve him of the misconception quickly.

He planted his hands on his hips, a move he knew from experience made his already imposing size seem even larger and he leveled an icy glare on the short, squat man.

"I don't know how you conduct business, sheriff and I really don't give a damn," Gary replied, giving attitude right back to him. "But you and your brother were found at the scene of a brutal homicide, your clothing is blood stained, you were wearing bloody gloves and in spite of the fact there were two people badly injured, you'd made no effort to call for help. That alone throws suspicion on your activities and justifies our having detained you. And considering you initiated an armed confrontation with FBI agents when you were told to 'freeze', you're damn lucky you're not dead or sitting in a jail cell. So, I suggest you lose the attitude."

53

Whether it was the dressing down or just Doug's erratic personality, Gary wasn't sure, but the sheriff's demeanor suddenly went from confrontational to condescending.

His surly gaze became even more churlish. "Besides advanced age, what are your credentials?"

For a beat, Gary allowed the insult to hang in the air between them. A lot of people took one look at his white hair and assumed he was older than his fifty-four years, but his hair had been white since he was in his twenties, a hereditary fluke, that had nothing to do with age. And Katie happened to love his hair just the way it was, so he'd never even considered trying to change it. Not that he intended to dignify McDougal's comment, but the arrogance of it spoke volumes about the man.

In spite of his three strikes against McDougal, Gary had been determined to form his own opinion of the sheriff. He wasn't given to making snap judgments, but this one hadn't taken more than a few seconds.

Mike's and Lucas' assessments had been spot on.

Doug McDougal was an obnoxious, egotistical jackass.

"My credentials aren't the issue here," Gary replied pointedly. "What's at issue is your father's murder. You might be sheriff of this town, but you do not have any jurisdiction at this murder scene and, in fact, were instructed to stay away. So unless you are here to answer our questions, I suggest you leave before I instruct these troopers to put you in cuffs and arrest you for trespassing."

A slow boil reddened McDougal's face as he silently glared at Gary.

If the look was meant to intimidate, it didn't work. Over the years, men far more dangerous and threatening than Doug McDougal had tried and failed to do just that.

He drilled Doug with a glare of his own and tapped the face of his watch. "The clock is ticking, Sheriff. Your decision is simple. Answer our questions or leave. Otherwise, you're wasting our time and interfering in a federal investigation."

The sheriff stared at him a moment before responding. "I don't know why I should answer any of your questions. This should be my investigation. Hell the man was stabbing my father when Ed and I arrived. No jury in the world will acquit him."

According to his signed statement, Edward McDougal had attested there'd been no sound of a struggle or fight when they'd arrived. Doug's statement had made no mention of a struggle either. Now the sheriff was claiming someone was being stabbed.

No way. The man was bluffing.

"You actually saw your father being stabbed?" Gary challenged.

"Yes!"

Mike had been quiet up to this point, but Doug's answer caused a reaction. Devlin took a step forward beside Gary. "Sheriff, when Special Agent Taylor and I first arrived, you were wearing your service weapon and after we confiscated that weapon, you made it perfectly clear that if you had it back, you'd execute the man. If you saw him stabbing your father when you first arrived, why didn't you stop him with the deadly force that would have been justified at that point?"

Doug's expression telegraphed his having been caught in a lie.

Even more irritated with Doug than he'd been before, Gary confronted him outright. "You didn't see anyone stabbing your father, did you? He was already dead when you arrived?"

The sheriff blew out an angry breath. "Yes. He was dead."

"Besides the man and the woman, was anyone else in the office with your father when you arrived?"

Still full of arrogance, Doug hurled his answer. "No!"

That answer had come just a little too quickly for Gary's liking. And the man diverted his gaze, avoided looking him in the eyes. Gary was no profiler, but he knew a lie when he saw one...and the sheriff was lying through his teeth.

But why?

What was McDougal trying to hide? Was it the fact he and Ed had seen what actually happened? Gary didn't think so. Not based on their statements. But his gut told him the brothers had seen or knew the identity of the real murderer.

"You're protecting someone. Aren't you? Who is it?" Gary demanded, knowing in advance he wouldn't get an answer. But he wanted the sheriff to know he was on to his lies. To give the man something to think about...to worry about.

Doug shoved to free himself from the grasp of the troopers still restraining him. "I'm not answering any more questions without my lawyer being present."

"That's your prerogative, sheriff." Gary had wondered when McDougal would wise up and seal his loose lips. But he narrowed his eyes on the man. "You're free to go...for now. But we'll expect you AND your attorney to be at the state police barracks for your formal interview tomorrow at noon."

Doug glared at him angrily for a heartbeat and then stormed out the door.

All of them stared after him until one of the troopers broke the silence.

"What a pleasant man," the trooper uttered with dead-panned delivery.

Not much about the murder or the murder scene was conducive to laughter, but the trooper's gross understatement succeeded in drawing a laugh from Gary and the others.

Shaking his head in dismay at Doug's nerve and arrogance, Gary turned back to the senator's office. "Come on, let's get back to work. I want to see that video of Ed and Doug again."

Ever since he'd watched the video of the brothers manhandling Jim, something had been niggling at Gary's mind. But his photographic memory had finally kicked in with the image and his gut told him they had another valuable clue to use in identifying the real killer.

Without questioning the request, Mike keyed up the video and passed the phone to him.

Yes. He'd been right. And Gary couldn't believe he'd missed it the first time he'd viewed the video.

Swinging his gaze up to the other agents, Gary turned the phone for them to see the freeze frame shot of Jim lying prone while Doug manhandled him. "Look at Jimmy's clothing," he instructed. "No federal agent would call on a U.S. Senator dressed in jeans and a tee shirt. And a hoodie? No way."

He glanced at the video frame again before continuing. "If we're right in assuming Clark sent Jimmy here to check out the threatening letter...then Jimmy would have been in a suit or at the very least khakis and a polo shirt...never jeans and a tee shirt."

His gaze lifted to the other agents again. "I think we've got a killer who changed clothes with Jimmy. And if I'm right, that means our killer and Jim are about the same size."

The three agents stared at him with dumfounded expressions for a moment.

Mike recovered first. "You're right! And dammit, I knew something was off about Jim's appearance, but I think I was so shocked to find him here and badly hurt, it didn't click what it meant."

Gary waved away his concern. "So we're most likely looking for someone about six feet tall and weighing about one eighty."

He noticed Lucas gazing between the freeze frame photo of Jim and the sealed evidence bag holding the clothing medics had cut off Jim. Shaw might have been out of the military for eight years, but he still had the clean cut appearance and impressively erect stance of the highly respected military officer he'd been.

"Something on your mind, Colonel?" Gary asked.

"Yes." Shaw pointed at the red hooded sweatshirt inside the bag. "The logo on that sweatshirt is an Army Ranger unit logo."

Gary did a double take at the sweatshirt and turning, he squatted down to examine it more closely.

The logo, which at a quick glance resembled a pirate's skull and cross bones image, was in fact that of crossed weapons and a dangerous looking winged soldier, wearing a cap emblazoned with the word *Ranger.*

Shaw was correct; then again, Gary had known he would be. No way would a man who'd spent sixteen years commanding special ops troops misidentify the logo of a closely associated unit.

Standing up, Gary turned back to him. "Good catch, Lucas. Will you run with that lead? Check our known suspects to see if any of them have an affiliation to the Rangers."

"Certainly," Shaw replied.

His mind already moving on, Gary turned to Zach. "Have the lab go over the inside of that clothing carefully for any hair or skin follicles that don't match Jimmy's," he instructed, as his cell phone rang. "If our killer wore it, his DNA is bound to be all over it. Maybe we'll get lucky and he'll be in our system."

Gary glanced at the display. "It's the hospital."

The call was brief and to the point and a moment later, Gary clipped his phone back into its holder. "Mike, take over here. I've got to run. Jimmy's out of surgery and the doctors want to see me."

Mike nodded. "Go…we'll finish up here and then head over to the barracks to talk to the mayor."

Chapter Six

Mike swung his gaze to the one-way mirror and took a moment to study the man currently sitting inside a state police interview room. After the encounter with Doug back at the law firm, Dev was half surprised the mayor had shown up for their meeting. But if Ed McDougal was aware he was being monitored by a closed circuit television camera, he didn't give any indication of it while conversing with the attorney sitting at his side.

Interested to hear Lucas' take on Ed, Mike turned back to Shaw. "Any suggestions on how Zach and I should handle Ed in the interview?"

"He's got a healthy ego…just like Doug. So play to it." A slow smile emerged on Shaw's face. "And watch for his tell."

The tip was the last thing Mike expected to hear. He couldn't believe their luck. If Ed McDougal had a nervous habit that emerged when he was lying, it would be an invaluable tool to know during the interview.

Shaw's smile widened. "Whenever he's bluffing, he scratches the crook of his left arm. Used to come in real handy when we played poker."

Mike shot a glance at Zach and saw him grinning. "Shall we go see what the mayor has to say?"

Zach nodded, but before they left the room, Mike's cell phone rang.

"Devlin."

"Mike, I couldn't get hold of Gary…"

Mike immediately recognized the voice. Maryland's Chief Medical Examiner, Dr. Georgiana Baker.

"He's in a meeting, Georgie, and probably has the ringer on his phone off," Mike explained.

"Oh, okay. Well, I thought you all would want to know..."

Mike listened in stunned silence as she informed him her preliminary autopsy had revealed a crucial piece of evidence. As he disconnected the call, Mike noticed Zach and Lucas staring at him expectantly.

"What does the good doctor have for us?" Taylor asked.

Mike swallowed his shock. No point in sugar-coating the news, so he just blurted it out. "We've got two perps and two weapons.

"Two?" Lucas questioned in disbelief.

Mike nodded. "Georgie is certain of it. The autopsy identified two different types of wounds. Those on the senator's back appear to have come from a small weapon."

"Like the letter opener we found by Jim," Zach uttered.

"Exactly," Mike concurred. "And Georgie said they were delivered by someone right handed. But the kill blows, the ones to the senator's chest all came from a lefty and were caused by a larger blade."

Lucas considered the information for only a moment. "If we're dealing with a Ranger, we're probably looking for a survival knife."

"Wow," Zach muttered almost to himself. "I wasn't expecting this."

"Neither was I," Lucas agreed. "And I think our job just doubled."

Mike couldn't argue with Lucas' assessment. But one thing was certain. Standing around in a daze wouldn't help them find their killers.

An hour later, as he and Zach walked out of the interview room, Mike shook his head in disgust. Generally speaking he didn't have much time for politicians. He'd suspected before the interview ever started that the mayor wasn't going to improve his opinion.

And Ed hadn't.

Weighing his every word so he could weasel out of responsibility on a technicality Ed had sorely tested Zach's and his patience with every question. A few times Mike had felt like reaching across the table and shaking a straight answer from Ed, but he'd managed to restrain himself.

He and Zach had conducted enough interviews to effectively handle a difficult suspect. They did just that. And either Ed had developed a serious case of poison ivy or he'd been lying through his teeth, because at nearly every question, the mayor scratched at the inside of his arm. In fact, it had taken Mike considerable self-control not to laugh at the man.

But perhaps the most beneficial result of Ed's interview, besides the fact they'd gotten him to confirm the Senator had already been dead by the time they arrived, was that they now had baseline information they could use to test the veracity of information they gleaned from their interview with Doug.

Since the brothers had been separated as soon as Zach and he discovered the crime scene, they hadn't had a chance to coordinate stories. And their statements already showed significant differences in their versions of events.

Mike's plan for Doug's interview was to identify those differences and nail down the lies.

BY THE TIME her door swung open again, thankfully some of the fog had cleared from her brain. Jamie still wasn't clear on a lot of things, but at least her memory was now more like Swiss cheese than the vacuum it had been when she'd first awakened. A good thing too, because she knew instinctively the two men who entered were the FBI agents the grouchy nurse had mentioned.

From the stern set of their faces, Jamie guessed it wasn't a social call. But then, she doubted visits from federal agents ever were.

The older of the two men appeared to be in his mid-fifties. A handsome man, but she was pretty sure if it weren't for his soft-looking snowy white hair, beautiful cobalt eyes and the laugh lines caressing his eyes and mouth, his mere height would make him thoroughly intimidating. It wasn't every day she saw someone duck to walk through a doorway, but there'd been only a sliver of daylight between his head and the frame.

He was huge. Not fat at all, just exceedingly tall and strong looking.

The other agent was also a lot older than her, probably mid-forties, but dear Lord, he was gorgeous. He looked to be about six-three and had the broad shouldered build of an athlete whose body was toned by physical activity. Maybe not classically handsome like a movie star, but in a rugged kind of way. Square jaw, chiseled features, tanned face.

But it was something else that captured and held her gaze.

Coal black hair threaded with silver at his temples was a stark contrast to the most striking baby blue eyes she'd seen in years. Like a deep crystal clear pool. And they were framed with the kind of long dark eyelashes most women would kill for.

Her gaze dropped to his hand and a rush of excitement pulsed through her when she found the ring finger on his left hand bare. All the better…he wasn't married.

She noticed him peering at her with interest. Unbidden, her heartbeat quickened and she gave herself a mental shake.

What in heaven's name was wrong with her?

Handsome or not, she couldn't believe she was fantasizing about a complete stranger, daydreaming like an adolescent. Still, try as she might, she could not drag her eyes off him.

Her gaze kept drifting back to his face. Something about his eyes tickled her brain. They looked so familiar. It was as if she'd been captivated by them before; at another time and place.

She gave herself another mental kick to rein in her wandering thoughts. And with her mind back on track, the attorney in her warned her to be quiet until they laid their cards on the table.

Thankfully they didn't keep her in suspense long.

Both men flashed their badges for her to see, but it was the older man who spoke first after giving her a brief nod of acknowledgement.

"Ma'am, I'm Supervisory Special Agent Thornton," he said in a voice so deep she half expected the windows to rattle. He indicated his companion before adding, "This is Special Agent Devlin. Are you up for answering some questions?"

Okay, so maybe the big guy wasn't as intimidating as she'd first thought. He'd actually sounded down right nice, like he was concerned for her well-being.

"My head hurts, but I can deal with that. What can I do for you?" She knew what she'd like to do for the younger agent, but kept those thoughts to herself.

"May I call you Mary?" the deep voiced giant asked politely.

"NO!" she snapped, surprising herself almost as much as she surprised him by the vehemence of her response. And she noticed immediately that both federal agents were peering at her curiously, clearly waiting for some explanation.

She heaved a weary sigh.

"I'm sorry. I didn't mean to take your head off. I dislike that name intensely. Please, call me Jamie."

MIKE STROKED HIS chin absently as he gazed down at Mary *"please, call me Jamie"* Kendrick.

Was Gary as confused as he was?

The employee list he'd seen earlier had listed two female attorneys. Mary A. Morrison and Mary J. Kendrick. Either way,

Mike had assumed his victim's name was Mary. Apparently he'd been wrong.

One thing was crystal clear though. Even a drab hospital gown didn't lessen her effect on him. In fact, he doubted a full suit of armor would provide enough protection against the effects of her beauty.

Anyway he looked at it, with sensual emerald eyes and short auburn locks that looked invitingly soft, Jamie Kendrick was a strikingly attractive woman. In fact, she reminded him of a younger, shorter version of Gary's wife. By any standards, Kate Thornton was beautiful and just about the sexiest woman he'd ever met.

Mike kept that last opinion to himself. A little voice in his head told him Gary wouldn't appreciate one of his friends voicing a lustful comment about his wife. And angering an armed, six foot six federal agent who was built like a pro-football wide receiver didn't seem like a particularly smart thing to do.

Thorny was one of the easiest going men he'd ever met, but still, Mike saw no reason to rattle his cage. And in all seriousness, Mike would never even joke about Kate, especially after what his own wife had done to him.

Abigail Staunton Devlin.

Damn. Even after five years, just the thought of his ex-wife, caused the acid in his stomach to begin an ominous swirl that unchecked, inevitably led to heartburn.

They'd been college sweethearts and he'd thought their marriage a good one. They'd rarely argued, shared common interests and had a healthy sex life...but after eighteen years together, Abby had drained their joint bank accounts and taken off with the insurance agent who'd sold them their last homeowner's policy. The ensuing divorce had proven to Mike that he'd been a complete idiot, living in a fantasy world. Abby had been cheating on him for years with an array of different men whenever the opportunity arose. And she'd given the insurance agent the shaft before the ink was even dry on Mike's divorce papers. Last he'd heard…not that he was keeping track of her…she'd taken up with an investment banker. Mike hoped the guy had a tight hold on his client accounts.

In retrospect Mike considered himself lucky to be rid of Abby, but still, for an FBI agent whose very life often depended on his ability to read suspects and situations, it had been humiliating to admit he'd been a naïve fool when it came to reading his own wife.

Something about Jamie gnawed at him though and he couldn't stop studying her. She seemed so familiar. But why? He was sure he'd remember her if they'd ever met before.

The trigger had been her reaction to her name. But why?

Shaking his head, he forced away the puzzle to concentrate on the interview.

THE BIG FBI agent gave her an amiable nod. "Jamie it is. Jamie Kendrick, correct?"

Jamie nodded, breathing a sigh of relief that he apparently wasn't holding her momentary loss of composure against her. But suddenly, something he'd said a moment ago registered in her muddled brain.

Devlin. He'd said his companion's name was Devlin.

Jamie's heart skipped a beat. Sitting up a little straighter, she looked at the younger agent again. His gaze collided with hers giving her a perfect view of those eyes and she nearly gasped aloud.

How had she missed that name the first time around? Probably because she'd been too busy undressing him in her mind.

But long ago, she'd been madly in love with an older man named Devlin, whose blue eyes Jamie had found incredibly intriguing because they'd contrasted so sharply with his pitch black hair and swarthy complexion. She'd fantasized about him endlessly and had cherished every moment she'd spent with him. But one month shy of her tenth birthday, Jamie's childish dreams had been shattered when he married someone else.

As devastated as she'd been, though she'd pumped her grandparents for information about him every chance she got, eagerly absorbing any news they shared.

And that's how Jamie knew he'd joined the FBI.

Was it only wishful thinking; or could this Special Agent Devlin be her Devlin?

She studied the federal agent with a critical eye, searching for anything that would tell her she was being a foolish dreamer. Hoping she was right while praying she was wrong.

After all, what woman in her right mind would want to meet her fantasy dream man when she looked her absolute worst? And Jamie knew she looked like a horror after the ordeal she'd been through.

Still...the little child in her couldn't resist.

"Mikey?" she said barely above a whisper.

Chapter Seven

The wave of emotion that tightened Mike's throat surprised him almost as much as the nickname he hadn't heard in over twenty years.

A fragment of his consciousness realized Gary had stopped talking and was watching him curiously. But Mike didn't care. He stared at Jamie Kendrick in shock as his brain snared a memory and reeled it in.

He could see it like it was yesterday. A tiny infant named Mary with tufts of red-hair, an infant he'd watched grow into a gap-toothed little green-eyed sprite during the summers she'd spent visiting her grandparents who lived next door to his parents.

The little girl had insisted on calling him Mikey.

He stared at the woman in the bed.

No...she couldn't be. Could she?

Mike thought back to the little girl who had followed him around like a puppy every summer from middle school through college.

He tried to envision what she'd look like grown up.

It was a lost cause. Computer programs that accurately age-enhanced someone's picture had nothing to fear from his brain. He couldn't picture the child as anything but a kid.

Had her last name been Kendrick?

Hell, he couldn't recall. He'd always just thought of her as Jamison's granddaughter. But the name Mary hadn't fit the little tomboy he'd known and she hadn't liked it either, so he'd given the child a nickname based on her grandparent's name.

Jamie. He'd called her Jamie. And she'd been so delighted by the nickname, he'd never called her by any other name.

Another memory popped to mind, this one of a stern, intimidating career military officer. The major, Jamie's father. Man, he'd been one cold unfriendly bastard, always too busy to do anything with the kid. He'd dumped her on his in-laws every chance he got. And the poor little kid had seemed so starved for attention that Mike had felt sorry for her.

What was the man's name?

Harold something. But what?

The name slammed into him with the force of a locomotive.

Kendrick!

It was her!

Mary *'call me Jamie'* Kendrick was his little Jamie!

Mike couldn't believe it. After all these years a stroke of fate had brought her back into his life. And even more unbelievable was the fact his pint sized red-haired shadow was all grown up, transformed into the beautiful, sexy woman lying in the hospital bed in front of him.

Mike shook away the thought.

Sexy? What kind of a pervert was he? This was Jamie. Practically a kid sister. And besides, at the moment, she was involved in his murder investigation. And he had yet to determine if she was a victim or suspect.

Still…she was Jamie. And apparently she'd liked the nickname he'd given her so much she'd adopted it permanently. Why that pleased him, Mike didn't want to evaluate too closely.

"What happened to the gap-toothed little girl I knew?" he asked, before his brain could censor his mouth.

"I grew up and got braces," Jamie chuckled. "It's so good to see you again."

Mike felt Gary's eyes boring into him and managed to put the brakes on his mouth long enough for his brain to kick into gear.

Although he and Gary were friends, Thorny was still his boss and getting pressure from all sides to solve McDougal's high profile murder investigation. If Gary perceived a conflict of interest, Mike might find himself tossed off the case.

The idea was totally unacceptable. Mike couldn't and wouldn't allow anything to interfere with his objectivity. Then again, nothing about this investigation was objective considering Jim Barrett's involvement in the case.

Mike let a smile curve his lips long enough to acknowledge her. "It's good to see you again, too, Jamie, but I wish we were meeting under other circumstances."

Wiping the smile from his face, he continued. "Agent Thornton and I are here on official business and now that I know there's a personal connection between us, Agent Thornton will be handling this interview."

JAMIE FORCED HER gaze away from Mike to meet the all business expression of the older man. She hoped she hadn't gotten Mike into some kind of trouble.

Before she had too much time to consider the matter, though, the big man spoke.

"Ms. Kendrick, as Mike stated, we're here on official business. We're investigating the murder of Senator Andrew McDougal."

Blindsided, Jamie heard her own gasp, knew her mouth was probably hanging open, but she was powerless to do anything except stare at him in disbelief.

Several heartbeats later she found her tongue. "Andrew? Murdered?"

She knew she sounded like a parrot, but she couldn't help it. Sure, Andrew had been a disgusting excuse for a man and she hadn't liked or respected him, but she certainly hadn't wanted him dead.

The older agent nodded. "Yes…murdered. He was stabbed to death. And Agent Devlin and I are hoping you can shed some light on what happened." He paused for a moment before continuing. "As an attorney I'm sure you know your rights, but before we go any further…"

Every molecule of air escaped Jamie's lungs and she barely registered him reciting her Miranda rights as her mind raced for a reason. She didn't know anything about Andrew's murder. Heck, she barely knew her own name and didn't have a clue how she'd landed in the hospital. Why was he Mirandizing her?

Somewhere she found the presence of mind to acknowledge him when he asked if she understood her rights. He paused for another moment and gazed at her with a look of concern. "What can you tell us about how you were injured?"

His kind, unthreatening tone eased some of her concern, but she gave a small shrug. "I don't remember anything about it. I assume with a concussion, I must have been in some kind of accident, but I don't remember it."

"You don't remember anything about being in Andrew McDougal's office? About some kind of an … an encounter there? A disagreement or struggle perhaps?"

Jamie's radar kicked in and she mentally sealed her lips. This definitely wasn't any casual visit. They didn't just think she might know something about Andrew's murder; they were placing her in his office when it happened.

"Agent Thornton, I meant what I said. I don't remember anything about how I was hurt."

She shifted her gaze to Mike, hoping to see some sign that he believed her, but he was merely looking at her with a strange expression, as if he was lost in thought.

Unfortunately Agent Thornton wasn't suffering the same affliction.

A deep breath lifted the big man's broad chest and he blew it out in a gush. "Okay, let's try this. What's the last thing you remember before waking up here at the hospital?"

That required some thought. Jamie closed her eyes, trying to concentrate around her headache and glanced up at him realizing she didn't have a clue how long she'd been unconscious. "What day is it?"

"Saturday...evening," he replied matter-of-factly.

"Then it was this morning. And I remember going to my office. I was behind on some paperwork because I'd been in court for two days and was trying to catch up."

"And?"

She looked at him blankly. "I'm sorry. I don't remember anything else."

Twin cobalt laser beams drilled her, questioning her veracity.

Jamie tried to steady her breathing, to not let him rattle her. It wasn't easy. Not only was Agent Thornton's size intimidating, so was the intensity of his gaze.

"Ms. Kendrick, you were found in the senator's office about five feet from his body, wearing only your underwear and covered in what is believed to be his blood. Does that jog your memory at all?"

No way! Underwear? Blood?

Jamie heard the older man's bass voice, but the pounding in her head made concentration difficult. In spite of the headache, she knew being found half naked at the murder scene of a notorious lecher like Andrew wasn't good.

If she was the district attorney or even the police, she would be her own prime suspect. She only wished she could remember why she'd been there. But that part of her mind was still mired in fog.

Still...a murder suspect? It was insane. Heck she went out of her way to avoid stepping on bugs and had been known to help turtles across the road so they didn't get squished. She would never harm another human being and if she had, surely she would remember it, concussion or not.

Mike stepped to the side of her bed and gazed down at her. Even as a teenager, he'd been more handsome than should be allowed by law. But apparently he was like fine wine, improving with age, because in the interceding years, he'd soared from the ranks of hunk into the realm of drop dead gorgeous.

"Jamie, if you are invoking Miranda that's fine; but if you're not and you remember anything, now is the time to tell us."

Jamie contemplated taking her own legal advice to a client and not saying a word until her lawyer arrived. But this was Mikey Devlin. Sure he was a federal agent and she hadn't seen him in years, but besides her grandparents, no one had had a more positive influence on her life than him.

Moving around the country from one military base to another, she'd had few friends growing up. The one constant had been those summers with her grandparents…and Mikey.

He'd been little more than a kid himself, but their twelve year age difference had made him seem like a man to her. A man who, unlike her father, had never disappointed her or made her feel stupid. Heck, he'd taught her to ride a bicycle, swim, whistle loudly and even how to spit. And if it hadn't been for him, Jamie would probably never have learned how to throw and hit a baseball, skills that had later earned her a college softball scholarship.

She'd fallen hard for him. And if she was completely honest with herself, she'd never gotten over him. Every man she'd ever dated had fallen short when she compared them to Mikey. And she always did. So it was no surprise she was still single.

Occasionally she'd wondered if elevating him to such a lofty pedestal had been a childhood mistake, but seeing him again, she knew it hadn't.

Mikey had known she idolized him, but he'd never done anything to take advantage of her, had never been anything but a kind and caring friend. And Jamie saw those same traits in him now.

He was the same honorable man she remembered. If he hadn't been, just now he would have tried to capitalize on their personal connection, to use it to gain the upper hand in their questioning. But he hadn't; he'd stepped back and given her the out of invoking Miranda. After all he'd meant to her, all he'd done for her, Jamie was in a sorry state if she couldn't trust him.

Still, she prayed she wouldn't regret her decision.

"I'll answer your questions," she said. "I'll help anyway I can. But I really don't remember anything. I..."

Something flickered through her mind and she stopped. With a start her gaze flew back to his. "Wait a minute... I do...I remember something."

And she did. She wasn't sure if the shock of being questioned about a murder had jarred her memory or if more of the fog had merely lifted from her brain, unveiling a hazy recollection of events.

"I decided to resign my job..."

The full intensity of two sets of eyes bore into her and she thought Agent Thornton was going to pounce on her statement. But to her surprise, it was Mikey who spoke.

"You were resigning? Why? Did you have a disagreement with Andrew or one of the other partners?"

Her head hurt badly, but she had a choice. Tell them the whole sordid, humiliating story of Andrew's harassment or remain quiet and let them think she was hiding something. The decision was a no-brainer. She told them everything.

After Andrew's latest proposition, she'd realized her chance of obtaining a partnership at McDougal and Associates was about as likely as seeing elephants parading down Main Street. And to be completely honest, her chance of seeing the pachyderms was probably more realistic, since there was always the possibility the circus would pass through town someday.

That startling realization had led her to an important decision.

"I finally realized I'd never make partner there because I had no intention of ever giving into his sexual demands. I remember typing up my letter of resignation."

Jamie glanced between the two agents and saw ire had deepened the big man's eyes to a midnight blue. Mike's expression looked just as thunderous.

Great, she'd just handed the FBI her motive for wanting Andrew dead. If she hadn't been a serious suspect before, she certainly was now.

Agent Thornton muttered an oath so softly Jamie thought she imagined it. But when Mike nodded agreement, she knew she hadn't. Both men were livid. And not at her; they were furious with Andrew.

Relief lifted a weight from her shoulders and for the life of her Jamie couldn't explain it, but she felt vindicated by their reaction. Now more than ever she wished she could help them further, but she couldn't.

She shrugged. "After that, it's all a blank," she concluded.

For a moment, Mike said nothing, his gaze never wavering from hers. But finally he drew in a deep breath and blew it out in a gush. "You don't remember anything else?"

Jamie shook her head.

Big mistake. Her brain sloshed from one side of her skull to the other, magnifying the pounding in her head and sending the room into a spin.

She dropped her head into her hands, cradling her temples and closing her eyes...and prayed desperately that the tidal wave of nausea erupting in her belly didn't cause her to throw up.

"Jamie, are you okay?"

The genuine concern she heard in Mike's voice made her love him all over again.

Slowly, she opened her eyes and lifted her head to find him leaning close, peering at her with alarm darkening his gaze.

"I think so. It was just a wave of dizziness when I shook my head, but it's passed." She blinked to clear her vision.

"Would you like me to ring for the nurse?" Agent Thornton asked, worry evident in his eyes.

She smiled up at him. "No. I'm okay. But thank you for offering."

He nodded slightly and glanced at Mike. "We're done here for now."

Mike gave him a nod, then turned back to her and Jamie's heart stammered when he smiled. "Try to get some rest, Jamie. We'll check back with you tomorrow and maybe we can talk more if you're up to it."

Jamie didn't want to give too much thought to why the idea of him returning to see her caused heat to course through her body. Seriously, she ought to be indignant, she ought to scream and holler that she was innocent and just wanted them to leave her alone.

But she'd been practicing law long enough to know that investigators never gave up until they found answers to their questions; she doubted two federal agents were just going to fade into the woodwork.

"Okay, Mikey. See you tomorrow."

THE MOMENT THEY stepped into the hallway and Jamie's door closed behind them, a deep chuckle rumbled from Thornton's chest.

"Mikey?" he uttered, amusement dancing in his eyes.

Oh hell! Mike groaned silently. Here he'd been concerned Thornton would be upset by the personal connection. He should have known Thorny had something else up his sleeve. But the last thing he needed was Gary sharing that nickname with the rest of the Baltimore field office.

He'd never live it down.

And God forbid his sisters heard it. As it was, it had taken him years to convince them to call him Mike instead of Mikey. He'd finally worn them down, only to have Jamie learn to talk and re-christen him with the name all over again.

Thankfully by then his sisters hadn't been around the house to hear it. But growing up with them had been a real challenge. The age gap between his sisters and him had seemed insurmountable back then; all of them older, Bridget by ten years, Kerry by nine and Regan by seven.

He'd had two parents and three mother hens. But as they'd matured and all followed their father's footsteps into careers with the Maryland State Police, the age gap that had once been a stumbling block to any real relationship between them had vanished. And although Mike had eventually opted to join the Bureau, he and his sisters were all extremely close now.

However all three of them already got far too much enjoyment reminding him of all the stupid things he'd done as a kid. The last thing he needed was for that nickname to resurface and give them more fodder for their cannons.

Mike glared at Gary. "If you repeat that name to anyone I swear I'll sue you for slander," he growled under his breath.

Gary barked a laugh. But a moment later he wiped away his smile, suddenly all business again. "I want you to find out everything there is to know about Jamie Kendrick. And when she gets out of here, I want you sticking to her like fly-paper until you've garnered every useful scrap of information from her regarding this case."

It was Mike's turn to stare. Was Thorny trying to kill him? Jamie had his libido so twisted into knots, he could barely think straight around her. Just the thought of being around her long enough to complete the assignment had him sweating bullets.

"Are you serious?" he asked hoping this was all some colossal mistake, that he'd heard wrong.

Gary narrowed his gaze on him and nodded. "Absolutely. Do we have a problem...Mikey?"

Mike muttered a curse under his breath. "No." Other than the fact he'd have to take out a second mortgage on his home to pay the water bill for all the cold showers he was going to be taking.

A smile crept back onto Thornton's face and chuckling, he turned away and headed to the elevators.

ED MCDOUGAL PULLED his car into the driveway and cut the engine, heaving a sigh of fatigue.

What a day!

After dancing around the FBI's questions, trying to give them answers that didn't incriminate anyone, especially him, he'd gone to see his mother. Ed couldn't believe how well she was taking his father's death. Almost like she was relieved the old man was out of her life.

Maybe she was. Their marriage had always seemed more like a business arrangement than anything resembling a love match. They'd put on a good display in public, but even when he was younger, Ed knew his folks fought like cats and dogs behind closed doors.

His old man had ruled their house with an iron hand...iron fist really, but he'd managed to keep his explosive temper hidden from outsiders. His constituents would never believe their beloved senator had a volatile streak, but Ed, his brothers and their mother, had all encountered it numerous times.

But while most women probably would have tired of their husband's abuse and philandering a long time ago, his mother had always been the glue that had held their family together. She'd been hyper-sensitive about their public image; even more so than the senator.

Ed guessed it was because she liked the status and wealth of being Mrs. Andrew McDougal.

Even now, with the old man gone, her sole focus was on preserving the dignity of the family name and Ed had no doubt she'd go to any lengths to do just that. In fact, she already had. It was her phone call that had sent Doug and him to their father's office and they'd been given strict instructions to do whatever was needed to cover up what some lunatic had done to their father.

Ed still couldn't figure that one out and his mother had been no help at all.

For someone who'd been sedated by her doctor, she'd been remarkably lucid, pumping Doug and him for details about what had transpired at the law office. But she adamantly refused to discuss her reasons for wanting them to stage the scene to throw off investigators. And he and Doug had learned early in life not to push either of their parents. The consequences were never pleasant.

Thankfully, his mother had eventually run out of gas and claimed she needed to lie down. Ed had jumped at the opportunity to leave and finally he was home.

He stared up at his darkened house, relieved for the solitude awaiting him inside.

With their sons both out of the house — Kyle in his own apartment and Chad away at college — Sharon and he were empty-nesters. And at the moment, Sharon wasn't home either, away on a three week tour of Australia with her bird-watching group.

Most times, he missed having his family around, but tonight Ed was glad they were gone. Having the whole place to himself would give him a chance to think.

The reality of what had happened; what he'd done felt like an anvil around his neck. But he'd had no choice. Whatever his mother's reasons, Ed could never have refused to help her.

And maybe he was as cold an SOB, as much of a hypocrite as his father, because he wasn't sorry the old man was dead. They'd never been close; Andrew hadn't let anyone get close to him, except the women he screwed and even they were only temporary distractions.

Of course, Ed wasn't in any position to judge his father for all the infidelities. He hadn't exactly been a model husband himself.

Not that his wife knew about his infidelities and other indiscretions. If Ed had learned anything from his old man, it was how to cover his own tracks. And fortunately, another lesson he'd learned from his father was that money could buy an awful lot of silence.

Ed was no saint; he admitted that. But today...man, he had no frame of reference to help him put it all in perspective. He needed time alone to process everything...and his role in it.

He and Doug had done a good job of covering any signs of what had really gone down at their father's office, but they'd been interrupted by those two pushy Feds.

And Ed couldn't help worrying.

If the Feds found something. Or worse, if the press learned what he'd done...he'd be finished. He couldn't let that happen. It would ruin all his plans and dreams.

For years he'd had his eye on a prize. The Presidency. He'd set a path for himself and had been working toward his goal for decades. After today, though, he could skip the run for governor he'd planned. With the McDougal name, Ed figured he'd be a shoe-in to fill his old man's vacant Senate seat.

He'd never considered that idea before, but the moment he'd been summoned to his father's office he'd seen the possibilities.

No sense in letting someone else profit from the old man's demise.

But it could all come crashing down around him if anyone learned of his part in the cover-up.

Ed scoffed a chuckle at the irony of his predicament.

Now more than ever he could use his old man's help. Ed had never seen anyone who could bribe a witness or finesse the press the way Senator Andrew McDougal had. The media ate out of his father's hand, hanging on his every word and turning a blind eye to all his faults.

Andrew would have definitely figured a way to sweep the brewing scandal under the rug. Now that the old man was gone, though, Ed was going to have to deal with this one on his own. But how?

Chapter Eight

J amie glanced at the clock and heaved a sigh of frustration. Two a.m. A half hour later than the last time she'd checked.

Try as she might, she couldn't sleep. Thoughts kept ricocheting around in her brain and she couldn't shut them down.

Her memory had picked one inconvenient time to return. If she'd remembered everything earlier, she'd be sleeping like a baby right now. But no...not her. She'd had to wait until visiting hours were over and the hospital was on night shift.

Sure, she was looking forward to morning, to seeing Mikey again and clearing her name.

That thought stopped her cold.

Mikey? Had she really called him that?

A moment of thought clarified the embarrassing truth and Jamie rolled her eyes wishing she could turn back the clock. Seriously, who in their right mind called a forty-five year old gorgeous, virile male...Mikey?

All these years she'd been dreaming that someday they'd meet again and he'd see her as a woman...a desirable woman instead of the little girl he'd known.

Jamie rolled her eyes again. Fat chance that was going to happen. He probably saw her as a complete idiot.

Tossing her legs over the side, Jamie slid off the bed and stood up. Maybe a walk would clear her head of the memories...especially of how she'd humiliated herself in front of Mikey.

Jamie blew out a breath of irritation. There she went again. Mike...his name was Mike, not Mikey. When was she going to get that through her thick skull?

She almost shook her head, but the memory of the room spinning before stopped her from making that mistake again.

A draft on her backside stopped her from making another one. She couldn't very well parade around the hallways in a hospital gown opened up the back. Talk about making a fool of herself. She'd never be able to show her face in town again.

Rummaging through the bedside drawer produced a fresh hospital gown still wrapped in plastic. Jamie looked at it briefly before an idea came to her. Quickly, she ripped open the plastic and pulled out the gown. Slipping it on like a coat, Jamie tied it in front.

Satisfied she was presentable to the world, Jamie swung open her door. She gave a start.

The state trooper was gone. He'd been like a fixture ever since she'd regained consciousness. He'd even moved with her when Dr. Wells had her transferred from ICU to a private room, a few hours after Mike and Agent Thornton left.

Dr. Wells had told her that if all went well overnight, she'd be going home in the morning and he'd given her consent to get up. But the missing trooper gave her pause.

Was she allowed out of her room without his permission?

Shrugging away the concern, Jamie strolled toward the nurses' station and then turned down an intersecting hallway where she found the ICU waiting room.

Her windows overlooked the hospital's massive air conditioning system. Maybe the view in there would be better.

Deciding to check it out, Jamie opened the door and slipped inside the black solitude. A deep sigh of contentment escaped her and she grinned, gazing out the wall of windows at the twinkling lights of Jacob's Valley that glimmered in the distance.

She might not have been raised as a native of the little valley town, but she'd always thought of it as home and had snatched the opportunity to return when she'd been recruited by McDougal and Associates.

Knowing Jacob's Valley was Mike's hometown had been an added incentive. Deep inside she knew she'd returned here harboring hope she'd run into him again someday. Being a chief suspect in a murder case he was investigating wasn't exactly how she'd imagined their reunion, though.

"Don't let us startle you."

The voice, spoken softly from somewhere behind her had the effect of doing just that. Jamie jumped and spun around. Adjusting to the darkness, her eyes made out a massive shadow in the far corner of the room. "I'm so sorry. Did I wake you?" she asked.

"No. I'm too keyed up to sleep," the woman said barely above a whisper. "I didn't mean to scare you, though. I just thought I'd better let you know we're here."

As Jamie neared the voice, a tiny thread of light peeking from the edge of a curtained window to the hallway softened the shadows and gave shape to a pretty woman on the loveseat. With a blink, Jamie realized the lady wasn't alone.

She was reclined against a man who was slouched on the seat with his arms wrapped around her. A dark suit jacket that had apparently been blanketing them from the coolness of the room had slid to the floor, but its absence hadn't bothered him in the least because he was out cold.

Jamie's gaze zeroed in on what she could see of his face and she gave another start.

It was the big FBI agent! Funny, but sound asleep he didn't appear the least intimidating. Jamie glanced at the woman curiously. "Are you Agent Thornton's wife?"

Why she made that assumption, she didn't know. But there was a kind of familiar intimacy in the way he was holding the woman and the way she was reclined against him. And Jamie had noticed the gold band on his ring finger when he'd been in her room earlier.

"Yes." The woman turned a loving smile at him over her shoulder. "He's had an emotionally charged day. He's tired."

Jamie stared down at him. He must be tired, considering he seemed oblivious to the fact the furniture in the waiting room was standard hospital fare, which didn't lend itself to long term comfort and obviously hadn't been designed for someone so tall.

The woman lifted her gaze with a questioning look. "How do you know my husband?"

Jamie figured there was no point in hedging. If he woke up he'd certainly reveal her identity to his wife. And after all, Jamie had wanted to talk to Mike and him, to tell them what she'd remembered. Maybe she could do it now, get things off her chest and finally get some sleep.

"He and Agent Devlin interviewed me this afternoon about a case they're investigating…or I guess it was yesterday at this point. My memory was really hazy at the time, but this evening I remembered some details that might help them. I was actually looking forward to talking to them again."

The pretty woman looked at her with interest and suddenly, to Jamie's surprise; she turned slowly in his arms and stroked her husband's face. "Sweetie, wake up. There's someone here who'd like to speak to you," she murmured softly.

Jamie almost chuckled at the endearment. Sure he was handsome and probably a nice man, but sweetie just didn't seem to fit such a giant.

"Is it the doctor? How'd the surgery go?"

The question came out in that rolling bass voice of his before he was even fully awake. And from the urgency of his question, it sounded like he was anxious about someone. Did they have a child who was ill or hurt? His wife had said she was too keyed up to sleep and had mentioned the emotionally charged day he'd had.

Concern worked its way through Jamie and she had second thoughts about bothering them.

"We haven't heard anything yet," his wife assured him.

His sleepy gaze lifted slowly and slammed to a stop when it landed on Jamie. A frown creased his forehead.

"What are you doing in here?" he snapped, releasing his hold on his wife and shifting quickly to straighten his position. An almost comical groan slipped from his mouth in protest. No surprise considering the way he'd been slouched.

Reaching to switch on the lamp beside her, his wife twisted back to look at him, clearly startled by his sharp tone. "Honey, this young lady is the reason I woke you. She'd like to speak with you."

He rose to his feet suddenly making the room shrink in size. The sight of the weapon clipped at his waist made him even more menacing than normal. For someone only five-two, Jamie had long ago gotten used to people being taller than her. But if she had to spend too much time talking to this man, she'd likely dislocate a vertebra in her neck looking up at him.

He stooped down, snagged his jacket off the floor and came up looking at her again. "Where's the state trooper who was assigned to you?"

Jamie merely stared at him, confused by his reaction to seeing her. She quickly realized silence wasn't the way to improve his mood because he leveled those cobalt eyes of his on her again. Annoyed at being made to feel like a criminal, she glared at him defiantly.

"I don't know. I decided to take a walk and he was gone. But don't worry. I'm not trying to escape and I certainly don't intend to hurt you or your wife."

When his wife gasped in horror, he shot a quick glance back at her. "You're okay, sweetheart." But belying his comment, concern creased his brow and as he quickly shrugged his suit coat on over his unbuttoned vest, he issued a warning. "Both of you stay here."

Jamie exchanged a look of confusion with his wife as he opened the waiting room door and strode into the hallway. Curiosity prodded her over to the door where she could see what he was doing.

He'd just passed the nurses station when the twenty-something trooper re-appeared carrying what looked to be a packet of cupcakes and a soda can.

She couldn't hear them, but Jamie could see their faces and she was glad she wasn't that state trooper. Whatever Agent Thornton was saying it was clear he wasn't happy. He emphasized his displeasure by poking his index finger at the guy's chest once and then pointing emphatically to the chair outside Jamie's room.

When the trooper, looking properly chastised, gave him an apologetic nod and walked back to his chair, Thornton shook his head and looked skyward, ramming his fingers through his hair in clear frustration. Finally he turned away, but instead of returning to them, he headed into the men's room.

When he came out a moment later and returned to the waiting room, the hair around the edges of his face was wet. He'd obviously splashed himself with water, but Jamie wasn't sure if he'd done it to wake up…or maybe to cool off.

The door clicked closed behind him as he drew in a deep breath and blew it out slowly. "I'm sorry I lost my temper."

An apology was the last thing Jamie expected, but it sounded sincere. "That's okay. You were awakened from a sound sleep," she said, giving him an out.

He gave her an appreciative smile. "Just so you know. That trooper isn't there to keep you inside your room; he's there to protect you. I was upset that he left you unguarded. But trust me, he won't do it again."

Jamie fought back a chuckle. After the dressing down the young trooper had received, she doubted the fellow would even try to take a bathroom break. Still it was rather unnerving to learn Agent Thornton felt she needed protection.

After introducing her to his wife, he waved one of his large hands, motioning for her to sit down.

"So what did you want to see me about?" he asked when Jamie took a seat across from their sofa.

"I remembered more details."

"Really?" he asked with interest, sitting down next to his wife again. Leaning forward with his forearms on his thighs, he laced his fingers together. "What?"

Before Jamie could say a word, her dream man walked into the room. Behind him was an equally gorgeous hunk of a man whose hand was linked with that of a pretty and very pregnant woman's.

Focused solely on Agent Thornton and his wife, none of them seemed to notice her. No problem there. It gave Jamie the opportunity to drink in another gander at Mike.

"Any word yet?" Mike asked, still not noticing her.

Agent Thornton shook his head. "No. Nothing yet." He gestured in her direction. "But Jamie was just telling me she's remembered more about what happened."

Mike spun around then, noticing her for the first time and smiled.

Jamie's heart skipped a beat. Thank heavens for the soft lighting because her cheeks flamed with embarrassment. Willing her mind and body to behave, she greeted the couple she learned from Agent Thornton were his son and daughter-in-law. Zach and Cassie. Apparently law enforcement ran in the family because she quickly discovered Zach was also with the FBI.

"We're not staying," Zach explained to his parents. "I need to get Cassie home and get back to work. Let me know if you hear anything."

From the drink containers they doled out to Agent Thornton and his wife, Jamie guessed they'd been down in the hospital cafeteria and returned with caffeine. But it was two in the morning. Was their son really going back to work?

Now that she thought about it, it made sense. The murder of a US Senator, even a lecher like Andrew, would probably have a lot of people in the FBI working overtime to bring the killer to justice.

For several moments while the group engaged in family conversation, Jamie gazed over at Mike. Thankfully, he was listening to his friends and didn't notice her gawking at him. But once the young couple left, Mike's gorgeous blue eyes turned to her.

"So, you remembered something?" he asked, taking a seat nearby.

Jamie nodded. "Yes. As I said before, I'd decided to resign. I walked out to the supply room to get a box for my personal belongings and I heard Andrew having an argument with someone...possibly two people."

Thornton jerked upright, obviously surprised by her news. "Who?" he demanded. "Did you recognize the voices or hear what they were saying? Could you tell if it was a man or a woman?"

Jamie thought a moment before answering. "The voices were deep, but Andrew's was the only one I recognized. I'm sorry, I really didn't pay attention. I just grabbed a box and went back to my office to pack my things."

"That's okay," Mike said calmly. "Did you see anyone?"

"Not then, I didn't. But later, when I was taking my things to my car, the bell over the front door jingled and I saw a man enter the lobby." He'd spotted her too and had given her a friendly wave before heading toward Andrew's office. She'd gone out the back door to her car.

"This man. What did he look like?" Agent Thornton asked.

Jamie shrugged slightly. She knew it was crazy, but he'd reminded her of an actor she liked. She chuckled softly. "He was a little taller, but picture young Robert Redford and that's what he looked like."

Agent Thornton's wife gasped softly and he turned a stern glance at her before continuing with another question. "Can you describe what he was wearing?"

"Well, he was pretty far away. All I can tell you is it was a dark colored suit and light colored shirt." She peered at him curiously. "That doesn't help much, does it?"

To Jamie's surprise, he glanced at Mike and they both smiled.

"Actually, it helps a lot," Mike answered. He thought a moment before continuing. "What time was that?"

Jamie shrugged. "Boy I'm not sure. I lost track of time. But my guess is it was around noon."

"And you're sure this man arrived after you heard Andrew's argument...not before?" Mike pressed.

She didn't have to think about that one. "I'm positive. I heard the arguing when I went to get a box and I saw the man when I was finished packing and taking things to my car. At least a half hour had lapsed by then."

Both men were silent for a moment, but finally Thornton's gaze met hers again. "Do you think you'd recognize this man again if you saw him?"

As an attorney, Jamie prided herself on her memory for details. "Yes."

Again he gazed at her silently for a moment, then reached down and retrieved his cell phone. He played with it a moment and then standing up, brought it over to her.

"Scroll through a few of these photos and tell me if you recognize anyone," he said.

Confused by the odd request, Jamie did as she was told. She flipped through a couple pictures that were clearly family photos and then came to a shot of a good-looking blond man playing softball. Jamie recognized him immediately.

"That's him!" she exclaimed, somewhat surprised to have found him among the agent's photos.

Thornton's only reaction was a nod as he slipped the phone back into its holder at his waist.

Curiosity got the better of her. "Who is he?"

Thornton hedged. "We'll get to that in a minute, Jamie," he said returning to his seat. "Let's get back to what you remembered. What happened after you went to your car?"

Air conditioning pouring through the vents above, raised goosebumps on her arms and shivering, she suddenly wished she had the fleece bathrobe hanging in her bedroom closet at home. Her moment of fleeting wistfulness came to a screeching halt when she was suddenly enveloped in warmth. Her gaze flew around in time to see Mike releasing the jacket he'd placed around her shoulders.

"Thank you," she said, surprised she'd managed a coherent thought with her senses completely surrounded by the warmth and arousing scent of his aftershave.

"Any time. You were going to tell us what happened after you went to your car," he prompted with a knowing smile.

Damn. He knew she was still affected by his mere presence. How embarrassing was that? Somehow she had to make Mike see her as a responsible grown woman, not an immature child with a crush on him. And one thing she knew might achieve that end was to help his investigation every way she could.

Determinedly, her gaze met his. "I put the box and my purse in my trunk and came back inside to deliver my letter of resignation and return my office keys."

He motioned with his hand for her to continue, so she did.

After slipping her letter and the keys under Bob's door, she'd heard a noise coming from Andrew's wing and noticed a light coming from under his private office door. She hadn't really wanted to see him again, but she'd felt she owed it to the firm to tell someone personally that she was resigning.

Another memory surfaced and she scrunched her nose against it. There'd been a gross odor in the hall near his doorway and just as she'd been ready to knock on his door, she'd heard a noise behind her and turned. "That's when something slammed into my head."

"Someone hit you?" Thornton's question came out a perfect blend of concern and excitement and poised on the edge of his seat the way he was, he looked like a large cat ready to pounce.

"Yes." Hard, too, now that she thought about it. No wonder she had a concussion. She reached back to gently touch the wound on the back of her head. "That's the last thing I remember before waking up here at the hospital."

"Think hard, Jamie," Mike prompted. "When you heard the noise and turned, did you see any part of the person who hit you before you blacked out?"

Jamie squinted through the haze of her blurred recollection, but suddenly her eyes widened. "I saw boots."

"Boots? What color? What style? Cowboy, dress, work, hiking?"

Kate chuckled softly and patted her husband's back. "Gary, slow down," she cautioned. "Jamie has a head injury. You're confusing her."

"Sorry," Agent Thornton apologized.

Jamie shot his wife a grateful smile and when her brain finally caught up, she met Thornton's inquiring gaze.

"Like work boots. They were black and now that I think about it, they looked like the kind of boots a soldier or police officer wears."

Again, the two men exchanged a look of surprise. Jamie wasn't sure if what she'd said was good or bad; but it was the way she remembered the boots.

When Mike pressed her for details, she tried desperately to remember something else, but finally had to admit she hadn't seen anything besides her attacker's shoes.

"That's okay," Mike said. "What was Andrew wearing yesterday morning?"

Jamie didn't have to think about that one. She'd gotten a good look at him while he'd been propositioning her and had been surprised by his casual appearance.

"He was wearing khakis, a light blue polo shirt and his shoes were…what do you call them? Uh…boat shoes."

For a moment, the big man sat silently, rubbing the five o'clock shadow on his jaw. Then his eyes narrowed on her suddenly.

"One last question…"

Jamie nodded, ready for whatever he asked, but unnerved by the intensity of the gaze he leveled on her. Nice man, but he'd definitely mastered a stare that could make a nun uneasy.

"…Were you having an affair with Andrew McDougal?"

Jamie stared at him in shock. She'd been so sure she'd convinced both agents she was innocent. And he'd seemed friendly even. But now this! After all she'd told him, how could he still be entertaining the idea she was involved in the murder?

"No!" She didn't even try to mask her anger.

"Fair enough."

His answer was so unapologetic Jamie wanted to clobber him. In fact she caught herself clenching her hand into a fist. But she figured she had enough trouble without adding charges for assaulting a federal agent to the list. Not to mention his body was so solid she'd probably break her hand.

Chapter Nine

Gary stood to stretch his legs and walked over to the window. Could a day get any more bizarre? He hoped not.

When he'd awakened this morning, he'd thought his day would consist of attending a wedding. Never something he looked forward to, but he'd agreed to go because Kate had asked. Even after thirty plus years of marriage, he still had trouble refusing her anything. But then the hospital had called with news that Jimmy had been injured.

So much for a relaxing Saturday. Instead of a wedding and reception, he'd found himself up to his elbows in an investigation involving the murder of a U.S. senator and he'd been going non-stop ever since.

And now that they knew their theory about the killer changing clothes with Jim was correct and that Doug McDougal, wearing his sheriff uniform boots, had most likely been the one to knock Jamie out; they had new leads to check.

Yes, from what they'd just learned from Jamie, Sunday wasn't shaping up to be any less chaotic than Saturday had been.

In spite of that prospect, Gary gave into the smile he'd been fighting to hold back. But it took considerable self-control to keep from laughing aloud.

Jamie Kendrick was adorable, especially when she was fired up. She was younger and much shorter, but she reminded him so much of Katie, it was impossible not to like her. And she was so easy to read it was almost humorous. She'd practically undressed Mike with her eyes when they'd first walked into her room. It didn't take a genius to realize whatever crush she'd had on Devlin as a child hadn't dissipated over time.

And then there was Mikey. In all the years he'd know Dev, Gary had never seen him so tongue tied or distracted over a woman. And his reaction to the job Gary had given him had been hilarious.

Katie was the only person who'd ever dare to call him a matchmaker and live to tell about it. Gary preferred to stay out of his friends' personal lives unless asked for an opinion, but some things were just too obvious to ignore. And yes…he'd had an ulterior motive for assigning Mike to Jamie.

For the past five years, since the ugly incident with his ex-wife, Dev had been drowning himself in work. It didn't take a psychology degree to realize he was trying to avoid the loneliness at home. Oh Dev would never admit it, but Zach had seen it, so had Jimmy. And Gary had definitely noticed it. Today was the first time since the divorce that Gary had seen Devlin actually show blatant interest in a woman. So he'd stepped across his self-imposed boundary and taken it upon himself to give Mike a nudge in the right direction with a legitimate work assignment.

If Devlin was smart like Gary knew him to be, he'd take that nudge and run with it. Because if he didn't, Gary was going to set Katie loose and no one stood a chance against her matchmaking endeavors.

In the meantime, there was a murder investigation ongoing and Gary had had a job to do with Jamie. And he'd done it. He'd intentionally saved the question about an affair for the right moment, lulling Jamie into a false sense of security just so he could get an honest unguarded reaction from her.

He'd gotten it too. In fact, she'd been so ticked off he'd figured it was in his best interest to put some distance between them, to let her cool off. She'd seriously looked like she wanted to slug him. And he actually wouldn't have blamed her if she had.

With his back to her, Gary gazed out into the night and shoved away his amusement, forcing his brain to process everything she'd revealed. One thing he knew for sure…she was no guiltier of murdering Andrew McDougal than he was.

But then he'd been convinced of that before they'd left her room earlier.

During his long career in law enforcement, he'd developed a finely honed ability to tell when someone was lying. Jamie had been completely truthful and open about her recollections.

Gary rubbed his forehead against the beginnings of a headache.

As contaminated as the scene was, solving this crime was going to be no easy task. But he had two prime suspects already in his cross-hairs.

Doug and Ed McDougal. After watching the short video Mike had recorded of the brothers' activities at the crime scene, there was no question in Gary's mind that the brothers had been up to no good. They were involved; if not in the actual murder, definitely in a cover-up and the attempt to frame Jim and Jamie.

Still, to catch the killer, he needed Jamie's cooperation, which meant an explanation was in order.

Behind him he could hear the others talking and he quickly realized Mike was trying to calm Jamie down. Bracing himself for a fight, Gary turned around. Immediately Jamie's gaze flew to him and she shot him a scathing glare. Yes, he definitely had some fences to mend.

Returning to the love seat, he sat down beside Katie again and leaned forward, propping his forearms on his knees while meeting Jamie's guarded eyes.

"Jamie, you asked me earlier who the man in the photo is. He's FBI Special Agent James Barrett…my former partner."

A look of shock washed over her face and even in the dimly lit room Gary recognized the angry flush coloring her cheeks again. Her gaze bounced to Mike and then locked back on him.

"First you accuse me of murdering Andrew, then you ask me if I was having an affair with him and now this!" she fumed, standing up and glaring down at him. "What kind of game are you playing? That man went into Andrew's office; I saw him. For all I know he's the killer and you're trying to frame me to get him off?"

She started toward the door.

Gary understood her feeling of betrayal and her concern for his motives, but he wasn't about to let her walk away. Not now. Not when she could be the key to clearing Jimmy and helping them solve Andrew's murder.

Moving quickly, he caught her by the arm before she could open the door. She turned with daggers flashing in her eyes, but he cut off her protest. "Jamie, I'm a federal agent, sworn to uphold the law. I'm not trying to frame or entrap you. Neither is Mike."

Gary indicated Kate by tilting his head in her direction. "My wife is your witness to everything being said here. So please…hear me out."

She shook off his hand and glared up at him. "Go on. I'm listening," she said, still clearly annoyed, but giving in to apparent curiosity.

"I don't normally lay my cards on the table this early in an investigation, but I'm doing it now because I'm convinced I'm right. Between the forensics we've already gotten back and what you've told us…you've cleared yourself of any suspicion in this case. I'm convinced you're an innocent victim in all this."

Astonishment replaced her glare and her knees seemed to give out because she sank into the chair behind her. Her gaze lifted to his. "You believe me? Really?"

"Yes, I do," Gary answered, sitting down as well.

She glanced at Mike to see if he agreed and he smiled. "So do I," he said quietly. "But, we still need your help."

"Why? I've told you everything I know."

Gary paused to gather his thoughts and rubbed tension from the back of his neck before answering. "Jamie, I've worked closely with Jim Barrett since he joined the FBI five years ago. I know him probably better than anyone. He's a good and honest man. And he's an outstanding agent whose earned commendations for helping the Bureau solve several major cases."

Gary wished he had some solid evidence to back up his next comment, but he didn't. Still, he knew he was right. "We need your help for the simple reason that Jim Barrett didn't murder the senator either."

"How can you be so certain?"

It was a fair question and her voice held no accusation, only curiosity. She barely knew him and didn't know Jim at all. And Gary was asking her to trust his gut. It was a lot to ask of anyone, but he hoped she'd understand.

"When you were found in the senator's office, Jimmy was unconscious a few feet away from you. At this point, I can only assume that the argument you heard was the prelude to Andrew's murder. And my guess is that Jimmy was ambushed when he walked into the senator's office and was already unconscious when they clobbered you or I guarantee you, he would have been putting up a fight that you would have heard."

Gary hauled in a deep breath, releasing it slowly. "Jamie, the reason Mike, Katie and I are here now, is because of Jimmy. He was in surgery for hours this afternoon to repair a collapsed lung and some serious damage to several organs from repeated stab wounds...and he's back in surgery now because of a brain aneurysm that resulted from a head injury caused by someone slamming something into the back of his head."

Horror widened Jamie's eyes. "Oh my God! Who attacked him?"

Gary let his brow lift and he gave a small shrug. "I think common sense says he didn't inflict the injuries on himself. And there is no evidence that would indicate either the senator or you inflicted them on him. And that leads me to believe you and Jimmy are both being framed by someone intent on throwing us off their trail."

Another look of horror twisted her pretty features. "Framed?"

"Yes," Mike answered. "Framed. And Jamie, you need to understand that you are still very much in danger. Whoever committed this crime is extremely dangerous and if they suspect you remember the incident, they're likely to come after you again."

Gary picked up the conversation again. "That's the reason we have a state trooper outside your room. He's there to protect you."

He pulled a business card from his breast pocket and handed it to her, then nodded to Mike to give her one of his cards.

"That's our contact information," Gary reiterated when she had both cards. "If you remember anything else…or if the trooper disappears again…you call one or both of us. I don't care what time it is…call. Okay?"

"Okay." Her answer was punctuated by a yawn.

Gary felt Kate's eyes boring into him without looking over at her.

"Unless you have something else you want to discuss," he said. "I think you should go back to your room and try to get some rest."

"Yes…she should."

Kate's adamant agreement pulled a smile from Gary and he shot a wink at her before turning back to Jamie to see the questioning look in her eyes.

"Katie is a retired trauma surgeon. And trust me…she has exercised great restraint letting us question you this long," he explained, offering Jamie a smile. "And if you don't mind, I suggest you follow her orders before she yells at me."

Jamie laughed aloud and nodded to Kate. "I am tired." Her gaze drifted back to Mike and him. "And I'd hate to get either of you in trouble." As she stood up, she said good night, but at the door she stopped and turned back to them. "I hope Agent Barrett is okay."

Gary nodded appreciatively. "Thanks."

The lingering look Jamie gave Mike after returning his jacket wasn't lost on Gary...or Kate based on her expression. And he watched with amusement as Dev stared after her as she left the room.

A smile tugged at Gary's lips. *Mikey boy, you are in serious trouble where that young lady is concerned.*

Chapter Ten

M ike raked his fingers through the strands of his hair and rubbed the sleep...or rather the lack of it from his eyes. Although Gary and Kate had remained at the hospital waiting to talk to Jim's doctors, Mike had returned home to take a much needed shower. After steaming away the scent of death he swore had been lingering on him from the gory crime scene, he'd fallen into bed with the intention of getting an hour or so of sleep. But he hadn't been able to shut off his mind. He'd tossed and turned until he couldn't stand it any longer and then gotten up.

Cursing, he balled up the clothing Zach had loaned him and tossed them into his hamper.

If it had been the murder investigation keeping him awake, he would have understood. But the problem hadn't been Senator McDougal's murder or even Jim Barrett's injuries. The problem had been Jamie Kendrick. He couldn't seem to stop thinking about her.

When had she morphed from a cute little tomboy into an intelligent, sexy, desirable woman? Her transformation was shocking.

He'd known Jamie practically since the day she was born; he'd watched her grow from infant to toddler to talking child. And he'd never thought of her as anything but a cute kid. His reaction today had been totally inappropriate, not to mention worrisome.

None of the handful of women he'd dated since the divorce had stirred his interest even a fraction of what Jamie had accomplished lying in a hospital bed.

What had he been thinking?

Okay...apparently he hadn't been thinking. But that was the point. His brain had literally short-circuited the moment he'd walked into her room. In the blink of an eye, Mike had mentally transported her from that stark hospital bed to his bedroom, envisioning her sprawled sensuously on his king-sized bed. And things had gone south from there.

Seriously, he must be having some kind of breakdown. Fantasizing about a girl who was practically a kid sister.

If that wasn't bad enough, she was twelve years younger than him.

What could they possibly have in common?

Another image of Jamie in his bed popped to mind, compliments of the evil twin in his brain.

Mike cursed.

God, he needed his head examined.

One thing was certain; he'd better get his mind back in the game before he saw Jamie again. Gary already knew there was a personal connection between them and nothing got past Thorny. Mike had a feeling if he didn't get his act together pretty damn quick, he'd find himself tossed off the investigation team.

No way did Mike want that happening. He owed it to Jimmy to help clear his name. And to be completely honest, now that he'd met Jamie again, he wanted to know more about her.

A vision of her naked, flashed before his eyes.

Mike smacked his forehead, hard, banishing the image from his brain. Muttering an oath, he headed into his bathroom. He needed another shower. A cold one.

His attempt at showering was about as successful as getting some sleep had been. Stark naked and soaking wet, he heard his cell phone ring. He was tempted to let the call go to voice mail, but he didn't. In the middle of a high profile murder investigation he couldn't afford to ignore anything. When he saw Sergeant Trinity Jackson's name displayed, he knew he'd made the right choice.

Checking Jamie's story from the previous night, Mike had requested that state police pop the trunk of her car. Inside they'd found the plants and boxed personal belongings she'd said she'd put in there. As she'd claimed, her purse was also there. And troopers had also found Jamie's resignation letter and keys on the floor inside Bob McDougal's office, which matched her contention that she slid them under his door.

Like Gary, Mike had already cleared Jamie in his own mind, but to make sure they'd covered all bases, they'd needed to double check her account. The state police had provided the confirmation they needed and Mike had no doubt the rest of her story would check out as well.

Dressing had also proved a challenge. First Gary called to tell him Jimmy had come through his surgery well. Doctors had caught the brain aneurysm before it burst or caused any permanent damage and barring complications, they expected him to survive. He was, however, still in a coma and that was worrisome.

Still processing Jim's condition, Mike's phone rang again; this time with a call from the hospital informing him that Jamie would be released at nine.

He glanced at his watch. It was only seven o'clock. That gave him plenty of time to drive over to her apartment building and scope out the security before picking her up at the hospital.

First though, he had to finish getting dressed.

An hour later, after picking up Jamie's purse from the state police, Mike pulled into the parking lot of the two story apartment complex. He stared at the building and shook his head.

Small world. No wonder the address on her license had looked familiar. His niece lived in the same building; directly below Jamie if the apartment number was any indication.

Since the place held only eight apartments, it didn't take him long to check the location of the two exterior doors and determine the security of the building.

It sucked.

The lock on the rear exterior fire door was so old a kindergartener could pick it. And although there was a keypad for residents to use to access the lobby, it was useless. As a test, Mike pressed a random doorbell and he was immediately buzzed into the building without anyone challenging his reason for being there.

Not good. Jamie was a key witness in their case. The Bureau couldn't afford anything else happening to her. Not to mention the idea of her being hurt any further twisted Mike's gut.

Since he knew his niece was in the Caribbean on vacation, he didn't waste time stopping to say *hello*. Instead, he made his way up to the second floor where Jamie lived.

The moment he entered the hallway, the hair on the back of his neck lifted, sending his senses into instant alert.

Jamie's apartment door was ajar.

She was in the hospital; she hadn't opened it. And she hadn't mentioned anything about a roommate when he'd called to ask for permission to enter her apartment.

But maybe the landlord was inside.

"Hello!" he called as he stepped into the door opening. The word died on his lips as anger ignited inside him.

The place had been trashed.

Pulling his gun, Mike cautiously stepped across the threshold, alert for any sign the intruder was still there. Moving quickly, he cleared the apartment.

The perp was gone, but Mike kept his gun ready in case the person returned. And seething with anger over the damage and the violation of Jamie's security, he walked through the apartment again studying the carnage and forcing his brain to process it from an investigative view.

Living room furniture had been upended with cushions slashed open and stuffing strewn everywhere. Her desk drawers had been tossed to the floor scattering papers across the carpet.

But her stereo, television and computer, while all ruined, were still there. Definitely not the work of an intruder looking for cash or something that could easily be hocked for drug money.

No. This was personal.

The place was a disaster.

Broken dishes and glasses littered the kitchen floor. And her bedroom hadn't been spared either, with the content of her closet tossed onto the floor.

As Mike turned to leave the bedroom, his gaze landed on Jamie's dresser and his heart dropped to his stomach.

Talk and you die, bitch!

The ominous message had been scrawled in lipstick on her mirror.

Yes, this was definitely personal.

In his nineteen years with the Bureau, Mike had seen just about every kind of evil mankind could commit, but this one unnerved him. It didn't take a genius to figure out the killer had left that message. The killer or someone connected to him, he amended mentally as he remembered the suspicious actions of Ed and Doug McDougal at the murder scene.

Hauling in a calming breath, Mike glanced around again.

If this had been just a routine break-in, he'd call the local authorities. But with that threatening message, he was positive this crime scene was related to the senator's murder. And he wanted the Bureau's crime unit on it.

A quick call summoned the help he needed and while Mike waited for the CSI's, he used his cell phone camera to snap a series of photos in each room, capturing a record of the damage and the message.

Sliding his phone back into its holder, he remembered his phone call with Jamie earlier that morning. Everything she'd been wearing or that had been found at the crime scene yesterday had been confiscated as evidence. She'd asked him to bring her something to wear home.

A quick search turned up a small overnight bag on a shelf of a guest room closet and as he returned to her bedroom, he mentally made of list of what she'd need.

Shoes.

He spotted a pair of flat navy pumps on the floor of her closet and tossed them into the bottom of the luggage.

Pants.

Something with legs in the heap of clothing on the floor caught his eye and he snatched it up. Navy, like the shoes. Nice. Oh, and they were the kind that had been chopped off right below the knees. He'd get a gander at her legs.

Focus, Devlin…focus!

Disgusted with himself, he folded the pants and set them on top of the shoes.

Top.

What would she wear with navy pants? He stared at the clothing hoping for some divine inspiration. Nothing leaped out of the pile at him, but he spotted a silky blouse with softly flowing long sleeves and lifted it out of the heap.

Oooh. V-neck. Sexy. And green like her beautiful eyes.

Mike shook his head in disgust again.

No. It did not remind him of her eyes or anything else and where the hell had the sexy thought come from. He'd picked it because green went with blue; that was it. Period.

Concentrate. What else did she need?

He shot a glance around the messy room, his gaze landing on the bureau.

Oh, damn!

Underwear.

Dreading what he was going to find, he yanked open one of the top drawers and breathed a sigh of relief.

Phew. Panty hose. Okay...this wasn't so bad. He could do this. Reaching in, he snared the top pair and tossed it into the bag.

With a deep breath to steady his resolve, he pulled open the next drawer and stared gape-mouthed at a pile of lingerie in every color imaginable.

Great. Just great!

His mind was already on a mental vacation, torturing him with thoughts of Jamie pulling on those nylons. Now he'd never be able to look at her again without imagining her wearing all this sexy stuff.

Cursing his luck and his wayward thoughts, Mike grabbed a matching bra and panties and tossing them into the bag, he slammed the lid shut. He wasn't even going to think about why his choice had been something black and lacy instead of the staid white nylon set he'd seen.

Man it was hot.

If he wasn't pressed for time, he'd be tempted to use her bathroom to take another shower...another cold one. But with his luck, he'd be butt naked when the CSI team arrived.

He hauled in another deep breath, grabbed a few toiletries from her bathroom and then took another look around.

Nothing left for him to do here. Better to get the heck out of the apartment and wait for the investigation unit in the hallway.

As he walked back into the living room and his gaze took in the total destruction strewn around him, a truth crystallized in his brain.

No way could he let Jamie return to this place. Not with the killer on her trail. If the perp had done this to her belongings, Mike could imagine what he'd do to her. And the building wasn't secure. Even with guards watching her 24-7, Jamie would be completely vulnerable here.

"Pick her up at the hospital. Stick to her like fly paper," Gary had said.

Man, he was going to kill Thorny when he saw him. He didn't care if the man was a friend...not to mention, his boss.

Mike heaved a deep sigh. No…he wasn't going to kill anyone, especially not Gary. He might be having trouble controlling his mind, but he hadn't lost it. Thorny was right. If they had any hope of keeping her alive, Mike had to stick to her like fly paper. And the only logical thing for him to do was to bring Jamie home with him.

His property provided the perfect place to hide her until the killer was behind bars. The farm was off the beaten path; his address wasn't published anywhere and the home had the best security system on the market.

There was only one problem. A big one.

This crazy obsession he had going for her.

What kind of sick dog did that make him? She was way too young for him.

Yes, that's right. Jamie…was…too…young.

Well, thank God he had enough working brain cells to remember that detail. While he was remembering, he'd better remember something else too. Never in his life had he gotten involved with someone connected to one of his cases. Right. And he had no intention of stepping across that forbidden line now. So no matter how badly he wanted her, he'd just have to suck it up and resist.

He was responsible for keeping her safe.

The problem was, having her around constantly would be shear torture. The temptation excruciating. Would he even survive?

Don't bet on it, buddy!

Cursing the taunting voice in his head, Mike stepped into the hallway. As he closed Jamie's door, another door opened behind him.

Reaching for his weapon, Mike spun around expecting to confront the intruder, but instead he locked gazes with a sixty-something blonde with massive rolls of cellulite dangerously testing

107

the seams of her spandex pants. Her owlish eyes peered at him with a look of pure suspicion.

"Who are you?" she demanded, planting her hands on hips that nearly spanned her doorway.

Releasing his grip on the butt of his weapon, Mike pulled out his identification and flipped the case open. "Special Agent Michael Devlin, FBI, ma'am. Do you know Jamie Kendrick?"

"Of course I do," she declared. "But she hasn't been home since yesterday morning. And after hearing the terrible news about our senator and knowing she was working yesterday, I've been worried sick about her. Especially after all the commotion over in her apartment last night. It's a mess in there."

Hope soared in Mike. Maybe this woman had seen the perp.

The woman continued to assess him suspiciously. "You're really an FBI agent?"

"Yes, ma'am," he replied, tucking his credentials back into his pocket. "And you are?"

"Claudia Parker."

He nodded acknowledgement. "Ms. Parker, did you by any chance see who broke into her apartment?"

Her expression grew indignant. "I certainly did. The ruckus over there woke me up and while I was peeking through my door viewer to see what was happening, I saw a man bolt out her doorway and run down the hall to the stairs."

She motioned toward Jamie's door. "He left that hanging wide open, so I walked over to close it. That's when I saw the destruction." She turned a shrewd gaze up at him. "From those police shows on television, I know not to disturb a crime scene, so I didn't go inside. And frankly I was afraid to go in, but I pulled her door shut to keep him from going back inside. I think he must have broken the lock, though, because it won't stay closed."

Mike glanced back at Jamie's door. He'd noticed the broken lock as soon as he'd gotten close to the door. The jamb had been shattered and the door itself was damaged beyond repair.

Someone…and Mike's money was on their killer…had been determined to get inside that apartment.

His mind instantly returned to investigative mode. "You said, *he*. It was definitely a man you saw?"

"Yes."

"Do you remember what time you were awakened?"

"It was around one a.m., but the intruder was over there for a long time. At least a half hour…maybe more. I called the police to report the break-in, but no one responded. In fact, you're the first law enforcement to show up."

"You called police while the intruder was still inside?"

"Yes!"

Mike understood that Doug McDougal was dealing with the death of his father, but the entire sheriff's department shouldn't shut down because the sheriff was on bereavement leave. Still he was glad the locals hadn't shown up, because it gave Bureau CSI's a chance to process the scene.

"This man you saw…can you describe him for me?"

"He was Caucasian, probably in his mid-to late-twenties." Claudia appeared to size him up; mentally comparing him to the man she'd seen. "He wasn't quite as tall as you, probably about six foot, but he was solidly built like you. Athletic looking…about one eighty to one ninety. His hair was brown and looked short, but I can't swear to the length because his head was covered. He had a cleft chin and blue eyes, though. I saw his face real clearly when he was under the lights in the hallway."

Mike mentally filed away details of the guy's physical description. The fact he was very similar in size to Jim Barrett supported their theory the killer had changed clothes with Jim. "What was the guy wearing?"

"Jeans, a tee shirt and a black hooded sweatshirt." She thought a moment. "Oh…and he had white sneakers on his feet."

Mike locked on the mention of the hoodie and his mind whirled back to the logo on the sweatshirt found at the murder scene. "Did the sweatshirt have any kind of distinguishing marks or designs on it?"

Claudia thought a moment. "Now that you mention it, there was. It looked kind of like a skull and cross bones."

The last comment hit Mike like a two by four and he could feel his blood pressure soar. To an untrained eye and from a distance, the Ranger logo could easily be confused with a skull and cross bones.

He grabbed his cell phone and within seconds brought up the photo he'd taken of the Ranger logo on the hoodie at the murder scene. "Did it look anything like this?"

Claudia's eyes widened in surprise. "Yes...it did."

That was way too much of a coincidence for Mike's liking. Between the logo and the message on Jamie's mirror, any question his mind had harbored, vanished.

Jamie's intruder was Andrew's murderer.

Questions bombarded Mike's mind and the first one was too much to hope, but he had to ask anyway. "Do you have any idea who he was?"

She shook her head. "No, I've never seen him before."

"Do you think you'd recognize him again, if you saw him?"

Claudia straightened as if he'd insulted her. "Of course I would. I can even tell you what he was driving."

Apparently Mike looked surprised, because she gave him a satisfied smile before proving her point. "I can see the parking lot from my living room and I saw him get into an SUV. A new model Subaru. I know it's new because it looks just like the one my husband bought last month. Ours is the silver one out in the parking lot. His was dark; under the lights it looked black or gray, but I'm not positive about that. But his license plate was from Maryland...one of those red, white and blue commemorative ones."

Jimmy's car. The killer was still driving Jim's car. No doubt about it. Barrett had just bought a charcoal gray colored Forester two months ago and his license was a Fort McHenry commemorative plate.

For a moment, Mike merely stared at her speechlessly. Nosy neighbors could be a pain in the neck, but this woman was a gold mine of information. She'd not only given them a description of their murderer, she'd confirmed he had Jim's car.

He felt like kissing her.

While he was still trying to find his tongue, she gazed up at him curiously. "Why is the FBI interested in an apartment break-in, though?"

He cracked a smile at that one. The woman had spunk; he'd give her that. But how much should he tell her?

Fortunately, the Bureau had been able to extract Jim and Jamie from the senator's office before the press became aware of the murder. And although the presence of two other victims had been leaked to the press late the previous evening, the person making the disclosure had either not known their names or had chosen not to disclose them. So Jim and Jamie's identities were not yet public knowledge.

That detail reinforced Mike's belief the intruder had been the killer or someone helping him. No one else would know about Jamie in connection to McDougal's murder.

Mike settled for a glossed over version of the truth, figuring the Parker woman would have no reason to doubt him.

"I'm not here on official business, Ms. Parker. Jamie and I have known each other since we were kids. She was in an accident yesterday and sustained a concussion."

Claudia clutched her heart in a show of concern. "The poor child! Is she okay?"

Mike nodded. "She's going to be fine. But doctors kept her overnight as a safety precaution. She's being released this morning. I just came by to get her a change of clothing before going to pick her up."

"Well, you tell Jamie if she needs anything, I'm just across the hall and to give me a holler," she replied.

Another smile tugged at Mike's mouth. "I will. But Jamie and I need your help. The guy that trashed her apartment is dangerous and needs to be caught. I'd like to have a police artist meet with you to come up with a sketch of the man you saw. Are you willing to do that?"

The woman straightened proudly again. "Certainly. I don't want him on the streets doing that to anyone else."

Mike nodded his appreciation. If she only knew what the guy was capable of doing, she'd be horrified. He didn't want to scare her, but he also wanted her to be cautious.

"You've been a tremendous help, Ms. Parker. But if he returns, don't confront him. Anyone who can do what he did to Jamie's apartment is dangerous." Mike pulled a business card from his pocket and handed it to her. "Just call me. And do the same if you think of anything else that might help us find him."

Claudia nodded, slipping the card into the bosom of her knit top as she shuffled back into her apartment. But as her door closed, Mike heard footsteps in the stairwell. On instant alert again, he spun around with his hand on the butt of his weapon. Relief flooded through him when he spotted two Bureau crime techs.

That was quick! But then again, they'd only been a couple blocks away at the senator's office.

After showing the techs inside the apartment, Mike shot a quick glance at his watch. Time to get to the hospital. He might not be looking forward to Jamie living at the farm, but he didn't want her at the hospital any longer than necessary. The state troopers guarding her had better things to do...like helping with the investigation of the senator's murder. And in truth, there was too much activity at the hospital to ensure complete security. It would be too easy for the killer to get to her in that environment.

With instructions for the techs to call him with any questions, Mike headed back to his car.

Elizabeth A. Wilson

Chapter Eleven

Fifteen minutes later, Mike strode down the hall toward Jamie's hospital room. As he neared, he heard the delightful sound of her laughter and felt a ripple of longing trip through him.

Get over it, Devlin. She's involved in your case. She's off-limits.

His brain back on track, Mike rounded the corner of her doorway and froze.

Jamie wasn't alone.

A thirty-something male with the tall lean body of a runner and the kind of blond haired good-looks women loved, was sitting beside Jamie's bed, holding her hand and gazing at her adoringly while they shared a laugh.

Mike wanted to plant his fist in the guy's face.

How dare he flirt with her! She was recovering from a head injury. She'd be susceptible to the smooth talking jerk.

Mike shook away the thought.

What was wrong with him? He'd never been the jealous sort, not even when he'd learned Abby had been cheating on him. Anger, yes; jealousy, no. Besides, Jamie was too young for him. He'd already reconciled himself to that fact…except he seemed to keep forgetting it. But she'd never be interested in someone forty-five when she could have the young stud hanging on her every word.

But if that guy didn't let go of her hand in ten seconds, he was going to need dentures.

Suddenly, both of them turned toward the doorway.

"Mike! You're here!" Jamie actually sounded pleased to see him and her smile glittered in her beautiful green eyes.

Mike felt a smile curve his lips and tried not to think about why.

"Come in," she said waving him inside. "Curt, this is the friend I was telling you about."

"Mike, this is Curt Rossi. Curt and I worked together; he's an attorney. And Curt, this is Mike Devlin."

The stud stood up, extending a hand toward him.

Mike swallowed the urge to deck him, forcing himself to shake hands politely instead.

"Jamie tells me you're with the FBI." Curt chuckled slightly. "I don't know what I was expecting but you don't fit my image of a Fed."

Mike eyed the man silently. *Mr. Faded Jeans and Polo Shirt* didn't look much like a lawyer either. With that blond shock of hair and golden tan, he looked more like a surfer.

More than anything Mike wanted to hurl the insult back at the moron, but he managed to swallow the urge. Instead, he ignored the comment and turned to Jamie with a smile.

"How are you feeling?"

Another smile lit her face. "Better. Sleep helped."

"Well, I've got to run," Curt interrupted. He turned a grin at Mike. "I've got a meeting with one of your colleagues this morning. A Special Agent Shaw."

Mike eyed *Surfer Boy* for a heartbeat.

Hmm. Lucas knew about a hundred ways to kill a man without leaving a mark on him. One phone call; that's all it would take.

Mike smacked himself mentally.

Where had that thought come from? What was wrong with him? It was like some kind of green-eyed monster had taken over his brain.

115

Man he was so screwed up over Jamie he didn't recognize himself.

He cleared his throat, forcing himself to be professional. "Just tell Agent Shaw the truth and you'll be fine."

Curt gave him a friendly smile. "Thanks."

Rossi turned back to Jamie and the smile broadened. "I'm glad you're on the mend, Red. I'd hate for anything to happen to you." Leaning down, he pressed a kiss on her forehead. "Take it easy and I'll see you soon."

Mike glared at him.

A kiss. The man had kissed her. Curt Rossi was a dead man.

Okay, maybe that was overreacting a bit. Well, maybe a lot. The kiss had just brushed her skin. Kind of brotherly like.

"You hurt her and you answer to me," Rossi muttered as he breezed past him.

It took a heartbeat for the comment to register and by the time Mike turned to confront the threat, the guy was gone.

JAMIE DIDN'T WANT to examine too closely the rush of pleasure she'd gotten when she'd spotted Mike in the doorway of her hospital room. A rush that had magnified ten-fold as Curt walked out the door and she realized she was alone with Mike.

He was so handsome; he took her breath away.

But what had all that male testosterone chest thumping been about?

She and Curt were just friends and work colleagues. They'd started at McDougal and Associates at the same time and had known each other for three years. But he wasn't interested in her romantically.

He was gay. And in all the time she'd known him, he'd never kissed her before.

Why now?

It was almost like he'd done it to make Mike jealous. But that was ridiculous. Mike would never be interested in her. To him, she'd always be that gap-toothed little girl he'd asked her about yesterday.

Then again, why had Mike acted so strange when he'd first walked into her room? He'd looked absolutely murderous, glaring at Curt. For a moment, she'd thought Mike was going to deck him.

What had that been about?

A memory crystallized in her mind. Her hand. Curt had been holding her hand when she'd first noticed Mike in the doorway. Had he seen that? Is that why he'd looked so angry?

If so, why?

Jamie blew out a breath of frustration and mentally shook her head.

Men!

"I hope the outfit I put together is okay."

Jamie's wandering thoughts fled at the sound of Mike's voice and she met his gaze just as he set an overnight bag on the foot of her bed. When he'd called earlier and asked permission to go into her apartment to check the security, she'd asked him to bring her some clothing. Jamie supposed she should be embarrassed that he'd gone through her things to pick an outfit for her, but in truth she was eager to see what he'd selected.

"I'm sure it will be fine. I'm just glad I don't have to wear this thing home," she said pointing at the shapeless hospital gown.

His chuckle sent a wave of heat through her body.

"You ready to get out of here?" he asked.

Jamie grinned back at him. "Definitely."

Mike nodded amiably. "I'll wait in the hall then; give you a chance to get dressed."

"You don't have to leave. I'm going to take a quick shower since I have clean clothing now. I can dress in the bathroom."

With stitches in the back of her head, she wasn't able to wash her hair very well, but the shower felt divine. Eager to get home, Jamie toweled off quickly and flicked open the suitcase.

A smile curved her lips as she gazed down at a pair of navy Capri's and a light emerald green v-necked blouse.

Jamie lifted up the garments, unwilling to examine too closely the pleasure that washed through her, knowing Mike had chosen them. She didn't know how he'd done it, but he'd managed to select two of her favorite pieces of clothing.

Still holding the outfit, her gaze dropped back to the suitcase and a scrap of black lace caught her eye.

Jamie's breath caught in her chest.

Dear lord. Had Mike really chosen that?

In disbelief she lifted the bra and panties and stared at them. Of all her underwear, he picked this? They were the sexiest thing she owned; the sexiest thing she'd ever owned. She'd bought them on a whim and afterwards had stuffed them in the back of her drawer, embarrassed that she'd even considered wearing them.

After all...she didn't have anyone to try to impress.

Her gaze lifted to the bathroom door, her thoughts turning to the man on the other side of it. Had Mike just picked the first thing he'd found? Or had he actually envisioned her wearing the little black scraps of nothing?

Heat filled Jamie's cheeks at the latter thought. Still, she couldn't stop another smile from creeping onto her face.

For so long, she'd held Mike up on a pedestal. Her childish crush, an unrequited love of a much older man. Somehow, though, their age difference didn't matter as much anymore.

Well...okay...it had never mattered to her, even when she was three. But at least now she was smart enough to know anything between them back then would have been criminal.

Now, though...they were both of consenting age. And the thought Mike might harbor even an inkling of desire for her filled her with such happiness, Jamie could barely contain it.

She glanced down at the suitcase again and found a hair brush and small make-up kit he'd thoughtfully packed for her.

A woman could learn to love a man like Mike.

Jamie chuckled silently. Who was she trying to fool? She'd never stopped loving him. And if there was even a chance for them; she wasn't going to pass it up this time.

Maybe she should just walk out there in the little scraps of lace he'd chosen. She'd give anything to see his reaction.

Chuckling at her wicked thoughts, she pulled on her clothing...all of them...and after running the brush through her hair and dabbing on a little make-up, she gave herself a once over in the mirror.

Not bad for a woman with a concussion, if she did say so herself.

Grinning like a fool, Jamie practically floated out the bathroom door.

The approving glance Mike shot her way slammed into her like a bolt of lightning, sending tingles coursing through her entire body. He didn't say anything, just gazed at her silently with...what?

Before Jamie could identify the look, he blinked and it was gone. But for just an instant she'd thought she'd seen hunger in his eyes. And not the kind of hunger reserved for food. No...what she'd seen had looked like pure male lust. And it had been directed right at her.

She gave a mental shrug. Probably just wishful thinking on her part.

"Your chariot awaits, ma'am," Mike quipped, pointing at a wheelchair that had apparently been delivered to her room while she'd been in the bathroom.

With a grin, she took Mike's hand and let him help her onto the seat.

"I can't wait to get home and sleep in my own bed," Jamie uttered as he wheeled her toward the elevators.

When Mike didn't respond, she turned a look over her shoulder and saw a strange expression on his face. He looked worried about something.

"Is everything okay?" she asked.

"Let's wait until we're in the car. We can talk there."

His cryptic answer did nothing to reassure her, but she took the hint and remained quiet until they were on the road. Then she turned to him.

"Can we talk now?"

The smile he'd given her when they'd pulled out of the hospital parking lot dissolved. And from the worry lines creasing his brow, she figured he had something serious on his mind. Considering the events of yesterday, it was probably something she didn't want to know, but since she had an insatiable sense of curiosity, she asked anyway.

"Is something wrong?"

Mike sighed deeply. "Someone broke into your apartment and they trashed the place."

Jamie gasped. "Trashed? You mean they broke things?"

She was hoping she'd misunderstood, but that hope shattered when he nodded.

"I'm sure your insurance will cover most of it, but the apartment is a mess and a lot of your things were destroyed."

"Oh my God. Who would do something like that?"

By the set of his shoulders, Jamie could tell he was worried. His next comment explained why. "My gut tells me it's the same person who killed Andrew."

Horror twisted Jamie's stomach into a knot. "Why? What makes you say that?"

"Because the person left a threatening message on your mirror."

Jamie could feel her eyes practically bug out of her head. "A threat? What did it say?"

Mike shot a thoughtful gaze at her. "Are you sure you want to know?"

The question gave her pause...but only for a second. She'd never been one to run from adversity. "Yes."

Those broad shoulders of Mike's lifted in a shrug. "It said, *'Talk and you die, bitch!'*"

Jamie was glad she was sitting down because the space around her started to spin and to her annoyance, tears sprang to her eyes. Had to be the concussion because she wasn't one to cry at any little thing. Of course, a death threat wasn't something easily ignored...but she had no frame of reference for how to process it. It wasn't like she'd ever received one before.

Mike glanced over at her and as they drifted to a stop at a traffic light, he draped an arm around her shoulders and pulled her into the shelter of his side. "Try not to worry. I won't let anyone hurt you."

For an instant her brain overheated at the contact of his body. Jamie gave herself a mental shake.

It was just a friendly hug, girl. Get over it.

Taking her advice, she turned her gaze up to his. "What am I going to do, Mike? What if he comes back?"

He gave her a gentle squeeze. "You're not going back there. At least not to stay."

Apparently confusion radiated from her face, because he quickly explained. "We'll go back long enough for you to pack more of your things and then you're coming home with me. You can stay as long as it takes for us to catch Andrew's killer."

Okay, first her head was spinning and now she was hallucinating. That's all there was too it. Because there was no way her dream man had just invited her to live with him indefinitely.

Had he?

"Are you serious?"

Mike shifted the car into drive again before glancing her way. "I've never been more serious about anything, Jamie. When you see your apartment, you'll agree. It's not safe for you to be there, especially not by yourself."

"But why would he threaten me? I don't know who he is."

Mike shook his head. "I don't know. Anyone who would do what he's done isn't thinking rationally to begin with. But my guess is he thinks you can identify him."

Jamie wracked her brain trying to remember anything other than the boots she'd seen. Nothing. She'd seen nothing except those damn boots. So why was the killer after her?

She heaved a frustrated breath.

The blast of fresh oxygen revitalized her brain and gave life to another memory. An unexpected one.

"Oh my God!" She'd been so sure the only thing she'd seen before face planting on the carpet had been a pair of boots. But unless her memory was playing tricks on her, she'd seen a lot more.

Startled by her reaction, Mike slammed on the brakes and pulled to the curb. "What's wrong? Are you okay?"

For a moment, she was too stunned by her revelation to answer. But his look of concern finally broke through her horror.

"I saw them!" She grasped Mike's arm and looked at him imploringly. "I did. I saw them. I didn't remember it until just now. But right before something hit me in the head, I caught a glimpse of Ed McDougal in his father's office and there was another man...a young man with him. The guy was covered in blood."

Mike stared at her speechlessly for a moment. "You're sure?"

Jamie nodded mutely.

"What did this fellow look like?"

Now that she's snared the memory, it was clear in her mind.

"He was about the same height and build as the mayor...about six feet, one eighty...and he had short brown hair. His eyes were light colored and he had a dimple in his chin. If he hadn't been holding a huge knife in his left hand, I'd say he was good-looking."

Mike's eye widened as if she'd totally blown him away. "His left hand? Are you sure?"

She'd never been more certain of anything in her life. The knife had scared the heck out of her. Even now the memory of the blood dripping from the blade sent a shudder rippling along her spine. Her eyes had locked on that deadly looking blade and she hadn't seen anything else until the boots had appeared in her peripheral vision.

She nodded.

Again, Mike merely stared at her for several heartbeats before a smile curved his lips. A smile. They were talking about a murder and he smiled. What was that all about?

"Unbelievable," Mike muttered, reaching for his cell phone.

A moment later, Jamie heard Agent Thornton's bass voice filter through the speaker.

"Thorny, you're not going to believe this," Mike said with barely concealed excitement in his voice. "Jamie has recalled more details about yesterday and she got a glimpse of our killer."

"Hot damn!"

The response surprised a smile from Jamie, but Mike pushing the phone in her direction, erased her amusement.

"Tell Gary what you just told me," Mike encouraged.

So she did.

"What was the man wearing?" Gary asked her as soon as she finished repeating what she'd seen.

Jamie summoned the memory again. "Faded jeans, a tee shirt and a red hoodie. His tee shirt and pants were spattered with blood."

Mike took the phone from her before Gary said anything. "There's more Thorny," he said. "Jamie's apartment was trashed overnight and one of her neighbors saw the intruder. Her description of the guy is almost identical to what Jamie just gave us. And the intruder left Jamie a threatening message on her mirror, telling her to keep her mouth shut or die."

Silence reigned for a moment and Jamie imagined the big man on the other end processing what he'd been told.

"I'm taking Jamie back to her apartment just long enough to let her get some things and then I'm taking her out to my farm," Mike added breaking the silence.

"Good," Thornton replied. "And I'm sure I don't have to tell you, but make sure you're not followed." Another moment of silence. "Mike, contact the state police and see if they can get someone out to your place. I know you've got good security there, but we've got interviews today and I don't want Jamie left alone. Tell Sergeant Jackson, if there's any problem, to contact me…and to send any overtime bill to me."

"Will do."

For a moment the two men discussed business, solidifying where and when they were meeting for their interviews and then the call ended.

Mike's gaze lifted to hers and his smile melted Jamie's heart.

"You just gave us a huge break in our case. Thank you!"

Jamie knew she should be pleased and she was. But she still had no clue how she'd ended up nearly naked in Andrew's office.

Another shiver tripped up her spine at the thought of some stranger stripping her clothing off. And the mere idea did nothing to ease her concern.

Chapter Twelve

Mike swore he could feel Jamie's presence in his kitchen. It was crazy. When he'd checked on her a half hour ago, she was sleeping like a baby in one of his upstairs guest rooms. So it had to be some kind of trick his mind was playing on him.

His mind had been doing that a lot in the last hour or so. The second he'd heard her turn on the shower back at the hospital, his mind had taken a mental vacation, envisioning her naked with water sluicing over her body. And just when he'd managed to banish those images, he'd remembered that damn black underwear he'd tossed into her suitcase.

He still couldn't erase thoughts of her wearing that stuff or of him tearing it off her just before...

Mike gave his head a violent shake.

Not funny, Devlin. Get a grip!

Jamie had been here for less than an hour and already he was strung tighter than a tennis racket. The woman did strange things to him without doing anything. Just her mere presence tormented him.

How he was going to get any sleep with her right across the hall from him was anyone's guess. And they'd be sharing a bathroom too.

Man, this was not a good idea at all.

He shook away the thought. Yes it was. It was a necessity and he was just going to have to handle having her in his home, because the psycho who'd trashed her apartment was clearly a threat to her safety. And even if she wasn't a key witness in their case, he didn't want anything else to happen to Jamie.

Crazy as it was, he thought of her as *'his'*. He'd realized it the moment he'd seen Rossi holding her hand and jealousy had swamped his body.

Whether it was their shared past or some weird possessive streak he never knew he had…or maybe just his screwed up head; Mike didn't know. But no way was anyone else going to hurt her; not on his watch.

Movement outside caught his attention and he glanced out to see a state police cruiser pull in front of the house.

Mike walked outside to meet the trooper who stepped from the squad car.

Bill O'Brien. Mike recognized him immediately.

Bill had been a year ahead of him in high school, but Mike had quarterbacked the school football team for three of the years Bill had been a star running back. They'd gone their separate ways after high school, but reconnected for a time during Mike's short stint with the state police before joining the Bureau.

Last Mike had heard, Bill and his wife had moved to Maryland's Eastern Shore, but apparently they were back in Jacob's Valley.

Mike greeted him with a handshake. "Hey, Bill. How have you been?"

"Good," Bill chuckled. "Can't wait to retire though. Cindy retired last spring and she's been after me to do the same thing so we can travel. But I've still got two more years before I can claim full benefits."

Bill glanced around before meeting Mike's gaze again. "So, you've got a witness out here that needs a protection detail, I hear."

Mike breathed a sigh of relief Bill hadn't asked about Abby. The last thing he wanted to do was discuss his ex-wife and their failed marriage.

"Yes...come on inside and I'll tell you all about her," Mike offered, leading the way to the front door.

"This is a great old home," O'Brien exclaimed as he stepped inside.

"Thanks."

"When I was a kid, my best friend's grandparents lived in one exactly like it about two miles from here," O'Brien said. "I seem to remember hearing that both homes were built by identical twins or something like that. But we used to love coming out here to play at his grandparent's home because of all the great places to explore. It was like a constant adventure."

Mike had researched the history of his home before he bought it and O'Brien was right. Jacob's Valley had originally been part of a 1600s land grant deeded by Lord Baltimore to Jacob Rush. Years later, long after Jacob's death, his identical twin grandsons Thomas and David parceled off thousands of the original acreage for the formation of the little valley town that came to bear Jacob's name. But the grandsons each kept healthy parcels for themselves and built matching homes on their property.

The history of the home had attracted Mike to the property almost as much as its location and character.

"If you want a tour, I'll give you one, but if you were familiar with the other home, I'm guessing you know your way around," Mike answered.

"I'm good," Bill replied. "So tell me about your witness."

For several minutes Mike brought him up to speed on the senator's murder, Jamie's involvement in the case and the subsequent break-in and threat left at her apartment.

Mike glanced at his watch. As much as he'd like to stay and shoot the breeze, he needed to get moving.

"Jamie is upstairs sleeping." he said, motioning toward the living room with a wave of his hand. "So make yourself at home. Help yourself to any food in the kitchen if you get hungry and if you need anything and can't find it or have any trouble, call me."

"Will do," O'Brien replied with a nod.

Satisfied Jamie was in good hands, Mike headed out the door to meet Gary for their interview with Doug McDougal and to see if Zach and Lucas had learned anything from the surveillance video state police had collected for them.

FROM WHAT HE'D learned of the sheriff's attitude at the crime scene and what he'd witnessed last evening, Gary expected the interview to be difficult. The last thing he'd wanted was to give the man an edge by being late. But the delay had been unavoidable.

His meeting with Director Everett had been interesting to say the least. Apparently word had gotten back to Everett about the problems Chuck Clark had been causing at the Baltimore office. Everett had taken swift action and given Clark a choice. Resign or be demoted back to Special Agent and re-assigned to the Vancouver field office. Clark had accepted the demotion and was already on his way to Washington State.

That was fine with Gary. One less headache to worry about.

And it wasn't like Doug would have been kept waiting for him. Mike had probably taken the interview. Or maybe one of the other guys. But he'd been looking forward to questioning Doug…especially after the incident last evening.

A half hour late as he pulled into the parking lot at the state police barracks, Gary hurried inside.

"Catch your breath, Thorny," Mike said by way of greeting. "Doug is a no-show."

Gary glanced at Sergeant Jackson, who had arranged the interview. "What happened?"

"We don't know," Zach answered for her. "He just didn't show up. No call, no nothing."

"We were hoping you knew where he was," Lucas added.

Anger seethed inside Gary. "No."

It was bad enough the McDougal brothers had been caught red-handed at the murder scene tampering with evidence, but then

Ed had danced around giving any straight answers during his interview yesterday, Kyle McDougal had been a no-show at his interview and Doug had tried to bully his way into the crime scene again last evening.

And then there was the senator's widow, whose doctor had deemed to be too distraught to talk to anyone. She'd looked perfectly fine to Gary when he'd watched her on a national news channel last evening and again this morning, blasting the FBI's involvement in the case.

In thirty years in law enforcement, Gary had never seen anything like it. It was as if the family didn't give a damn that the senator had been murdered.

The investigation was barely twenty-four hours old and already he was sick of the entire McDougal clan. And dammit, he didn't care if they did own the town; no one was going to impede his investigation, especially not Sheriff Douglas McDougal.

Gary leveled his gaze on Sergeant Jackson. "Find him. I don't care what it takes. And unless he's got a damn good reason for blowing off this interview, I want his ass hauled in here in cuffs. If you need a reason…it's obstruction of a federal investigation."

The young sergeant and her troopers had been an enormous help at the crime scene and in gathering evidence. Zach and Mike had both commented how efficient and cooperative she'd been. But now she was merely staring at him questioningly.

Gary wasn't sure if it was his size or the fact he was furious, but she seemed a bit uncertain if she should leave. So he helped her along. "Let us know as soon as you learn anything."

Jackson seemed to snap to attention and gave him a curt nod. "Yes, sir."

As she left the conference room, Gary turned back to Lucas. "Please tell me we've got something useful on film."

Zach and Lucas glanced at each other and smiled.

"Oh yeah," Lucas replied. "Have a seat. We've already got things cued up for you to see."

SITTING ON THE edge of his seat, Mike propped his elbows on the conference room table and watched as the first images from the surveillance cameras displayed on a large flat screen television mounted on the wall ahead of them.

"First off, the law firm's cameras haven't worked for months," Lucas explained. "So we don't have anything from there."

Mike chuckled silently. Of course not. That would have made their job too easy and Old Murphy and his Law always seemed to make sure that didn't happen.

"The first video clip is from a doctor's office across the street from the rear of the law firm," Lucas continued, warning them before starting it that it wasn't a lot of help to their investigation.

Still, Mike watched the short clip intently for any clue.

When the clip ended, Mike heaved a frustrated sigh. Lucas had been right. The video hadn't been the smoking gun they needed. But it did afford a few details that helped and one that raised a question.

The video provided a distant view of the law office parking lot, but they were able to see the stolen black Honda pull into the lot, joining a silver VW bug and another vehicle, an expensive looking gold car.

"Is that a Porsche?" Mike asked.

"Not sure," Lucas replied. "It looks like one, but this is as clear a picture as we have and it's impossible to tell."

"Trinity has her people checking to see if they can identify that car on any other video in the area," Zach added. "And she's checking DMV to see what is registered to the senator."

Refocusing on the video, Mike concentrated on what they could see. Especially on the two people who exited the car and entered the senator's office through the fire door, shortly before Jamie reported hearing Andrew arguing with two people. Unfortunately, distance and the glare of the sun made any identification of the people impossible. Hopefully the lab would be able to enhance the image to identify them.

"Do we have anything showing the killer leaving the building?" Gary asked.

Zach shook his head. "Not on this camera. The sun glare completely washes out everything by the time anyone left and I'm not holding out much hope the lab will be able to do much with the video."

"Damn," Mike muttered, sure the others were as frustrated as he felt. If only the law firm's cameras were working, they'd probably be able to identify and nab their killer immediately.

"Okay, this film is from a business directly across the street from the driveway up to the law firm," Lucas stated, clicking a few keys to bring another video to the screen.

Again, Mike studied the footage carefully, watching as Jimmy's SUV appeared and turned into the McDougal and Associates driveway shortly after noon. Forty minutes later, the video caught Zach and him arriving in Zach's car.

Just when Mike was beginning to wonder why they were watching the video, Lucas froze the camera image.

A car...Jim's SUV appeared on the image, exiting the law firm driveway shortly after Zach's car had entered. And the camera had captured an image of the person driving.

From the dead silence in the room, they all knew they were looking at the face of their suspected killer. The person Mike suspected had left the senator's office through the fire door as Zach and he had entered the building. The same man who had trashed Jamie's apartment and scrawled a threat on her mirror.

"Lucas and I went by Jamie's apartment building after Dev told us about the break-in," Zach said, before anyone could comment on what they'd just seen. "The convenience store across the street from the apartment has cameras everywhere and we lucked out."

Lucas tapped a few keys on the computer and an image from the convenience store parking lot appeared on the large screen in the conference room.

"That's Jimmy's SUV," Zach said, pointing at a car pulling into the lot. "We've confirmed the license plate."

The time stamped on the video displayed 1:45 AM. The time wasn't lost on Mike. Claudia Parker had told him the break-in had occurred around 1 AM and lasted at least a half hour. So, the fact Jim's SUV, which they knew the killer had driven from the murder scene, was at a convenience store across from Jamie's apartment around the time of the break-in, was pretty damning evidence the killer was her intruder.

Mike shook his head, watching a male in jeans and black hoodie — the exact clothing Claudia described — exit the SUV and enter the store. Apparently destroying an apartment had made the guy thirsty, because he walked directly to the refrigerated cases and pulled out two bottles of water.

With another click of his computer keyboard, Lucas switched feeds to another camera angle, this one inside the store. And he froze the image as their man walked through the front doors.

Mike wasn't sure if it was arrogance or ignorance, but the guy looked right up at the camera lens. And it was the same man they'd seen in the earlier video driving Jim's car from the murder scene, only this image was perfectly clear.

"It took our lab all of ten minutes to get a hit on facial recognition," Zach announced.

"Who is he?" Mike asked.

"Scott Cooper," Zach answered. "We're running background checks on him right now."

Gary drummed the fingers of one hand on the table. "Do we have a DMV photo of Cooper? I'd like to see the comparison."

Lucas nodded. "Give me a second." Within moments another image, this one clearly a driver's license popped up on the screen adjacent to the convenience store close-up.

Mike stared at the DMV license and then at the close-up. If it wasn't the same man, it was his identical twin. And the DMV description of a Caucasian male, age twenty-five, height five-eleven, weight one eighty was also very similar to the descriptions they'd gotten from Jamie and Claudia Parker.

"Do we have anything else on Cooper?" Mike asked.

He'd no sooner asked when Zach's and Lucas' cell phones chimed back-to-back alerts for incoming texts.

Zach glanced at his phone. "We do now," he said with a chuckle. "This is the result of our background check. Talk about timing."

Mike waited impatiently while the two men read their texts. He shot a glance over at Gary to see he'd pulled a laptop closer and was intently working on something. Knowing Thorny, he was probably checking financial information for anything else related to Cooper.

Finally Zach glanced up from his phone. "Okay…Cooper is the only son of a single mother. He grew up in Baltimore and went to public schools. Apparently he was a good student; he skipped tenth grade and graduated near the top of his class at sixteen. Then he attended NYU as a film major…"

"New York University," Mike echoed. "Tuition there is steep. How's a guy from a single parent home afford it?

"I think I can answer that." Gary shifted in his chair to look at Zach. "Is his mother Stephanie Cooper, by any chance?"

Zach glanced at the message again. "Yeah. How'd you know that?

Gary's gaze met his son's, then scanned to Lucas and back to Mike. "Last night while I was going through Andrew's financials, I found a trail of payments that the senator has been making to a former housekeeper named Stephanie Cooper. The first of those payments was $10K and every month afterwards a $5K payment was transferred from the senator's account to the Cooper woman. Those payments began almost exactly nine months before the date of birth on Scott Cooper's DMV license and as of this month, are still occurring."

Mike whistled softly. Neither he nor any agent he knew believed in coincidences and that one was a whopper.

Thornton's voice pulled Mike's attention back to the conversation. "My gut tells me there's got to be a connection between twenty-five year old Scott Cooper and those payments. And if I'm right, he had plenty of money to afford tuition anywhere."

"So are we going on the premise the senator was this kid's daddy and he was paying the woman to keep her quiet?" Zach asked.

Mike snorted a laugh. "That would be just like the old man and it would certainly explain the payments."

"I thought so too until I saw the perp's photo," Gary interjected. "But look at him. Am I the only one who thinks this guy is a dead ringer for Ed McDougal?"

Lucas swore aloud. "Oh my God, Thorny! You're right. He even has the same cleft in his chin as Ed. I can't believe I didn't notice it immediately. Put a cadet uniform on him and he'd be Ed back when we were at the Academy." Shaw stared at Cooper's photo and swore again. "Twenty-five years. That would have been our second year at the Academy. I wonder if that scandal I told you about had anything to do with Cooper's mother."

Mike couldn't answer Shaw's question, but his mind was already forming a scenario. "An illegitimate kid could be a skeleton in the family closet the senator and Ed didn't want to become public knowledge. So, if Stephanie is in fact Scott's mother, those payments the old man was making to her could be hush money or blackmail to keep it quiet."

"Bingo!"

Mike chuckled at Thornton's simple reply. The puzzle pieces all seemed to fit nicely. Now all they had to do was prove it. Simple? Somehow he didn't think so.

"What else did we get on Cooper?" Mike asked.

Zach glanced at Lucas. "You want to take it from here?"

Shaw nodded. "Cooper enlisted in the Army when he left NYU. A Ranger unit."

The room got so quiet for a moment, it was as if no one was breathing. Then Lucas spoke again.

"And get this, his specialty was a knife."

An expletive escaped Gary's mouth. "That can't be a coincidence."

"Yeah," Lucas agreed. "His military record is interesting, too. His service was pretty routine...at least as routine as it gets for a Ranger...for about four years. Then his original commanding officer was reassigned and a Captain Martin Zerphy was assigned to command their unit. There's nothing in here about Zerphy, but apparently the Captain didn't agree with Cooper's battle tactics. In an official report, Zerphy called Cooper a *psychopath* and accused him of *enjoying the kill too much* and *of using tactics that bordered on torture against civilians allegedly to get intelligence on enemy combatants.* The Army apparently agreed with Zerphy because six months ago Cooper was stripped of his rank of corporal and given an OTH discharge."

Shaw glanced at the other agents. "OTH means Other Than Honorable. It's not quite as serious as a Dishonorable Discharge, but still, not good. Most likely Cooper was denied any VA benefits. And get this...Captain Zerphy was found murdered a week later. He'd been tortured and his throat had been cut."

Thornton's brow cocked upward. "Sounds like our boy's M.O."

A silent nod was Shaw's answer. "That's the army's take on the murder."

Not that his interest and attention had waned at all, but adrenaline spiked inside Mike. "And Cooper is still walking around free? Why?"

Lucas turned to him. "The army can't find him. Apparently Cooper has the resources and wherewithal to move around a lot."

Mike nodded. "So we've identified Cooper as our killer. We've placed him at the law firm at the time of the murder, which gives him opportunity. And as a Ranger, he definitely had the means to commit the kind of violence we saw at the crime scene. What we don't have is motive. Why'd he do it?"

"Exactly." Thornton's gaze turned to Zach and Lucas. "Keep digging into Cooper's background. We need more than our hunch about the payoffs. See if you can find anything that proves why Andrew was paying the mother. And what he has been doing since he was booted from the army. Anything that will give us his motive."

Lucas gave a curt nod. "Will do."

With Lucas and Zach continuing to dig into the background of their prime suspect, Gary turned to Mike. "The merry widow has been talking to everyone but us, so what do you say we go see if we can rectify that situation. Maybe she can shed some light on Cooper for us."

Chuckling at the irreverent reference to Lauren McDougal, Mike nodded. "I'm ready when you are."

Chapter Thirteen

Hostile witness. The phrase immediately popped into Mike's mind seeing Andrew's widow sitting in an antique wingback chair, her back ramrod straight and not a hint of a smile on her face. But for the life of him, he couldn't figure out her attitude.

Her husband was dead. It seemed logical she'd do anything to help find his killer. But she acted as if Gary and he were nuisances who were taking up her valuable time.

With a regal carriage, Lauren McDougal looked like she'd never worked a day in her life and probably hadn't, considering both she and the senator came from extremely wealthy families. Vanity had dyed any hint of gray from long black tresses she wore in a tight knot at the back of her scalp. And a good plastic surgeon had removed all but the smallest age lines from the porcelain skin of her flawlessly made up face.

An immaculately tailored rose colored silk suit and creamy high-necked silk blouse showcased her tall, trim figure, as did the black spike heels on her slim feet. From head to toe, her appearance screamed affluence.

But even her wealth and flawlessly applied makeup couldn't conceal a large bruise on her left cheek; a bruise that oddly, resembled the imprint of knuckles.

Mike filed the observation away for later, when the widow finally deigned to acknowledge them.

Her cold gaze traveled between Gary and him.

"As my housekeeper told you, I have a previously scheduled appointment." Lauren's throaty voice was void of any civility. And as if to emphasize her urgency, she lifted back the edge of her sleeve and peered at her watch. "I don't have time for mundane questions."

On the drive out to the mansion, he and Gary had decided he would play good cop and begin the interview in a non-confrontational tone, allowing Gary to observe Lauren for her reactions. But surprise stole Mike's response for a heartbeat.

Mundane? Really?

They hadn't even started the questions and already the woman had an attitude. Yes...she was definitely going to be like a hostile witness.

Recovering quickly, Mike nodded. "We understand your concern, ma'am, but this is important. We'll try to be brief."

"See that you do."

Disregarding her condescending attitude and the fact she hadn't offered them seats, Mike made himself at home on the sofa across from where she was perched, as if sitting on a throne. Gary opted to lean against the mantel, off to the side.

"Mrs. McDougal, were you aware that shortly before his death, your husband had received a threatening letter?" Mike asked.

"No," she replied with absolutely no emotion; her entire demeanor screaming a lack of interest. "Andrew rarely discussed such matters with me."

Mike paused only a moment before posing his next question. "Can you think of anyone who had a grudge against your husband?"

"My husband was a politician," she paused to light a cigarette and blew the smoke directly at Mike's face. "He was bound to upset some people."

Mike brushed the smoke away and narrowed his eyes on her. "Would any one of those people, specifically, have wanted to kill him? Perhaps a business associate or personal...acquaintance?"

He'd had to search for a diplomatic way of referring to McDougal's numerous mistresses. Acquaintance had seemed innocuous enough.

"I believe you already have the murderer identified and he's one of your own agents," she answered coolly, taking another puff of nicotine. "There was a woman there too and she could very easily be involved. There's no need to defame anyone else."

Ignoring her attitude, Mike pressed forward. "What was your husband's relationship to the people found with him? How did he know them?"

"How naïve can you be?" the widow replied disdainfully. "It's obvious. Ms. Kendrick is a very ambitious junior attorney at the firm. I have no doubt she was willing to offer sexual favors to my husband in exchange for a promotion. For all I know your agent could be involved with her…a jealous boyfriend."

"Do you have any proof that she and your husband were having an affair?" Mike asked, ignoring her speculation about Jim, which he knew was baseless.

Her expression looked like she'd swallowed something distasteful. "Of course not, sonny. My husband was discreet."

Mike let her comment slide and moved on. "What can you tell us about your husband's relationship with Joseph Kanell? We understand there was bad blood between them."

Although they had no proof Kanell had been at the scene of the murder, the former law firm partner clearly hated the senator and it was entirely possible the widower had hired the killer.

"Joseph Kanell had nothing to do with my husband's murder," Lauren replied harshly. "He wasn't the one found with a bloody letter opener in his hand and my husband's blood on his clothing. Your agent is the murderer and the only reason you haven't arrested him, is because you're trying to cover up for him."

FROM THE MOMENT they'd entered the parlor, Gary had been studying Lauren McDougal, watching for signs of grief that would indicate they should back off the interview. So far all he'd seen was an arrogant, confrontational bitch.

During the past twenty-four hours, Gary had reviewed every shred of information accumulated on McDougal's employees, former employees and known mistresses. And he'd spoken with several employees himself. He'd also spent the better part of his night reviewing the senator's financial records.

With several degrees in forensic accounting and years of practical experience putting his knowledge to work, it hadn't taken much effort for him to find some very interesting entries in those financial records.

At this point, he knew pretty much everything there was to know about all the characters with possible connections to the case. And he knew exactly what answer Mike should have received from the widow.

Gary had to hand it to Mike. Dev's patience with the woman's haughty attitude was admirable. But the bored expression plastered on her face, did nothing to foster compassion. Gary had had his fill of her insults and her stonewalling.

If Lauren McDougal was truly a grieving widow, he'd never consider doing what he was about to do, but as far as he could tell, she had ice water running through her veins. She thought she was above cooperating with law enforcement and he intended to correct her misconception...quickly.

He might have his head handed to him by the Director tomorrow, but he was going for the jugular.

With a subtle gesture to Mike, Gary took over the interview.

"We're not covering up anything," he rebutted forcefully.

The woman jumped as if she'd forgotten he was in the room. Her gaze swung to him.

"The accusation that we are, is both insulting and inflammatory." Gary pushed away from the mantel and drilled her with an unyielding glare. "Your hostility and condescending demeanor toward Agent Devlin is also puzzling, Mrs. McDougal."

She squared her shoulders. "I'm sure I don't know what you are talking about."

"Perhaps you've forgotten we're conducting a murder investigation. Maybe this will help you remember it." Gary paused for a heartbeat. "You have the right to remain silent..."

A very brief flicker of alarm flashed in her eyes as he recited her Miranda rights, but she recovered quickly. After acknowledging her rights, she merely glared at him.

Again, her entire demeanor did nothing to cause him a moment of compassion.

"You have a choice here," he continued. "Have your attorney present and consult with him before answering our questions, or talk to us on your own. But let me make one thing perfectly clear." While Gary kept his voice intentionally calm, his tone was anything but friendly and his eyes bore into her. "You **will** answer my questions or I'm going to arrest you for obstructing a federal investigation."

Fury burned in her ice blue eyes. "Ask your damn questions and get out," she snarled.

"Fine. Who is Scott Cooper?"

For only an instant the woman looked like a deer caught in headlights, but Gary had to give it to her, she recovered quickly and the same icy expression she'd worn since they arrived slid back into place.

"I...I don't believe I know anyone by that name," she stuttered.

"Really?" Gary challenged, onto her lie. "Perhaps you should think about the name a little longer. Cooper."

"Like I said. I don't know anyone by that name."

So...she was going to maintain her charade, was she? Well, that was fine. He'd help her out.

"Have you've forgotten Stephanie Cooper, the woman who worked as a housekeeper for you? I believe she was an underage minor in your employ for over a year about twenty-six years ago."

141

Cornered, she finally relented. "Now that you mention it, Stephanie did work for us. But it was a long time ago and I barely remember her. And I'm certain she couldn't have been an underage minor. But what can she possibly have to do with my husband's murder?"

Gary doubted she was telling the truth about remembering the woman, but since she'd opened the door for him to connect the housekeeper to the murder, Gary walked through it, more than happy to oblige her, if for no other reason than to see her reaction.

"For one," he said. "Scott Cooper is her son. And for another, your husband has paid Stephanie Cooper over one and a half million dollars in the past twenty-six years. Ten thousand dollars when she left your employment — which curiously was nine months before Scott was born — and five thousand dollars a month ever since."

He drilled her with the full intensity of his gaze. "That's a lot of money to pay a former housekeeper, especially since it wasn't workman's comp. I checked. And the timing is curious, isn't it?"

Lauren's face flushed with rage. "What are you implying?"

Instead of answering her question, he spent the next several minutes blistering her with questions about Joseph Kanell and a litany of women, all of whom were receiving financial payments from Andrew McDougal. From the frequency of the payments, it didn't take a genius to figure they were pay-offs.

"These women were all former mistresses of your husband, weren't they?"

Gary already knew they were. With a little leg work the investigation team had already contacted the women and all had admitted having engaged in affairs with the senator.

To Gary's surprise, Lauren nodded and for the first time she looked as if the last twenty-four hours had taken an emotional toll on her. But Gary was beyond caring at this point. He couldn't find anything to like about the cold, conniving woman and even less to like about Andrew McDougal. The powerful senator had been nothing more than a self-indulgent unscrupulous cheat.

Gary wasn't sure if Lauren McDougal's cool demeanor was one of the reasons her husband treated his marriage vows so cavalierly or if she'd merely developed the screen out of self-preservation after years of humiliation.

At this point her reasons were irrelevant. What mattered was getting straight answers from her and so far they'd gotten few.

"Now that we've broken the ice on the other women in your husband's life, let's get back to Stephanie Cooper."

Gary watched the color drain from her face. Good. Keep her off balance.

"For a while, I thought Scott might be the product of an affair between your husband and Ms. Cooper. But then we found photos of Scott. And it's odd. The young man is a dead ringer for your son, Ed. And that makes me wonder if all that money your husband has been paying the Cooper woman was to keep her from making Scott's connection to your family public."

"You can't prove any of that," she challenged. "And if you insist on pursuing the subject, I'll sue you for liable and slander."

Gary stared at her...hard...for several heartbeats. "You're right. I can't prove it...yet. But DNA will tell me quickly if my hunch is correct or not. And it's only a matter of time before we have that DNA."

"Edward would never consent to such a test."

He let a sly smile curve his lips. "Perhaps not. And he'd be smart to avoid it if he's trying to protect secrets. But DNA can be obtained easily from blood and there was plenty of that at the murder scene. And if Scott Cooper has any biological connection to your family, it will come out in the results of our DNA tests."

For a moment, Gary enjoyed watching her squirm. But he'd made his point. Time to move on.

"You and your family have spent the past twenty-four hours blasting the FBI for not making an immediate arrest in your husband's murder. But in order to make an arrest, we need a motive for the crime. And contrary to your contention Ms. Kendrick was having an affair with Andrew, there isn't one shred of evidence to support that claim. And the man in the office has no connection to Ms. Kendrick or your husband. He has absolutely no motive for the crime. But all those women you just confirmed were former mistresses of Andrew's...all of them...and their husbands or boyfriends...they all have potential motives. Scott Cooper...if he's a skeleton in this family's closet...has a motive for murder. And if I may be so bold...you have a motive yourself."

Gary ignored her startled gasp. "After all, you've put up with Andrew's affairs for years. Perhaps you finally had enough."

She glared at him silently for a moment. "But none of them, nor I, were found in his office covered in his blood, holding the murder weapon."

"That's true," Gary conceded. "However, crime scenes can be staged, which is why we carefully investigate all angles."

Keeping Lauren off guard, he pressed her for details on when she'd last been at her husband's office and where she'd been at the time of the murder.

In both instances her answers were lies.

Her own sons, Bob and Colin confirmed she'd been at the office on Friday, the day before the murder. But Lauren claimed she hadn't been there in weeks. And she'd also claimed to have been shopping at the time of the murder, but when pressed, couldn't produce one receipt or name any store she'd visited.

Everything about the woman from the moment they'd entered the house had succeeded in jumping her to the top of Gary's suspect list, right alongside Scott Cooper. And it hadn't escaped his notice that she was right-handed. An interesting coincidence considering Scott was a lefty and the coroner had told them Andrew's wounds had been inflicted by two different people, one a lefty and the other a righty.

Granted they had no proof she was involved in the murder, but her behavior was bizarre to say the least. And Lucas had said she was fiercely protective of her family. So, if Scott Cooper was in fact a skeleton in the family closet, perhaps she'd gone to confront the senator and snapped when the truth had been revealed.

Clearly he and his team had a lot of leg work to do yet, but Gary wasn't about to give the woman a pass, merely because she'd just lost her husband. He seemed more concerned about that detail than she did.

If he thought they'd get anything resembling the truth from Lauren, Gary would keep pressing. But at this point, the likelihood of learning anything useful from her was slim to none. Continuing the interview was only wasting his and Mike's time.

Better to keep digging. They could always come back again.

He shifted his gaze to Mike, giving a subtle signal he was ending the interview. When Dev suddenly stood, the widow glanced between them, clearly surprised.

Gary gave her a curt nod. "Thank you for your time, Mrs. McDougal. We'll be in touch with further questions." His tone was intentionally dismissive and his words designed to keep her off balance. Let her wonder what they'd ask the next time.

Without waiting for her reply, Gary spun around and headed to the door.

"Man, you really have that 'bad cop' routine of yours down to perfection," Mike chuckled as they walked to their car.

Gary stopped and looked at him before glancing over his shoulder at the house. "She made it easy. Seriously, have you ever seen a woman whose husband has been brutally murdered, exhibit less emotion? Katie shows more concern when I cut myself shaving!"

Mike chuckled at his blatant exaggeration. "It's like the whole family doesn't care he's dead."

"Exactly," Gary agreed, glancing at his watch. Two o'clock.

By his estimate, he'd gotten about ten minutes of sleep last night; the cat nap Jamie Kendrick interrupted in the hospital waiting room. He was used to working an investigation on little sleep, but without food, he was worthless. The raisin and cinnamon bagel he'd eaten at five that morning before leaving the hospital had been good, but hours had passed since then. And right now he was running on empty.

"I don't know about you, but I'm starved," he said. "Let's get something to eat and if we're lucky we won't get indigestion talking about these morons."

Mike chuckled. "The day I turn down food, someone needs to check me for a pulse."

"Let's go then."

Mike grabbed his arm suddenly. "Thorny, look at that car over there," he said pointing to his left.

Gary's gaze slid that direction and landed on a gold Porsche being washed by a man in coveralls.

"That looks like the car in our video. The one sitting in the law firm parking lot," Mike offered.

Striding over to the worker, they flashed their badges. "Whose car is that?" Gary asked.

The man shot an uneasy glance toward the house as if he was hesitant to answer. But then he evidently thought better than stonewalling two federal agents. "It's the senator's car," he answered. "Why?"

For several seconds Gary tried to make sense of why the car seemed important. But his hunger was affecting his thought process because nothing came to mind immediately. "No reason, just wondering," he replied. "Nice car."

"It was the senator's baby. He loved this car," the man said, choking up as he spoke.

Gary stared at him a moment. Finally, one person who actually seemed to be mourning the man's death.

Nodding to Mike, Gary spun on his heels and headed to his car.

As he shut his car door, his cell phone rang. Gary glanced at the display before answering. "Hey, Zach. What's up?"

Zach got right to the point. "We're at Doug McDougal's home. You and Dev need to get out here, now."

Gary blew out a breath of frustration and glanced at Mike. So much for lunch.

"On the way," he answered.

Chapter Fourteen

The sheriff's den reeked. Mike's nose immediately identified the odor even before he saw the evidence.

Booze. Lots of it.

A half empty bottle, expensive whiskey based on the label he saw, sat in the middle of the large mahogany desk comprising the centerpiece of the room. A tumbler lay tipped on its side in a puddle of mostly dried liquid, staining the blotter. Another bottle, an empty, had been tossed casually into the trash can beside the desk.

But it was the man sitting behind the desk that captured Mike's attention.

Slumped forward in his desk chair with his head face down on the blotter, Sheriff Doug McDougal was quite obviously dead. Between the gun still clutched in the dead man's right hand and the tissue matter scattered across the desk and floor, Mike didn't need the coroner to tell him the cause of death.

The sheriff had blown his brains out.

Doug's body was in full rigor, so he'd been dead at least twelve hours, putting time of death at some time last night.

Leaning closer, Mike peered at the gun curiously. Doug's service revolver had been confiscated at the crime scene. Mike wasn't sure if state police had returned the gun yet, but this one was definitely a different caliber weapon.

Mike immediately keyed on the weapon that had been missing from Doug's ankle holster. Using search warrants, state police had been all through Doug's home, office and cars searching for that missing weapon. They'd found nothing.

Was it possible this was the weapon they'd been searching for?

Mike's mind flashed back to his conversation with Jamie's doctor about her head injury. Wells had been positive the wound was caused by the butt of a gun. In between hunger pangs, Mike's gut told him he was looking at the gun in question.

He turned to one of the Bureau CSI's who'd just arrived. "Make sure you bag and print this gun."

"Got it," the man replied, pulling out an evidence bag and dropping it inside after carefully extracting the weapon from the deceased sheriff's hand. "You want the standard tests?"

Mike nodded. "Yes, but I also want the grip checked for any hair or blood that doesn't match the deceased's. And I know you just got here, but I need the results, ASAP," he added as the CSI tagged and initialed the sealed bag.

"On it," he replied.

"This makes absolutely no sense."

Gary's voice drew Mike's attention and he turned to see Thorny standing a few feet away, staring at Doug.

"What do you mean?" Mike had a feeling he already knew, but he was curious to hear Thorny's take on the scene.

"Unless there's something more we aren't aware of yet, I just can't see Doug McDougal killing himself. All we have on him at this point is possible tampering with evidence and given the family's money and power, I'm guessing the worst he would have gotten was a slap on the wrist and a hefty fine."

Thorny was right. The same thought had popped into Mike's head when he'd first walked into the sheriff's home office. "Is there a suicide note?" he asked, glancing to Zach and Lucas for an answer.

"We haven't found anything yet, but the crime unit just got here. They've got a lot of ground to cover," Lucas replied.

Shaw glanced over at Doug's body. "But frankly, if he drank as much booze as it appears he drank, I doubt he could have held a pen long enough to write anything."

Good point. Which also raised the question of how the man had held a gun steady enough to fire such a deadly shot. Mike scanned the room until he found Maryland's Chief Medical Examiner, Georgiana Baker. He'd heard her voice and knew she'd arrived on scene, but she hadn't yet made her way over to the deceased.

He motioned her over. "Georgie, we're going to need a blood alcohol test run on him. I want to know if he was physically capable of holding and firing a weapon."

Georgie glanced at the body and then peered at him curiously. "You think this might not be a suicide?"

Mike shrugged. "At this point, I'm not willing to rule out anything. So just work your usual magic and let us know as soon as possible what you find."

"Anything for you, Dev," she quipped with a smile.

The woman was an unapologetic flirt, but as a medical examiner, she had no peers. Georgie worked tirelessly and always nailed *cause of death* with her autopsies. He had no doubt she'd be able to determine if Doug's death was in fact a suicide or not.

"The minute the press gets wind of this, it's going to be a nightmare." Gary muttered the comment to no one in particular. But then his gaze snapped up to Zach and Lucas. "Have we made notification to the family yet?"

"You probably passed Sergeant Jackson on your way here," Zach replied. "She and one of her men headed over to the senator's home to notify Lauren as soon as we got here. And she sent other troopers out to notify the rest of the family."

Gary nodded. "Seal this place off like Fort Knox. I want this room gone over with a fine-toothed comb. If there's anything in here to explain why he killed himself, I want it found."

150

Zach's cell phone rang as he nodded acknowledgement to Gary's order.

While Taylor answered his call, Mike continued to study the crime scene. A loud curse caused him to turn back to Zach. Gary and Lucas both spun around to look at him too.

Zach and he had worked together for so many years, Mike knew immediately something was wrong. Taylor's expression looked like he was going to be ill.

"You're kidding, right?" Zach said to whoever was on the other end of the call.

With a muttered reply, he disconnected the call and for a moment he merely stared at his phone. Then his gaze lifted slowly.

ANOTHER BODY? NO WAY!
First, the senator, then Doug...and now Ed McDougal.

"They found the mayor's body in his den," Zach explained. "No sign of a struggle, no nothing. Just dead. Murdered."

Mike flicked a glance at Gary and Lucas. Both men looked as stunned as he felt. They weren't anywhere near solving the senator's murder or finding their chief suspect, and now two of their key witnesses and suspects were dead. The word unbelievable didn't begin to express the situation.

Fifteen minutes later, Mike drove onto the mayor's estate and parked behind several state police cruisers already on the scene. Zach pulled in behind him. As they stepped out of their cars, Gary arrived and joined them in the driveway. Lucas had remained behind to oversee the crime scene at Doug McDougal's home.

Ahead of them, bright yellow police tape, waving in the breeze, clearly identified the property as a crime scene.

Flashing their badges, they made their way to the front door where they were met by a petite female who looked too young to be a state trooper, but her crisp uniform said otherwise. With a grim expression, she directed them to step carefully when they entered the home office.

151

While this crime scene wasn't as gruesome as the previous two, it was nevertheless a stark reminder of the devastation bullets could cause to a human body.

Edward McDougal lay in a crumpled heap less than five feet inside the door of a cozily furnished den, with two point blank shots to his heart.

As they'd been told, no sign of a struggle or break in was evident anywhere. Preliminary indications pointed to the mayor knowing his killer or at least feeling comfortable letting him inside.

Like Doug, though, Ed was in full rigor, so his murder had occurred sometime overnight and the killer was most likely long gone.

"You've searched the house to make sure no one else is here?" Mike asked the middle-aged male trooper they'd found standing guard over the body.

"Yes…it's clear," he replied.

Staring down at Ed McDougal, an image of Jamie flashed through Mike's mind. And on its heels the threat written on her bedroom mirror blared in his head.

A chill ran the length of his spine. Their witnesses were all dying and their killer was still out there somewhere. Was Jamie the next target?

Pulling out his cell phone, Mike punched in Bill O'Brien's number.

O'Brien answered on the second ring. "Jamie's fine," he confirmed in response to Mike's question. "She came down for some lunch shortly after you left, but went back upstairs to bed again. Other than her headache, she said she feels okay…she's just tired."

Quickly Mike summarized the situation with Doug and Ed. "Our killer is out there somewhere and it's entirely possible he's got Jamie in his cross-hairs. So stay sharp."

"Will do, Mike," O'Brien replied.

"Thanks."

As soon as he disconnected the call, Mike placed another call to the ICU unit at the hospital to check on Jim. With terse orders to the state trooper guarding the door to Jim's room not to leave him unattended for any reason, Mike disconnected the call and returned his focus to the crime scene.

"Hey! You can't go in there."

The loud protest as Mike clipped his cell phone back into its holder spun him around in time to see a young man blow past the female trooper trying to detain him at the front door.

The guy didn't get far.

He ran smack into Gary, who'd stepped into the foyer to find out what was happening.

"NOT SO FAST," Gary said, snagging the young twenty-something male by the scruff of the neck and pressing him against the wall. The kid strongly resembled their suspect, Scott Cooper, but his size was off. Still, Gary had no intention of letting him get away.

"I'm Supervisory Special Agent Thornton, FBI. Who are you?" he demanded, easily containing the fellow while searching him for weapons. "And what are you doing here?"

The kid yanked and pulled against Gary's iron grip.

"What's it to you? Ow! Hey dude...take it easy."

Gary heaved a resigned sigh and applied more pressure on the kid's arm, effectively restraining him, while deciding the guy wasn't too bright. At five-eight and maybe one-fifty dripping wet, the kid was trying to out maneuver a trained federal agent, easily ten inches taller and eighty pounds heavier. The odds of getting free were slim to none.

"I'm a federal agent. Stop resisting," Gary replied sternly.

"Let me go," the kid shouted with the same petulance of a child throwing a temper tantrum.

With an active crime scene less than five feet away, no way was Gary allowing anyone inside unless they had a legitimate reason for being there and he was sure they didn't pose a threat to anyone.

Finished frisking the kid for weapons, Gary spun him around, but kept him pinned against the wall. "I'll let you go as soon as you explain who you are and why you're here."

"I'm Kyle McDougal, bro" the kid snapped, still struggling to get free.

Gary recognized the name. The mayor's son. A no-show for his interview with Zach yesterday.

According to background information the Bureau had pulled on him, twenty-one year old Kyle had graduated the previous spring with a pre-law degree from University of Maryland. His reward for a less than stellar academic career that had included two underage DUI arrests, had been a law clerk position at McDougal and Associates.

"What are you doing here?" Gary fired back.

Apparently the kid finally realized he wasn't going to win a battle of strength and stopped squirming. But the defiant glare remained in place.

"This is my parent's home. And not that it's any of your damn business, but my Uncle Doug killed himself and he and my dad were close. I know my dad's gonna take the news about him hard and I wanna check on him. So, get out of my way, dude."

If Kyle McDougal was trying to score points with his communication skills, he'd have to do a damn sight better than dude and bro. But his explanation sounded credible and he hadn't given any indication he already knew his father was deceased.

Even so, until Gary was satisfied Kyle had no involvement in this crime or the senator's murder, he was a suspect and would be treated as one.

"Why did you blow off the interview you were supposed to have with us yesterday? And where have you been since then?"

The fellow gave a cocky shrug. "What business is that of yours?"

Gary answered his question with a hard, silent stare for several beats before replying. "If you're smart, you'll lose the attitude and answer my questions."

"I don't like being ordered around by anyone, bro...especially Feds, so I left. I've been with my girl the whole time. Why?"

Gary continued drilling the kid with an unyielding look. "I'm the one asking the questions and I want a full accounting of your time from then until now. Every minute."

A look of confusion lit in the kid's eyes, but at least he answered without further argument. "When I left the law firm, I picked up Angie and we met some friends at Giuseppe's for dinner. Afterwards we bar hopped to a couple clubs, danced and had some drinks. They kicked us all out at closing and Angie and me went back to her place. I was there all night."

Smugly, Kyle stared at him. "Would you like me to spell out for you in detail what we did, dude?"

Gary listened to him and gave a mental shake of his head. Unbelievable. The kid's grandfather had been brutally murdered and Kyle's reaction was to spend the better part of the evening and night partying with friends.

Why that surprised him, Gary wasn't sure. So far he had yet to meet any of the senator's family who seemed to be at all broken up over the murder. It was like none of them gave a damn.

But the kid was sorely testing his patience and he drilled Kyle with another unwavering glare.

"You might think this is a joke," Gary replied icily. "But keep it up and you're going to find yourself in handcuffs. I am not your *bro* or a *dude*. I am a Supervisory Special Agent with the Federal Bureau of Investigation and you may either call me Agent Thornton, Mr. Thornton or sir. But one more dude or bro and we're going to have a problem. Got it?"

Kyle stared at him a moment, weighing how far to push and apparently decided it was in his best interest to lose some of the attitude. His shoulders sagged slightly and he heaved a sigh.

"Got it," he relented. "This morning we got up, went to late mass at St. John's and then to lunch at Mickey D's. Angie's a nurse at the hospital and after lunch, I dropped her off at work. I was on my way home...I live in the apartment over my grandparent's garage...when I got the call about Uncle Doug and I came over here."

Gary considered Kyle for a moment. The kid was a cocky smart-mouth idiot, but every vibe he was getting told him Kyle wasn't involved in his father's death. But he wasn't ready to sign off on that hunch quite yet.

"When was the last time you talked to or saw either your father or your uncle?"

"What's going on, dude?" Kyle challenged.

Without a word, Gary stared at him, hard, and reaching into his suit coat pocket, he pulled out a pair of handcuffs and dangled them from his hand.

Kyle's eyes widened, apparently realizing what he'd said and for the first time, he actually looked contrite. "Sorry. It slipped out. I won't do it again, promise."

Gary accepted the apology with a nod and returned the cuffs to his pocket. "Now answer my question."

"I talked to Dad yesterday after learning Grandpa had been murdered, but I didn't see him or Uncle Doug 'cause they were tied up with the cops. But Dad and I went to an Orioles game together Friday night." Kyle thought for a moment, clearly trying to recall something and shook his head. "I don't know when I saw Uncle Doug last. Honest...but it was probably a week ago...maybe more. I usually just see him around town, but it's not like we hang out or anything."

Between surveillance cameras at the bars, restaurant and the baseball stadium, the kid's alibi would be easy enough to check.

Satisfied his gut instinct had been correct, Gary released the kid and took a step back.

"I apologize for grilling you, but I had a reason for everything I just did."

"What? Has something happened?"

Seeing the look of concern creasing the young man's brow, Gary didn't keep him in suspense any longer.

"Kyle, there's no easy way to say this, but your father is dead. He was murdered here in the house sometime overnight. That's why state police are outside and my agents and I are here."

The kid's jaw dropped open and tears that no one could fake, flooded his eyes. "Dad...dead?"

He tried to push past Gary, but Gary grabbed his arm and easily held him back before he could enter the den.

"You can't go in there. It's a crime scene."

"But he's my dad," Kyle cried with unabashed grief.

"I know, son, but you don't need to see him like that," Gary replied, putting a comforting hand on his shoulder. "Is there anyone I can call for you?"

"No...I'll be okay," Kyle answered.

As Gary watched him, something crossed the young man's features that spelled trouble. A look. Revenge? Was Kyle planning on acting as judge, jury and executioner for someone? It sure looked that way.

And no way was Gary letting him leave without challenging him on it. He had to be careful though. Kyle had just lost his father and two other relatives. And when he'd first arrived at the house, Gary had traumatized him further by treating him as if he was a potential criminal. He didn't want to seem insensitive to the kid's loss.

"Kyle, I've been at this job a long time. I've gotten very good at reading people," Gary said gently. "And you've got something on your mind; something you're keeping from me. Something important. I can see it in your eyes and on your face. Whatever it is…if it has anything to do with your father's or grandfather's deaths…or even your uncle…now would be the time to tell me, because nothing good will come of it if you leave here and go vigilante on us."

For several long moments, Kyle looked as if he was going to deny the accusation, but then he pulled himself together with a deeply drawn breath and after swiping the tears from his eyes, he steeled his shoulders and met Gary's gaze with a steady one of his own.

"You're right," Kyle announced to Gary's surprise. "I do know something…and I wanna help." Anger had clearly replaced his grief. "I know who did this. I know who killed my dad. Or at least I'm pretty sure I know…and I think it's the same guy who killed Grandpa. I dodged the meeting with you yesterday because I didn't want to point the finger at someone if I might be wrong. But now…well, I think I know who did it."

If he'd announced that aliens had just landed on the roof, Kyle couldn't have surprised Gary more. "Mike…Zach…get out here," he bellowed.

The moment they stepped into the foyer, Gary motioned them all into the living room. As he followed them into the room, his cell phone rang.

Before answering the call, Gary introduced Kyle to Mike and Zach and then explained. "I've got to take this call, but Kyle says he knows who killed his father. Get his statement."

While they sat down, he headed back into the foyer to take the call.

The display identified the caller for him.

Wells. Jimmy's doctor.

Gary prayed whatever the doctor had to say wasn't bad news. He'd had a belly full of that in the past twenty-four plus hours.

Thankfully the call was brief, but his hope for good news had been premature. Jimmy needed more surgery and the doctor wanted him at the hospital immediately to sign the necessary papers.

Gary's gut twisted. How much more could Jimmy take?

Muttering a curse, he walked back into the living room. Conversation stopped when they saw him, so he got right to the point, directing his comment to Mike and Zach.

"That was Wells. He needs to see me about Jimmy, so I've got to run." He turned to Kyle. "I'd like to stay to hear what you have to say." He flicked his index finger indicating Mike and Zach. "But these men are the best. Tell them everything you would have told me."

Kyle nodded. "Okay."

"I'm sorry about your father, Kyle and if I can help in any way, please let me know."

All traces of the arrogance the kid had worn like armor before, had vanished, replaced by solid determination. Kyle met his gaze. "Just find his killer."

Gary gave him a curt nod and then left.

Chapter Fifteen

Although Kyle had volunteered to make a statement, Mike still advised him of his Miranda rights. Before asking any questions, he pulled a small tape recorder from his pocket and switched it on.

"You know who murdered your father?" Mike asked.

"Yeah," Kyle replied. "I live at my grandparent's estate…in the apartment over their four car garage. Yesterday morning, I was on my way over to the main house to talk to my grandmother about something. I saw some guy over there and when the maid opened the front door, he sort of forced his way inside. He was really angry and that worried me. So I went in through the kitchen door to see what was happening. I didn't mean to eavesdrop, but it was hard not to hear the guy."

Kyle heaved a breath. "He had my grandmother cornered in the hallway, yelling at her that he was *Scott Cooper*. My grandmother said she didn't know him, but when he mentioned his mother's name, Stephanie Cooper…my grandmother acted like she knew her. And she told Tillie…the maid…to leave them alone. As Tillie walked away, the guy turned slightly and I saw his face. I know it sounds kinda bizarre, but he looked a lot like me. A little older and bigger, but the same color hair and eyes…and the same hole in his chin as me and my dad."

Fidgeting slightly, Kyle appeared uncomfortable disclosing what he knew, so Mike nodded encouragement. "You're doing fine, Kyle. Just tell us what you heard or saw."

"This Scott guy claimed that Grandpa had raped his mother when she was sixteen, and that she got pregnant and he was the kid. Grandma turned white as a sheet at first, and when he yelled at her to admit she knew about it, she kept denying knowing anything about him or any rape. But then, all of a sudden, she stared at Scott and I heard her swear at Grandpa. In all my life, I've never heard Grandma swear about anything, but she was furious. She said she'd *had enough of his philandering and this was the last straw*. And then she told this Scott guy that they were going to Grandpa's office, so she could hear what he had to say about the whole thing."

"Did you see them leave?" Mike asked, trying to contain his building excitement over what could potentially solve their entire murder case.

"Yeah…they left through the front door and got into a black Honda the guy was driving."

Mike glanced over at Zach and flicked his brow up. They'd known two people were in a black Honda that had pulled into the law firm parking lot, just before the time of the murder. But the glare of the sun had made it impossible to identify either occupant of the car on the video. And Jamie had told them she'd heard Andrew arguing with two people, but she hadn't recognized the voices. So, even though they'd established Scott Cooper had left the murder scene in Jimmy's Subaru and that a stolen Honda had been found in the law firm parking lot, they'd had no solid leads as to the identity of the other occupant of the Honda.

Kyle had just identified both occupants for them.

"What was Scott wearing when you saw him?" Zach asked calmly.

Kyle shrugged. "Baggy jeans, a white tee shirt and a red hoodie and I think he had sneakers on his feet. I'm not sure about that, though." He thought a moment longer. "Oh…and when he and Grandma turned to leave, I saw a large knife hanging on his belt.

Zach studied him for a moment. "Kyle, what makes you think this fellow killed your father?"

The kid rubbed an itch away from his nose and sucked in another deep breath, clearly upset by what had happened.

"Man…this is going to sound so bad, and I don't want to hurt my dad…especially since he's not here to defend himself. But this guy…Scott…looked just like me and my dad. A couple years ago, I heard my dad and Grandpa arguing about money Grandpa was paying to some woman. And I heard Grandpa tell my dad that it was all his fault…that if he…dad…hadn't raped the woman, they wouldn't have to pay to keep her quiet." Kyle looked down at his feet as if something interesting was on his shoes, and then with a look of embarrassment glanced back at Mike.

"Like I said…this guy looks so much like dad and me, I think he's my brother…or half-brother…or whatever you call them."

"And you think he murdered your father because of that?" Zach persisted.

"I think this Scott guy murdered Grandpa thinking he was his daddy…like he'd told my Grandma. But I know my dad and Uncle Doug walked into Grandpa's office after he was killed and they saw Scott and Grandma there. If Scott saw my dad…well…it wouldn't take much for him to think he'd killed the wrong man. And he was so angry…I think he came after Dad and killed him, too."

Mike was stunned to silence for several seconds, processing the kid's claim that his grandmother had been in the senator's office during the murder. That in and of itself was a revelation they hadn't known. And now they had confirmation of that and of their theory that Scott Cooper was an illegitimate child of possibly Andrew, but more likely Ed McDougal.

"Kyle, we're going to have this statement of yours typed up for you to sign, but Zach and I thank you for coming forward with this information. And I know Agent Thornton will thank you, too. You've been a tremendous help."

Kyle glanced down again. "I wanted to help my dad. But if this Scott guy is my brother, I feel bad ratting on him. Still, if he really did kill Grandpa and my Dad...I want him to pay for what he's done."

"You didn't *rat* on anyone, Kyle," Zach assured him. "If it makes you feel any better, we already had Scott Cooper identified as a suspect in the senator's murder. You've only helped us confirm our suspicions. And trust me; if we establish Scott murdered your father and grandfather, he's going to be spending the rest of his life behind bars."

Before Mike could agree with Zach's comment, his cell phone rang. Spotting Lucas Shaw's name on the caller ID, he took the call.

"What's up, Lucas?"

"Mike, CSI's found blood and hair on the butt of the revolver in Doug's hand. And the blood type doesn't match Doug's," Lucas explained. "They also did preliminary GSR tests on Doug's hands and found something interesting."

So, Mike's suspicions about the gun had been right. He'd be willing to bet the blood and hair matched Jamie. But the Gunshot Residue test, he hadn't expected anything unusual with that one.

Lucas didn't keep him in suspense. "The back of Doug's hand doesn't have any blood spatter or GSR powder on it. They spotted the lack of spatter with their naked eyes and that got their curiosity up, so they did the prelim test right here before Georgie took the body back to the morgue. There is no residue on the back of Doug's hand."

For a moment, Mike let the news roll around his brain. On the surface, it didn't make sense. Anyone committing suicide with a gun would have GSR all over their hand, due to its close proximity to the gun's discharge. And there would also be blood spatter on their hand. Doug had none of that.

His thoughts jumped to another detail.

If Jamie's hair and blood was on that gun, then it had initially been at the crime scene. But it hadn't been on Doug when he'd been searched and it hadn't been found during subsequent searches by state police. So where had Doug found it?

Mike's gaze drifted to the young man seated across from Zach. If Kyle was right, Scott Cooper had killed two people in cold blood. And Scott knew Doug; they'd met at the murder scene. Was it possible Scott was eliminating anyone who could identify him? Could he have staged Doug's death?

The more Mike thought about it, the more it made sense. If Doug drank all the booze they suspected he'd drunk, he would have most likely passed out. It was doubtful he could have held a gun steady enough to shoot himself. Someone using their own hand to hold Doug's hand steady long enough to fire a gun, would explain the lack of GSR on the back of Doug's hand.

The question was…how did they prove Doug's alleged suicide was actually a homicide staged by Scott Cooper or someone else?

Off hand, Mike didn't know. But he knew the first step.

"Lucas, call Georgie and make sure she does thorough tests on Doug for residue and blood spatter. Have her check all the places it should be for a suicide."

"Will do, Dev."

Before ending the call, Mike gave Lucas a brief summary of what they'd learned from Kyle, but his phone signaled another incoming call. Mike glanced at the display to see who was calling.

O'Brien.

Mike's heart leaped into his throat and he quickly ended his call with Lucas.

"What is it, Bill?" he asked without even saying hello. No way was the trooper calling to shoot the breeze. "Is everything okay?"

"Mike we've got trouble." Concern was evident in the man's voice and his next words explained why. "There's someone outside trying to get in, but the guy's like an apparition. One minute I see him and the next he's gone. I called for back-up, but between the senator and sheriff and now the mayor…our unit is spread really thin. I don't know if…or how much help is on the way."

Apparition? No…more like a former Army Ranger on a mission. And Mike's gut told him exactly which Ranger was outside the home.

Mike didn't hesitate. "It's probably Cooper, Bill. Be careful. I'll get there as fast as I can."

JACOB'S VALLEY WASN'T a large town, but at rush hour, the trip out to his farm took longer than Mike wanted. By the time he finally reached his driveway, he'd tried to call O'Brien and his house phone twice, with no answer either time.

With three active crime scenes, the state police weren't the only ones stretched thin. So was the Bureau. And with the pressure to solve the Senator's murder quickly, Mike didn't have the authority to pull Zach and Lucas off the crime scenes they were overseeing. That responsibility sat with Gary, as head of the investigation.

First chance he got at a traffic light, he sent Thorny a short, concise text.

Cooper spotted outside my house; O'Brien not answering calls; need back-up ASAP.

The time that passed between O'Brien's call and Mike arriving at the turnoff for his farm lane were the longest seven minutes of Mike's life. He floored the accelerator as soon as he turned off the main road and skidded to a stop in front of his home seconds later.

The state police cruiser was still parked in front of the house and everything appeared normal, but Mike pulled his gun and flicked off the safety, nevertheless. The minute he opened his front door, he knew everything was not all right.

Bill O'Brien's body was crumpled at the bottom of the staircase, lying in blood pooling from the gaping slice cut across his throat. Mike didn't even need to check to know the man was dead.

Guilt tore through him, while he winced at the gruesomeness of the wound. Bill had been so close to retiring and now he was dead, all because he'd been trying to help Mike and the Bureau keep a witness safe. Where was the justice in that?

Mike shook away the thoughts. He didn't have time for anything except staying focused right now.

Cooper could still be in the house. If Jamie was alive…and he prayed she was…he had to find her quickly.

No easy feat considering the size of the home.

A quick but careful search of the downstairs told him it was empty, which left the basement, second floor and attic. Mike opted for upstairs first. As he ascended the stairs silently, Mike was thankful he'd refinished the hardwood when he moved in. He knew where all the squeaks were located and carefully avoided them.

By the time he reached Jamie's bedroom, he'd cleared two other guest rooms, both of which had been ransacked by someone clearly looking for something…or someone….Jamie. The bathroom had also been empty. That left her room and his.

Mike hauled in a calming breath and nudged open Jamie's bedroom door, which was slightly ajar.

He breathed a sigh of relief. At least she wasn't lying on the floor like O'Brien. But this room had been torn apart, too. Quickly he searched the closet and under the bed to make sure he hadn't missed Jamie somewhere. He hadn't.

Where was she? Had Cooper taken her out of the house? Did he have her down in the basement or up in the attic? Had she gotten away?

Somewhere downstairs a step squeaked. Mike spun toward the bedroom door with his weapon leveled. Whoever was out there was trying to be quiet, but didn't know the house the way Mike did. Silently, Mike slipped into the hallway and crept closer to the staircase.

His gaze landed on Gary, who with gun drawn and ready, was nearly to the top of the staircase. A gush of air rushed out of Mike's mouth in relief.

A few more steps and the two men were standing side by side.

"Lucas and Zach are clearing downstairs and the basement," Gary whispered. "What's the situation up here?"

"My bedroom still needs to be cleared," Mike whispered. "Then the attic. And it's a mess up there. The previous owner left a ton of furniture and crates behind. I haven't had time to clean everything out yet. Zach and Lucas are going to find the same kind of mess in the basement. Someone could hide either place and be hard to detect."

Gary nodded. "Let's go. You take the lead; I'll watch your back."

Thankful for the help, Mike headed down the hall toward his room.

SCOTT COOPER WATCHED the Fed moving slowly, methodically through the room.

Knock yourself out, sucker. Ain't gonna work. You were as good as dead the moment you stepped in here.

His time as an Army Ranger had honed all his survival skills to perfection.

Kill or be killed. His mantra had served him well over the years. And he'd killed. Often. Never blinking, never letting emotion creep into his soul, never feeling anything except the satisfaction of a mission accomplished.

His specialty was Ol' Bessie...his knife. And his targets rarely ever saw him coming. Even if they did, they were dead before they had a chance to react. Just like the sucker walking toward him now.

Scott fondled the hilt of his survival knife. Ol' Bessie and him were ready and waiting. Just a little closer and the guy would be history.

Just like the senator...just like the state trooper. The cop hadn't known what hit him...and neither would this moron.

He didn't feel even an ounce of remorse for anything he'd done, either.

He never did. No sir…over the years he'd become an expert at compartmentalizing his emotions. He had the Rangers to thank for that talent, too.

Carefully lifting crate lids and peering into storage closets as he passed them, the guy closed in on Scott's position. Another couple steps and the guy would be dead.

Excitement poured into every cell of Scott's body. He always felt a rush just before a kill. And this one was going to be fun, 'cause he recognized the guy as one of the two Fed's who'd arrived at the senator's office just before he made his getaway.

In about two seconds there'd be one less man on his tail. Then he'd take care of the rest.

Chapter Sixteen

"**B**reathe and you're dead. Drop the knife."

Scott froze at the menacing threat, which had come an instant after an arm had snaked around his throat and with lightning speed, he'd found himself in a dangerous head lock.

How had anyone gotten that close to him without his realizing it? Sure he'd been focused on the Fed in front of him, but no way could anyone sneak up on him like that. He was a Ranger. His senses were sharp and yet somehow, the guy behind him...whoever it was...had gotten a clean drop on him. How?

Scott blocked his brain from questioning the situation.

At the moment, *how* didn't matter. What mattered was eliminating the threat and Scott wasn't surrendering Bessie to anyone. All he needed was a split second chance and he'd turn the tables on the guy behind him. The man would be dead before he knew it.

"Don't even think about it. One move and I'll snap your neck like it's a toothpick," the menacing voice hissed. "If you want to die, just flinch; I'll be happy to oblige you. Otherwise drop the knife."

Whoever the guy was, it was obvious he wasn't some normal cop. Scott had never known anyone who could move like this guy. He was a phantom and the hold he was using was definitely a lethal one. Scott ought to know; he'd used it often enough. If he so much as cleared his throat, his neck would snap.

Well, he hadn't planned on this development, but Scott knew when to concede defeat. Better to live out the moment and plan for the next.

He dropped Bessie.

"Smart move."

The guy didn't release even a fraction of the pressure on his neck, so Scott let the taunt pass.

"It's clear Zach," *Deadly Guy* called out.

Suddenly the man Scott had been stalking appeared and Scott found himself with a gun pointed at his chest.

"Now...slowly," *Deadly Guy* warned. "Hands behind your back. One false move and you're dead." As if to reiterate his threat, the man tightened his choke hold to the point of pain.

Scott wasn't a fool. He knew he was beaten...at least for now. So, he slowly moved his hands behind his back, mentally ticking off the seconds when *Deadly Guy* would have to loosen his hold to handcuff him.

When that happened these two clowns would be dead, because he and Ol' Bessie never traveled alone. His hands, arms and feet were killing machines just like Bessie...and Scott could retrieve the back-up blade he had strapped to his calf in under a second.

The guy with the gun moved cautiously beside him and handcuffs suddenly appeared in his hand.

Wait a minute. The guy with the gun was holstering his weapon to cuff him? *Deadly Guy* wasn't going to do it? Who the hell would have anticipated that move?

"You thought you'd gain an upper hand, didn't you?" *Deadly Guy* taunted in his ear. "Think again, Cooper. You're through. You might as well get used to it."

Before Scott could even think of a response, the cuffs clicked around his wrists and a second set was snapped on for good measure. A moment later, Scott realized he couldn't move his arms more than a couple inches away from his body because at least one set of the handcuffs had also been looped around his belt.

Damn. So much for the move he had planned to get his hands in front of him again.

While Scott tried to come up with a plan to turn the tables on them, the guy with the death grip spoke to his companion.

"Grab that box over there. You're going to need it."

The one named Zach turned, spotted a small carton and pulled it over. Then he snapped on a pair of latex gloves and without touching the handle, he tossed Bessie inside the box.

"Be careful; they'll be sharp," *Deadly Guy* cautioned as he coached his buddy where to look for hidden weapons.

Held the way he was, Scott was powerless to do anything but watch as he was practically stripped of his clothing and the search commenced.

Two ballistic knives taped to his legs and the razor blades taped to his arm, joined Bessie in the box. So did the guns at the small of his back and taped to his ankle. Next went the four throwing star knives clipped to a chain around his neck and taped to his chest. A switchblade, knife ring, brass knuckles, mace, several zip ties and a garrote were tossed from various pockets. And then his shoes were yanked off and more zip ties hit the floor.

When the one called Zach finished, he hastily refastened Scott's clothing, but didn't return the shoes. They went into the box.

Scott seethed inside.

Unbelievable. They'd found every one of his toys. All of them.

He was still trying to determine how *Deadly Guy* had known where to look, when the iron grip around his throat loosened.

Sucking in a good gulp of air, Scott turned around and came face to face with a tall, trim, silvery haired man with gray eyes.

Scott felt his jaw drop.

The guy had to be in his forties! At least!

No way. He'd been bested by this guy? How?

A badge and credentials appeared in the hand of the one named Zach.

"Special Agent Zach Taylor, FBI" the man stated firmly. He pointed at his deadly companion. "This is Special Agent Lucas Shaw. And you're under arrest."

Scott stared at Shaw, still trying to figure out how an old guy had gotten the drop on him.

Shaw stepped close again and stared him down, those gray eyes of his absolutely icy. Scott had seen that same look often enough when he'd been a Ranger, always from some army brass. Before he even spoke, Scott knew Shaw had military training. The man had it written all over his stance and carriage...not to mention the way he'd manhandled him.

"Lieutenant Colonel, U.S. Army Special Operations, Retired," Shaw said, deadly earnest lasering from his eyes.

Before Scott even realized what was happening, he found himself wrapped in another arm lock. Scott had to give the man credit; he had some neat tricks up his sleeve. If his life depended on it, Scott wouldn't have been able to do anything except move the way the man steered him.

"Gary....Mike...down here," Agent Taylor hollered as soon as they stepped from the basement into the kitchen. "We've got Cooper contained."

Horses coming down two flights of steps from the attic would have made less noise than the two men who suddenly appeared in the kitchen. One of the guys was a giant of a man who had to duck slightly to come through the doorway.

Scott assessed his situation.

Outnumbered four to one, especially with Shaw's deadly talents and this new giant, Scott figured it was in his best interest not to mess with any of them at this point.

"Where is she?" asked the one who introduced himself as Special Agent Devlin.

Scott recognized him too. The other Fed who'd come to the senator's office with Taylor. An edge of panic laced Devlin's voice, giving Scott renewed spirit. And he changed his mind.

Messing with this guy would be fun.

"Where's who?" Scott shot back.

Devlin stepped into his space at the same time *Deadly Guy* locked him in another death grip.

"Where is she?" Devlin growled through clenched teeth.

Scott let him sweat a moment.

Apparently a second too long.

"Answer him or I'll snap your neck in a tragic accident," Shaw hissed in his ear, so quietly Scott was sure no one else heard him.

Scott heaved a disgusted sigh. This guy was no fun at all. Where the hell had the Feds gotten him?

"I don't know where she is," Scott admitted when the pressure on his neck became almost unbearable. "When I got here, I ran into the cop. He wouldn't tell me where she was. So, I dispatched him and went looking for her. Then you guys showed up. I never did find her."

The giant took a step closer, looking absolutely murderous, but he nodded at Shaw. "Let him go, Lucas," he said.

"Who are you?" Scott asked curiously.

"Supervisory Special Agent Thornton," the man replied in an incredibly deep voice.

Scott eyed Thornton with interest. So...the big guy was the boss. He filed that piece of information away. It might come in handy later. The bass voice, though...that reminded him of Captain Martin Zerphy. Man, he'd hated Zerphy. The SOB had gotten him kicked out of the Rangers. Zerphy had paid for that decision with his life, but not before Scott had made him regret messing with him. He could learn to hate this Thornton guy, too...just because of that voice.

The pressure eased on his neck and Scott sucked in a couple gulps of air, as the big guy fired off a couple more orders.

"Zach...Lucas...get this piece of crap out of here," Thornton said, making it clear Scott was the crap he was referring to. "Lock him up securely and then get back here. Mike and I are going to tear this place apart until we find Jamie and we may need help.

And just that quickly Scott found himself being hauled out to a car and unceremoniously dumped into the back seat, where restraints kept him from so much as moving an inch in either direction.

Oh…if he only had Ol' Bessie. He'd make short work of these two jackasses. In fact, all four of them were now at the top of his hit list.

IT WAS SO dark Jamie couldn't see the hand in front of her face.

She had no idea where she was. Well, that wasn't exactly true. It was some kind of secret passage behind the walls of Mike's home.

But everything had happened so fast, she'd been completely caught off guard.

One minute, Bill O'Brien had rousted her from a sound sleep and the next he'd dragged her into Mike's bedroom. The only thing she remembered him saying was that Scott Cooper was somewhere outside and she needed to hide.

Her mind had still been struggling to rid itself of slumber and she'd barely registered his words, when he'd slid back a long piece of wood on the side of the fireplace hearth in Mike's room and lifted a large lever hidden inside.

She was sure her mouth had gaped open when part of a bookcase grinded open with a protest of metal, revealing a gaping hole and a secret chamber behind the bedroom wall.

Jamie had seen something like it once when she'd caught an episode of an old 1950's television show called, *Zorro*. But she'd never imagined anything like it existed in real life.

Bill had fished a small penlight from his pocket, shoved it into her hand, pushed her into the abyss and with a caution to be quiet; he'd pushed the lever down and the door grinded closed, sealing her inside.

She'd been so shocked, she hadn't had time to react before she found herself alone in the cold dark stone wall enclosure.

Fright didn't even begin to describe what she'd felt. Panic was more like it. Her heart had pounded so hard, she'd felt her pulse in her ears. And like an idiot, she'd taken a couple tentative steps before remembering the flashlight.

Lucky for her, she'd flicked it on when she had or she would have tumbled face first down a flight of stairs several feet away. Actually there'd been two flights of very narrow stairs. One leading up and the other going down.

She'd spun around to look behind her and saw nothing but the short dark hallway back to where she'd begun.

Thankfully Jamie had managed to rein in her runaway emotions. And although she had still been scared silly, her curiosity had gotten the better of her. Instead of waiting for Cooper to find her or Bill O'Brien to free her, she'd decided to explore.

Figuring Cooper was likely downstairs, she'd decided to go up the stairs and see where they led.

Between cobwebs and just the eeriness of the tunnel, she'd almost turned back. But she'd forced herself to keep going, to learn as much as she could about the place where she was trapped.

At the top of the stairs she'd found a small room, but for the life of her she hadn't been able to spot anything that even remotely resembled a doorway or lever like what she'd seen in Mike's bedroom.

They had to be there; she'd known that. But she hadn't found them. And unfortunately for her, she'd spent so much time searching; the penlight battery had died, leaving her stranded in the dark with a flight of steps one direction and solid walls everywhere else.

Frustrated, Jamie had sat down, trying not to think about all the creepy crawlies that were probably scurrying all around her.

She'd awakened with a start, shivering at the thought that some critter or insect skittering over her, had pulled her from sleep. She appeased her overactive imagination by telling herself the only thing that had gotten her awake was just that...her overactive imagination.

If she could just see, she was sure she'd be able to figure a way out of her predicament. But no matter how adjusted her eyes became to the lack of light, it was still too dark to see anything.

She appreciated that Bill had thought to give her a flashlight, but couldn't he have at least made sure it was one with fully charged batteries?

Ignoring the protest of her muscles, Jamie struggled to sit up. Between the cold dank stone and the hard unforgiving surface, it took a good minute or two for her circulation to return to normal and her muscles to stop screaming at her.

Yes...she'd definitely been asleep. But for how long?

That was anyone's guess.

In the eerie solitude, Jamie lost all track of time. She wished she had her watch. Besides knowing the time, she'd also have the illumination from the display to help cut the isolation of darkness. But she'd taken it off when she'd first arrived at Mike's home, when she laid down to sleep. And it was still lying on the bedside table beside her cell phone...another thing that would come in handy in her predicament.

Just her luck!

Determined to keep moving, Jamie felt her way back down one flight of the stairs to where she'd started, mentally kicking herself with every step.

Why hadn't she thought to look at the wall Bill had closed behind her? Surely there was some kind of lever on the inside that she'd be able to use to re-open the door and get out. But she'd been so startled by the whole experience, she hadn't looked.

Instead, like an idiot, she'd traipsed up the stairs, the flashlight had died and now she was trapped...not able to see anything.

Brilliant move, Kendrick!

She couldn't hear anything either. It was like being in a void.

Unbidden, a short story from high school English class popped to mind, sending an icy chill up her spine.

The Cask of Amontillado...if she remembered the title right.

Jamie shook her head, trying to will away the thought. Stubbornly, it refused to leave and instead the storyline played out in her mind. A twisted story by Edgar Allen Poe about a man chained inside an old tunnel, while a man he thought was a friend entombed him behind a wall of brick or stone.

Jamie couldn't remember which. But the similarity to her situation was more than a little unsettling.

What if something happened to Bill? What if she couldn't get out? She'd die inside these walls and no one would ever know it.

Stop. Just stop.

She wouldn't solve anything by panicking. The reprimand succeeded in settling her nerves and giving her a plan.

Maybe if she made it down to the first floor, she'd be able to figure a way out.

Good idea, Jamie. Keep moving. That way the chill won't seep into your bones and you won't have time to think about all the little critters sharing your space.

Steeling her resolve with another deep breath of stale air, Jamie felt her way forward again, using her hands and toes to feel for any hidden obstacle. She knew the steps were somewhere ahead, she just wasn't sure exactly where. And she had no desire to take a header down the stone flight of steps.

One concussion was enough, thank you very much.

She wished she knew what was happening out in the house. She'd been so terrified at first, especially when the flashlight died, that she'd almost screamed. But thankfully she'd managed to clamp her mouth together and stifle the yell.

She still didn't trust that it was safe to make noise.

The only reason Scott Cooper would be at Mike's home was to come after her...to make good on his threat. And a yell, or any noise for that matter, might give away her hiding place.

Carefully she picked her way down the stairs and discovered yet another small room, like the one she'd first entered and the one she'd found at the top of the steps.

If she ever got out of here, she was going to have to come back again…with a plentiful supply of flashlights…and explore this place. While she wasn't pleased by the idea of being trapped in it, the mere existence of the tunnels intrigued her. She'd love to be able to explore them when she could actually see something.

As she'd done in both the other rooms, she felt all around searching for some kind of mechanism that would open a hidden door. Unfortunately, like before, she found nothing.

Time lost all meaning in the dark. What felt like a year later, she suddenly heard a noise. Faint…but a noise.

Her heart leaped to her throat and beat wildly again, making such a loud racket in her ears she couldn't hear anything else. Willing her heart to calm down, she hauled in a deep breath and listened.

"Jamie!"

Her name! Someone had called her name. She was sure of it. Well, she thought she was sure; maybe she was hallucinating. And even if she wasn't, the sound was so far away, she had no idea where it originated. With all the stone surrounding her, the noise could be bouncing around from several stories away.

"Jamie!"

No…there it was again. And louder this time.

"Jamie! Holler if you can hear us."

Someone was out there. The voice was deep…very deep. Was that Agent Thornton?

Jamie wished she could hear the person more clearly so she could be sure who it was. But the voice sounded as if it was in the next county. The walls must be a foot thick or more to dull the sound so much.

She opened her mouth to holler back, but clamped her lips closed. What if it wasn't Gary? What if it was the killer? She didn't know Scott Cooper's voice. It could be him trying to lure her out into the open?

The thought sobered her enough that she was afraid to move.

"Jamie...it's Mike. Can you hear me? Holler if you do!"

Jamie's heart leaped for joy. That voice she recognized. It was Mike.

"I'm in here!" she hollered at the top of her lungs. "In the tunnel behind the wall."

Chapter Seventeen

S tunned, Mike turned to Gary. "Did she really say she was in a tunnel behind my walls?"

Thorny shook his head in disbelief and gave a nervous chuckle. "If you're hallucinating, we both are. I heard the same thing. And I take it you didn't know you had a maze behind your walls."

"Uh uh," Mike mumbled. "But we've got to get her out. I'll knock the damn wall down if I have to."

Thornton had the nerve to give him a strange look, as if he'd lost his mind. Maybe he had. But Jamie was stuck in there and he wanted her out.

"Let's try something a little less drastic, first," Gary suggested. He walked over to the wall where Jamie's voice seemed to be coming from. "Jamie, how did you get in there? Is there a door somewhere? If so, where?"

Mike gaped at Thornton. How could the man think so clearly at a time like this? A better question was why hadn't Mike thought to ask the same thing?

Unfortunately, Mike knew the answer to that one. He'd been having problems with rational thinking where Jamie was concerned since the moment he laid eyes on her in the senator's office.

Jamie's voice filtering through the plaster snared Mike's full attention.

"Get Bill. He can show you where the door is. He put me in here when he discovered Scott Cooper was breaking into the house."

Mike stared at the wall of books. Bill put her in there? How? And why?

"Jamie, Bill can't help us," Gary answered before Mike found his tongue. "Cooper killed him. So, tell us how he got you in there and we'll get you out."

"I was sleeping upstairs in my room. Bill got me awake and took me into Mike's bedroom. At the side of the fireplace he moved a piece of wood and exposed a lever of some kind. He pulled it and the bookcase made a grinding noise and moved back to expose an opening. He gave me a flashlight, but the battery died and I can't see anything at this point. I have no idea if there's a matching lever on this side of the wall. But there's a tunnel and steps leading from the attic to this level. I don't know if it goes to the basement."

Mike shook his head, trying to wake up from what he was sure was some kind of bizarre nightmare. This couldn't be happening. Jamie's voice had quivered with fear when she'd answered Gary. It was no wonder. She had to be scared to death being trapped inside a secret tunnel no one but Bill knew how to access.

His home was old and full of character; Mike had known that. But tunnels behind the walls? Any other time, he'd probably find the idea intriguing, but not with Jamie trapped inside. He wanted her out. Now.

They were standing in front of a fireplace similar to the one upstairs in his bedroom. Maybe they'd get lucky and find the same kind of lever.

"Check that side of the fireplace," Mike told Gary. "I'll look here. See if anything is loose or can be moved."

Working in silence, they searched and prodded the sides of the wooden fireplace mantel. Suddenly, a long slab of wood moved beneath Mike's fingers.

"I think I found something," he said, feeling a surge of adrenaline fill his body. Gary was at his side in a flash and together they examined the area and spotted the threaded panel.

"It's stuck," Mike muttered in frustration.

For several seconds, the two of them fumbled with the thing, trying to figure out which way to slide or lift it. Suddenly it slid out, revealing an iron lever.

With a glance at Gary, Mike lifted the handle and stared wide-eyed as the bookcase in front of them began to move. Startled, Gary stepped back; so did he while holding his breath, praying the thing opened enough for Jamie to get out.

Several heart-stopping moments later, Jamie appeared in the opening. Looking a little shell-shocked, she stumbled into the room, blinking against the sudden assault of light. Mike was at her side before she'd taken two steps and swept her into his arms, afraid she was going to collapse.

Ever since he'd gotten the call from Bill, he'd been half crazy with worry. He'd been petrified Cooper would get to her, kill her. And even once Zach and Lucas had taken Cooper into custody, he'd still been panicked, wondering where she was.

All sorts of thoughts had been torturing him. Had Cooper lied? Had he killed her and left her body somewhere? Was she hurt and unable to call for help? A litany of possibilities, none good, had raced through his mind.

Never in his wildest dreams had he thought he'd find her in a secret tunnel behind his walls. But he'd never been happier to see someone in his life.

Mike crushed her to him, half afraid to let her go for fear she wasn't really there. As he caressed her face with his hands, the shaky smile she gave him drew his eyes to her lips. He dipped his head, the need to kiss her stronger than his need for another breath.

Gary cleared his throat. "Are you okay, Jamie?"

Mike suddenly snapped to his senses, realizing what he'd almost done. He straightened.

Bad idea, Devlin. She's still a witness in your case.

If that wasn't bad enough, he'd been so focused on holding her and almost kissing her, Mike had never even asked if she was hurt. Gary had done it.

Get your damn head on straight you moron!

Mike blinked against his mental reprimand, but it cleared his head. Releasing her, he took two steps back so he wouldn't be tempted to haul her back into his arms. "Are you hurt?" he finally managed to ask. "Do you need us to call an ambulance?"

Jamie smiled at him. "I'm fine, thanks to you." Her gaze swung to Gary. "Both of you."

And as if to affirm her words, she brushed a kiss on his lips, but before Mike could recover and pull her back for more, she stepped away. She turned to Gary and stretched up onto her tiptoes, but couldn't quite reach him. Realizing her intent, Thorny smiled and leaned down while she pressed a kiss on his cheek.

Mike saw red. He didn't care if it had been a platonic kiss. She shouldn't have done it. Thorny was married. And how dare Gary encourage her.

He opened his mouth to protest, but the words got stuck in his throat.

Get a grip, Devlin. It was a simple kiss. Nothing more. And Jamie isn't Abby. She wasn't making a play for Thorny; just thanking him for helping to rescue her. Not only that, but she isn't yours; so why do you care who she kisses?

The thought sobered Mike for the heartbeat it took for him to collect his composure.

Gary's smile turned his way. "Well, I'm not needed any further, so I'll get out of your hair." He turned back to Jamie. "Glad you're okay, Jamie."

As Gary passed her, he whispered something Mike couldn't hear and winked at her.

Winked! Sure Thorny had done it discreetly. But not discreet enough.

Jealousy flared again bringing a scowl to Mike's brow. Was Gary flirting with her? The scowl grew deeper when a sly grin curved Gary's mouth. Like he knew something no one else knew. But before Mike could call him on it, Thorny was out the door.

Mike contemplated going after him and giving him a piece of his mind, but a soft hand laced fingers with his, short-circuiting his annoyance. A wave of awareness washed through him and Mike turned to see Jamie gazing at him adoringly.

"I'm so sorry about your friend. Bill was such a nice man." She caressed his cheek. "But you're my hero. Do you know that?"

How was he supposed to respond to that?

Okay…he knew how he'd like to respond to it. By hauling her up the stairs, tossing her on the bed and making love to her until they were both too weak to move.

Fight it, man. Fight it.

"Thank you for rescuing me…again," she added, dropping another quick soft kiss on his lips before he could react. "But I am really exhausted and my head hurts. I'm going to go lay down unless you need me for anything."

Oh he needed her alright. If she only knew.

Yeah, right. She'd probably laugh.

When was it going to get through his thick head? He was too old for her. Old enough to be her…well…old enough to be her much older brother.

He hauled in a breath to clear his mind and nodded. "Do you want anything to eat first?"

Jamie thought about it a moment and gently shook her head. "Not if you don't mind me raiding your refrigerator in the middle of the night."

He chuckled. "Go. I can take care of things down here. And you are welcome to anything you can find in the kitchen."

Before they left the study, he made Jamie close her eyes, so she wouldn't see the pool of blood that remained in the foyer. Taking her elbow, Mike led her up the stairs.

At her bedroom door, he gave her a wink of his own. Hey, if Thorny could do it, so could he. "Holler if you need anything."

She gazed at him a moment and then turned and walked into her room.

SHUTTING THE DOOR to her bedroom, Jamie turned around, biting her lip to keep from laughing aloud.

Mike was jealous. He was. And of Gary Thornton. The idea was hilarious.

She didn't know Gary well, but even a blind person could tell he was hopelessly in love with his wife. But the big guy also apparently had a wicked sense of humor.

The smile he'd had on his face before he'd winked, had told her he'd known Mike was struggling to keep his hands off her. And he'd winked intentionally to get a reaction.

Boy had he gotten one. The outraged surprise on Mike's face had been comical. And Jamie had almost lost it when Gary passed by her on his way out the door and whispered for her to *'go easy on Mike; he's had a rough day.'*

The man was playing matchmaker. She loved it.

What Jamie couldn't figure out was why Mike continued to fight against the attraction he obviously felt for her. She certainly wasn't going to rebuff anything he did.

She'd wanted him for so long, she'd probably faint if he ever kissed her and die of happiness if he made love to her. The mere thought of the latter left her a little weak in the knees.

But she also didn't want to cause him trouble. The poor man had his hands full with three murders…well, actually four counting Bill. The last thing Mike needed was her pressuring him into a relationship when he wasn't ready for one.

Then again, if she left things up to Mike and his hang-ups about their age difference, they'd never get together…or if they did, they'd both be too old to enjoy themselves.

185

One of these days, the timing would be right…and then Jamie was going to tell him exactly how she felt about him and what she wanted from him. Then she'd know if there was a chance for them. Because he'd either walk away or kiss her senseless.

She shook her head wistfully. She knew which option she hoped happened, but it wasn't going to happen tonight and she was beat.

After a quick trip to the bathroom to wash her face and brush her teeth, Jamie slipped back into her room.

Glancing at the clock, she saw it was nine p.m.

What a day? Had she really just gotten out of the hospital twelve hours ago? It seemed more like a week, with all that had happened.

Stripping off her clothes, Jamie pulled a nightgown over her head and wearily slipped into bed.

MIKE WATCHED AS Jamie disappeared into her room. He heaved a frustrated sigh.

His damn jaw hurt from clenching his teeth against the need that surged through him every time the woman was in the same room. And nothing he did seemed to help.

But why was he still obsessing about her?

Jamie was too young. She deserved someone closer to her age; someone she could grow old with. Not him and all the trust issues he'd developed, thanks to Abby.

Shaking away his wayward thoughts, Mike headed downstairs, his gaze dropping to the blood staining the floor at the landing. Bill's blood.

Instantly another wave of guilt filled him.

He hadn't killed Bill and wasn't responsible for it. Rationally he knew that. But rationale didn't help. His friend was dead, killed in his home, guarding his witness.

Mike heaved another sigh.

Get to work, Devlin.

The medical examiner had long ago removed Bill's body and the crime unit was finished inside the house; but there was a mess remaining.

Grabbing a bucket of water, rags and cleaning solution, Mike set out to clean up the pool of blood. But after five minutes, he realized he wasn't equipped to handle the task. And after tossing out the rags and dumping the soiled water down the toilet, he washed his hands and did what he should have done in the first place; he called a professional firm the Bureau had used for similar situations.

They'd be there first thing in the morning.

In the meantime Mike fished out a piece of plastic and an old sheet he used as a drop cloth for painting and covered the stains. At least Jamie wouldn't see it if she came downstairs.

With one more glance at the area, Mike went into his den to study the secret panel beside his fireplace.

He still couldn't believe tunnels snaked behind the walls of his home. What he wouldn't give to see the architectural design for the home. Then again…did they even have those things in 1774 when the house was built?

Considering the home's age, the access panel was a marvel of engineering. Gears, cogs and a chain, all controlled by a lever turned the heavy wooden bookcase into a doorway leading to the tunnels.

And because he wasn't able to resist, Mike grabbed an LED flashlight and set out to explore. With each step his fascination grew.

The small chamber on the other side of his study wall was about five feet deep and ten feet long. And as Jamie had said, at one end a narrow stone staircase traveled from the attic to the basement, with exits at each level.

Mike could only speculate as to the tunnel's original purpose.

To his knowledge there hadn't been any violent Indian raids in Maryland back when the house was built, but that didn't mean robbers and scavengers hadn't been a problem. And the heavy old shutters that adorned all the windows had narrow slits wide enough for the barrel of a musket to fit through in times when the home needed to be defended.

The tunnels would have come in handy in those instances, too. Mike could easily envision the original owners using the tunnels as a secure place to hide themselves and their valuables in the event of an emergency.

With the help of the bright light, he was finally able to locate levers that released the door from inside. Cleverly, they were secreted behind loose stones that were hinged. No one not knowing to look for them would ever spot them, they were that well camouflaged.

Mike supposed it had been done in case someone, like Cooper, had managed to get into the tunnels, to prevent them from finding their way into the house.

Thankfully, he didn't discover bones of any wayward visitor though, so Mike contented himself with studying the latest novelty of his home.

Mike's thoughts snagged the conversation he'd had when Bill first arrived at the home. O'Brien had commented about the fun he and his best friend had at that kid's grandparent's home, saying it had *great places to explore* and had been *like a constant adventure.*

Mike hadn't understood what Bill meant at the time. He'd thought Bill was just referring to the old home's character. Now he knew better. And while he still felt terrible about Bill's death, his sadness was tempered by gratefulness to the man.

Of all the cops and state troopers in Maryland, the odds of Bill being the one assigned to guard Jamie were infinitesimal. But thank God he had been. Because probably no one else would have known the house had secret tunnels.

A blood curdling scream reached Mike's ears as he stepped from the tunnel back into his study.

Jamie!

Grabbing his gun from the holster at his waist, Mike flew out of the study and up the stairs at a dead run, panicked by the thought that Scott Cooper had somehow escaped custody and was inside the house again. He skidded down the hall with his gun ready to confront any threat and threw open Jamie's door, bursting inside without hesitation or thought to what might await him on the other side.

Mike stopped dead in his tracks.

Breathing hard, Jamie was sitting up in bed with her covers carelessly tossed aside as if she'd thrashed them off. From the terror etched on her face, Mike thought his initial fear had been realized. That Cooper was back.

But a second look at Jamie's face told him the truth. She'd been awakened from a dead sleep by a nightmare.

He lowered his weapon, watching her take a mental inventory of her surroundings. She hadn't even noticed his presence yet.

Suddenly, her eyes met his and she gasped in surprise. "What happened?"

You gave me a heart attack. That's what happened.

Mike kept the thought to himself. "You screamed," he answered. "I think you were having a bad dream."

She looked doubtful, but took another survey of the room. "No one was here? Are you sure?"

Instead of verbal reassurance, Mike led with his weapon and walking across the room to the closet, he tossed open the door. To satisfy her fear, he searched every crevice of the empty space, even pounding on the walls to make sure they were solid and not another secret panel.

Nothing.

Returning to her bedside, he got down on his knees and peered underneath the bed.

Again, nothing.

His inspection of the windows showed them to be closed and securely locked.

"Honey, it had to have been a nightmare," he said gently. "You've been through an awful lot in the past day and a half. It's no wonder you had one."

Her breathing seemed to slow a little and some of the fear drained from her eyes. "It was so real. Scott Cooper was here; he had a knife at my throat."

Mike sat down beside her and gathered her into his arms. But he wasn't about to minimize her fears or make her feel foolish. Everything she was feeling was well justified by what she'd been through.

Phone calls to Zach and Lucas satisfied him that Scott Cooper was in jail at the Jacob's Valley Sheriff's Office. The Bureau was scheduled to transfer him to a federal prison the next afternoon. And Lucas was guarding Cooper overnight, so the killer wasn't going anywhere.

When he disconnected the call, Mike turned to Jamie. "Feel any better?"

"I think so." The brave smile she attempted wasn't convincing.

Mike gave her a nod of encouragement. "Try to get some sleep. I'll be right across the hall if you need me."

Before he changed his mind and did something they'd both regret, Mike rose and walking across the room, reached for her door knob.

"Mike...would you please stay with me until I fall asleep?"

Chapter Eighteen

First she'd jumpstarted his heart with her scream and now it skidded to a stop with her question. The woman was trying to kill him.

Every fiber of his being told Mike to keep walking, but he couldn't do it. Instead, he gave himself a mental shake.

Get a grip, Devlin. That was an innocent plea by a frightened woman, not an invitation to satisfy your wildest fantasies.

And in truth, she sounded so scared and looked so small and young in the large bed without a trace of makeup on her face, Mike couldn't help but remember the lonely child she'd been.

So many times Jamie had been let down by her old man. Mike couldn't...no...he wouldn't be another man to disappoint her.

Against his better judgment, he returned to her side and slid onto the bed beside her. Wrapping his arm around her shoulder, Mike made himself comfortable. Well, as comfortable as he was likely to get lying on a bed next to Jamie.

"My hero," she whispered, as she snuggled against him and draped her arm across his chest. "Thank you."

Every muscle in Mike's body tightened to the point of pain and his heart kicked into high gear. Oh, man...this was going to be shear torture.

"I'll be able to sleep knowing you're here," she murmured, closing her eyes.

He groaned silently. At least one of them would be getting some sleep; he sure wouldn't. He'd be too busy trying to control his body and the totally inappropriate reaction it was having to her being so close.

MIKE AWOKE WITH a start to pre-dawn darkness hovering over the room. He blinked to clear his vision and tried unsuccessfully to move.

He was pinned to the mattress by a mass of warm soft curves.

It took all of two seconds for his brain to register where he was and a curse screamed in his head.

He was lying in bed, with Jamie sprawled atop him, her lush red hair tickling his naked chest and shoulder.

Naked?

Panicked, Mike lifted the sheet slightly, praying he'd see pants on his body.

He muttered another curse. It was worse than he thought. He was wearing only his boxers.

Oh...this was so not good.

A moment of thought produced a memory. Cold permeating his body had awakened him in the middle of the night. He'd been so tired, but comfortable, he'd pulled off his clothing and climbed under the covers, never really waking up enough to give thought to what he was doing.

The evil twin that had taken up residence in his head taunted him with doubt about the veracity of his recollection. But he was sure it had been completely innocent on his part. At least that was going to be his story.

And no way had anything happened between them. He'd definitely remember if it had. Heck, he'd been daydreaming about getting her into his bed ever since seeing her two days ago. But no matter how much he wanted her, he'd never take advantage of her. They were all wrong for each other. He knew that in his soul. And more to the point, she was recovering from a concussion.

Glancing over at Jamie, his concern shifted focus.

She was contentedly sleeping, totally unaware of the misery he was in. And brother was he ever in misery. In fact, if he didn't get out from under her before she woke up, the state of his body would embarrass them both.

Hauling in a breath and praying he wouldn't wake her, he gently lifted her arm from around his waist. Carefully...very slowly...he slid out from under her, biting back a moan of pain radiating through him.

The moment he was free, Mike grabbed his clothing and practically ran from the room. A minute later he was standing under the cold spray of his shower, cursing his stupidity. He was still cursing himself several minutes later when he stepped from the shower.

Determined to refocus on the day ahead, he dried off, then wrapped the towel around his hips and slathered shaving cream on his face.

His cell phone rang.

Mike glanced down at the cream all over his hands. Great timing, phone.

Shrugging, he rubbed the froth off his hands onto the towel, then grabbed his phone and looked at the display.

Gary. Didn't the man ever sleep?

"Hey Thorny!" he greeted.

"'Mornin' Dev. You ready for a good head scratcher first thing?"

Not really. It was five blasted o'clock in the morning. He was barely awake and the *Team Jamie* hormones still grossly outnumbered the *Team FBI* brain cells in his body. But he couldn't very well tell his boss that.

"Sure," he said stupidly. "What do we have?"

"I just got off the phone with the lab and the bullets that killed Ed and Doug McDougal came from the same weapon."

Mike wasn't sure if it was lack of sleep or a water-logged brain, but Gary lost him on that one. "Are you saying Doug killed Ed and then shot himself?"

"That's the logical conclusion, but there's more," Gary replied cryptically. "There are traces of hair and blood on the grip of the gun that match Jamie."

That got Mike's attention. When he'd been staring down at Doug's body, he'd wondered whether the gun the sheriff had used to kill himself was the one that had been used to knock Jamie out."

Mike was still trying to figure out where and how Doug had retrieved a weapon, that everyone and their brother had been searching for and no one had found, when Gary spoke again.

"And we got a gift wrapped bonus from the lab," Thornton said, sounding entirely too wide awake for such an ungodly hour.

"It seems our good sheriff had a new patio poured just outside his home office on Saturday morning. The crime scene team found a set of beautiful footprints in the nearly hardened cement. And guess who those prints match?"

Mike rubbed his chin thoughtfully, trying to come up with an answer and quickly realized all he'd succeeded in doing was getting shaving cream all over his hand again.

Moron!

He swiped his hand on his towel again while processing the information.

The only conclusion Mike could draw, was that after Doug had clobbered Jamie with it and before Zach and he arrived, someone other than Doug had secreted the gun out of the senator's office.

Mike's eyes widened, his brain suddenly fully engaged. Cooper! The man who'd killed the senator and Bill O'Brien in cold blood and whom they suspected of killing Ed McDougal. It had to be him.

"Scott Cooper," he said, fully confident he'd reached the right conclusion.

"Bingo!" Gary replied. "The cement must have been set enough that Cooper didn't realize he was leaving a trail, but the sneakers he was wearing when he was arrested are a perfect match for the sole imprints found in the cement. And the lab found traces of the cement in the groove pattern on the bottoms of his shoes."

Mike chuckled. "We've got him dead to right."

"Exactly," Gary replied. "Those prints and the cement on his shoes prove he was at the sheriff's home. The set time on the cement gives us an approximate time of day, which closely matches the estimated time of Doug's death. He killed the old man, then killed both Ed and Doug and staged Doug's death to look like suicide, to throw us off."

"His interrogation this morning should be fun," Mike said, causing Gary to laugh.

"For sure, because we've also got a blood match on the drops by and on the fire door. They are a type match for Cooper. Don't know if you noticed or not, but he had a nasty gash on his hand when he was arrested yesterday."

No, Mike hadn't noticed. He'd been too worried about Jamie. But the wound only added to the mound of evidence they'd accumulated to nail Cooper's coffin shut.

After a few more minutes of conversation, planning their interrogation strategy, the call ended and Mike finally was able to shave and get dressed.

After checking to make sure Cooper was still tucked away in his cell, Mike penned a quick note to Jamie telling her that since she didn't have a car at his home, he was leaving her keys to his SUV.

He hadn't driven his vintage Mustang for a while and the weather was ideal. He'd take the Mustang and Jamie could use his SUV if she had any errands to run.

Satisfied she'd be fine, Mike set the security system and left the house.

SCOTT COOPER STARED across the table at the two Fed's. So far they hadn't said a word. He knew their trick. They were playing mind games, going for the psychological edge.

Let 'em try. It wouldn't work. He'd been trained by the best and knew how to avoid being broken during interrogation.

Name, rank and serial number.

The Rangers had drilled that into him early and fast.

He'd thought he'd miss army life, but he didn't. Scott was still making a living using his skills, only now he freelanced. Instead of being paid by Uncle Sam, he gave his services to anyone willing to pay his price.

Killing Andrew McDougal had been different though. No one had paid him for that kill, although he would bet there were plenty of people out there who would gladly pay for what he'd done.

But Scott hadn't wanted or needed money for that one. It had been personal.

Revenge, pure and simple.

No one messed with him and got away with it. And the old man had done a hell of a lot more than "mess" with him.

The not-so-honorable U.S. Senator from Maryland had been the lowest kind of scum on the earth. A lying, blood-sucking leech, feeding at the public trough for decades, while adding to his obscene wealth by screwing over people who were stupid enough to trust him or too weak to fight him. People like his mother.

And for that, Andrew J. McDougal had deserved to die.

For years the old man had fooled everyone, swept all his secrets into a closet. But no longer. Now that McDougal was dead, the truth would come out. Scott intended to make sure of that.

He snorted a silent chuckle. It might be fun to toy with these Feds, though. Feed them a few morsels of information; satisfy their curiosity so they could fill out some government forms. Make them think they'd won, that they'd beaten him.

They hadn't, though.

He might be behind bars, but he wasn't finished. They just didn't know it yet.

He planned on being free before sunset, before they transferred him anywhere. He'd be gone before they even realized it. And no one was better than him at becoming invisible, at disappearing into the night. The army had been trying for months to find him, but he'd always managed to stay several steps ahead of them. He could do the same thing with these morons.

Suddenly the big guy spoke. "You've been advised of your rights and you have consented to meet with us without presence of counsel. Is that correct?"

"Yeah. Not sure how much I'll tell you, but I've got nothing better to do."

"Before we start," old white hair stated in a completely business-like fashion. "You should know that we've got an eye-witness who positively places you in the office of Senator Andrew McDougal at the time of his murder. And DNA we found places you there as well."

No surprise in that. They were talking about the woman.

He should have eliminated her when he'd first had the chance. His mistake. He wouldn't make it a second time. Just give him Ol' Bessie and two seconds alone with the woman and she'd no longer be a problem.

"So this is your one chance to come clean," the big guy continued. "Tell us what we want to know and we'll help you."

Yeah, right. When pigs fly, they'd help.

"You might have white hair, but you ain't Santa Claus," Scott fired back.

Thornton's eye's darkened with a glare. "And you aren't stupid. I've seen your school records. So, you might want to rethink your position, Scott. You're being held on capital murder charges in the death of a U.S. Senator, the murder of Trooper Bill O'Brien, the attempted murder of a federal agent…"

Scott schooled his expression to show no reaction but inside his gut twisted.

The Fed wasn't dead!

How was that possible?

No one could have survived the injuries that man had. Damn! He'd been so sure he'd finished the guy off.

Maybe the big guy was bluffing. Except, he didn't look like it.

"And as of this morning, we've also added first degree murder charges for the deaths of Ed and Doug McDougal," Thornton continued calmly.

"I heard the sheriff committed suicide," Scott retorted, unwilling to show he was ruffled by the charges.

"Heard?" Thornton countered. "If you heard anything, it was the gun going off as you helped an unconscious man pull the trigger. And don't bother denying it. We've got you placed at the scene at the time of his death."

The big guy paused and stared at him with a look Scott assumed was meant to scare him. It didn't.

"You're looking at death row, Scott," Devlin interjected. "They're going to strap you on a table and shove a needle in your arm. And in a few months everyone will forget you ever existed."

Scott shook his head against the picture Devlin had just painted, but he couldn't ignore the words. He'd never bargained on death row. Then again, he'd never bargained on being caught. And he still had plans in the works to turn the tables on the Feds and make his escape. But just in case, maybe a deal wasn't such a bad idea.

"So what are you offering?"

A glance passed between the two agents and the big guy nodded so slightly Scott almost missed it.

"If you tell us everything we want to know," Agent Devlin answered. "We'll take the death penalty off the table."

Scott mulled the offer over for a moment. "Not good enough. I want your assurance in writing that the military has no jurisdiction over me for anything I may have done up until now."

With another glance at Devlin, Thornton slid his chair back and standing up, he walked out the door. Scott wasn't sure if he'd pushed too far and the interview was over or if the move was some kind of mind game, but Devlin just sat there staring at him.

Refusing to be baited, Scott rattled the chains on his feet and the one around his waist binding his hands. He took perverse pleasure when the guard outside the door, burst inside with his gun drawn.

As if the Fed there couldn't take care of himself.

Several minutes passed before Agent Thornton appeared again. "You've got a deal…but only if you come clean. If you play us, or give us any trouble, the deal is off."

Scott considered his options. At this point nothing leaned his way. And although he knew that would change shortly, he had nothing better to do at the moment. He might as well humor them. And frankly, he wanted people to know what he'd done and why.

His goal had been to make Andrew McDougal pay…and what better way than letting the world know why he and his sons were dead.

"You got a deal. But I wanna talk to Lt. Colonel Shaw," Scott challenged. "No one else…just him."

Thornton and Devlin shared another glance and to Scott's surprise, they both rose and left the room.

Were they actually going to give into that demand? He'd thrown it out there never really believing they'd agree to it. But he'd given it a try, because as far as Scott was concerned, Shaw was the only Fed worthy of hearing what he had to say. No one else would have ever gotten the drop on him the way Shaw had…and that earned him a degree of adversarial respect.

Chapter Nineteen

Barely a minute passed before the tall silver-haired man with the light gray eyes appeared in the doorway.

Lt. Colonel Lucas Shaw, U.S. Army, Retired. Yeah, the man oozed military brass right down to his bones.

"I understand you want to talk to me," Shaw said icily, taking the seat Devlin had vacated. He set a tape recorder on the table and started the recording. "Let's get started. Talk."

And Scott did. Spilling his guts to a man he begrudgingly admired.

"My mother died two months ago…"

"Sorry to hear that," Shaw replied, sounding like he actually meant it.

Scott nodded, but continued talking. "…while I was going through her papers I found a ton of documents and cancelled checks….all signed by Andrew McDougal," Scott explained. "From the documents, I learned that at age fifteen…fifteen…my mom had started working as a housekeeper for McDougal's family. A year later, she was raped by someone in the household. I am the product of that rape."

Rage simmered inside Scott as he related how the senator had used money and power to bully his mother into silence. How Andrew had even tried to force her to abort the baby. But she hadn't and the senator had been paying her lots of money ever since to keep her quiet about the rape.

The more Scott had read those letters, the more furious he'd become. And everything about the documents pointed to Andrew being the rapist.

"We know about the payments, but where are these documents?" Lucas asked.

Scott knew the mirror on the wall was two way and that he was being watched. He looked directly at the window figuring Thornton was back there somewhere. "I left them in the SUV I borrowed from Special Agent Barrett. His badge and wallet are in the car, too. The car is in an alley two blocks behind the sheriff's home. You're going to need a locksmith, though, because I locked his keys inside."

Confirming his suspicion about being watched, Shaw slid a quick glance at the mirror before nailing him with those gray eyes again.

"Okay...keep going," Shaw instructed.

"After everything I'd seen, I decided the man had to pay."

His first plan had been to eliminate both the senator and his wife, because Scott was sure Lauren had known all about the rape and payoffs. But as soon as he'd met her, he'd realized she was clueless; she hadn't known anything about him or the rape.

"Lauren was almost as pissed as me. And when she offered to take me to the senator's office, I agreed. It played right into my plan. I confronted him and at first he denied everything, but then he finally admitted the payoffs. But he blew off the rape as if it had been insignificant. Then he slapped his wife hard for bringing me there."

The arrogance of the man had infuriated Scott and first chance he'd gotten, he and Ol' Bessie had gone to work to wipe the smirk off the supercilious man's face. Everything had been going along like clockwork until the Fed had caught him in the act of stabbing the old man.

"For a couple seconds I thought I was history when Agent Barrett arrived," Scott admitted.

Ol' Bessie was serious business and in close order combat, Scott would pit his skills against anyone. But at a distance, his knife was no match for a semi-automatic pistol.

He nearly chuckled aloud remembering what had happened next.

As much as he disliked working with amateurs, he'd gotten help from an unexpected source. And man, watching that Fed crumble to the floor like a rag doll had been a beautiful sight.

"I never would have guessed old Lauren McDougal could swing a golf club so well. Man, she laid Barrett out cold. And I decided to finish him off."

He'd been doing that when all of a sudden the sheriff and mayor showed up. Scott hadn't realized Lauren had called them, but she had.

"When I saw the mayor, I realized I'd killed the wrong man. Ed McDougal and I look exactly alike. I knew the minute I saw him that he was my father. Don't get me wrong…Andrew deserved to die. But Ed needed to pay too. I was going to confront him then and there, but the Kendrick woman appeared in the hallway. Doug clobbered her with a weapon he pulled from an ankle holster."

Once she was out cold, the sheriff had taken charge. He'd ordered Lauren to leave. Then he and the mayor decided they should stage everything to look as if there'd been a love triangle between the senator, the woman and the Fed.

"Why would Doug and Ed help you cover up what you'd done?" Shaw inquired.

Scott considered the question a moment before answering. "You'll have to ask Lauren that. But my take is she was so upset about having a grandson she never knew about, that she was willing to do anything to protect me. And her boys went along with her because she insisted. Plus that, she was there and they probably didn't want her blamed for anything." He shrugged. "Only way to keep her clean was to frame someone else...like Barrett and the Kendrick woman."

Scott tipped his chin toward the two way mirror again. "I stayed to help Ed and Doug until I saw your buddies Devlin and Taylor arrive, then I bolted out the back door and took Barrett's car to get away."

"Why'd you take his car?"

Scott shrugged at what he considered an insignificant question. "The Honda I was driving was stolen and I figured it was time to change wheels. Barrett's keys were in his pockets."

"And after you left the senator's office, you went to Jamie Kendrick's apartment that night to eliminate her, didn't you?"

Scott nodded. "Yeah, I wanted to kill her right away after Doug knocked her out, to eliminate her being able to identify me or anyone else. But Lauren wouldn't let me. She said Andrew and Barrett were enough blood for one day. Anyway, the Kendrick woman wasn't home, so I left her a message and some proof of what would happen to her if she talked."

"Then what? You went to Ed McDougal's home and killed him next?" Shaw stated, making it more an accusation than a question.

"You're pretty good at this," Scott noted.

Shaw acknowledged the compliment with a silent nod.

Figuring that was as much reaction as he was going to get, Scott continued.

"Yeah. I went to his house to confront him about what he'd done to my mother. The bastard told me he'd been home on break from West Point and had gone out drinking with some buddies. He claimed he'd been drunk and didn't remember much about that night except that my mom had helped him up the steps when he'd stumbled in the front door. He claimed he didn't know she was sixteen and that she looked sexy in her maid uniform. He actually told me she had the body of a goddess and eyes and a smile to tempt a saint. Do you believe it?"

203

Just thinking about Ed's arrogance made Scott livid all over again. If Ed were alive now, he'd kill him all over again.

"Ed told me that the next morning after it happened, his old man stormed into his room, yanked him out of bed and beat the crap out of him for raping my mom. Ed claimed again he didn't remember any of it, but that her torn dress was still lying on his bedroom floor, so he guessed he'd done it."

Completely unremorseful for any of it, Ed had told him Andrew had arranged to pay her off to keep the incident from becoming public because the senator was up for reelection. A scandal would have hurt him.

"You killed him with a gun registered to the sheriff. How'd you get it?"

Scott shifted his eyes to the mirror. Old white hair Thornton hadn't lied. They did have everything pretty much all figured out. Pulling his gaze back to Shaw, he shrugged.

"After Doug bashed the Kendrick woman on the head with his gun, he gave it to me and told me to get it out of the senator's office; he didn't want to be caught with it. So I took it with me. My plan had originally been to cut Ed's throat; it's my trademark. But that gun was just too tempting and I decided to use it instead. I mean, Ed had to pay for what he'd done to my mother. It was just a matter of how."

"What about Doug," Shaw asked matter-of-factly. "We know it wasn't a suicide. But why did you kill him?"

What the hell...he was in for the whole ride at this point, Scott figured. Might as well tell them everything.

"I figured when Doug heard about Ed that he'd throw me under the bus and I wasn't going to let him do it. So I went to his house to shut him up. I took the gun because I was dealing with a man I knew would be armed. But when I got there, he was dead drunk and passed out cold. The plan to make his death look like a suicide just came to me when I saw him like that. I figured everyone would think he'd killed his brother and then committed suicide."

"And why would we think that?" Lucas asked flatly.

"Because ballistics for the gun would show it was a match to the bullet that killed Ed. And the Kendrick woman's hair and blood were still on the handle."

Scott had expected some reaction to his admission, perhaps even a hint of admiration for a well thought out plan. He got nothing. Just those icy gray eyes.

"And yesterday, you killed Bill O'Brien because he wouldn't tell you where Jamie Kendrick was hiding?" Lucas asked.

"Yeah," Scott replied. "He was in my way."

For several moments Shaw studied him intently. Scott tried to figure out what he was thinking, but it was impossible. So, he stared back at him.

The lull ended with another question. One Scott hadn't expected.

"Tell me about Captain Martin Zerphy. Why and how did you kill him?"

The question caught Scott off-guard and that annoyed him. He thought about refusing to answer, but then he remembered the deal on the table. Answer all their questions and the death penalty wouldn't be a factor in his future.

"Zerphy took over command from our original unit commander. Lt. Rockford was a great guy and a good commanding officer, but the army decided to transfer him and Zerphy was assigned. He didn't like me from day one and made it his mission to make my life miserable. He had the gall to call me a psychopath and he got me tossed out of the Rangers."

Scott chuckled, remembering the look on Zerphy's face when he'd walked into the trap set for him. "I got my revenge, though. Tortured him for hours and watched him bleed and scream before I slit his throat and put him out of his misery."

Shaw stood up suddenly. "We're through here," he announced. He started to leave, but turned back to face Scott. "You think you're some kind of super soldier, but you don't deserve the title of Ranger. You're an embarrassment to the name and honorable service of that group…to the entire army for that matter. And if they hadn't stripped you of your rank, I'd yank it off your sleeve right here and now. Zerphy was wrong. You're not a psychopath; you're a sociopath. You belong in a cage, Cooper, and that's exactly where you're going to spend the rest of your life."

As Shaw spun around and walked out the door, Scott stared after him fuming too badly to say anything. He'd trusted the man, thought they had a bond of some kind due to their similar service background. But Scott had misjudged the man. Shaw was no better than any of the others he'd met. And when he got out of here, he was going after all of them. He'd make them all pay for the trouble they'd caused him.

STANDING IN THE observation room next to where Scott Cooper was weaving an unbelievable story of cold-blooded murder, Mike, Zach and Gary listened in absolute silence, all of them stunned to speechlessness by Cooper's unremorseful delivery.

Mike glanced over at Zach, who just shook his head in disbelief. Mike agreed. Cooper seemed to have no conscience whatsoever.

But as horrifying as it had been listening to Cooper, a sense of relief filled Mike. It was over. They had the senator's murderer in custody and Cooper himself had provided them with his motive.

Revenge.

The only thing left, other than paperwork and making sure they had all their *i's* dotted and *t's* crossed, was Cooper's trial, which Mike fully expected would be a publicity nightmare bordering on a three-ring circus.

The door opened and Lucas walked in. He looked at all of them and shook his head in disgust. "I had to get out of there before I lost my lunch." He shook his head again. "I've met some cold individuals in my life, but that guy takes the cake. He brutally murdered five people...that we know of...and talks about it as if he's discussing the weather."

Mike nodded. "And he probably hasn't lost a second of sleep over any of it?"

Zach scoffed a humorless chuckle. "Right."

"I want Lauren McDougal found and brought here, now,"

The sudden change of subject drew their attention to Gary. His gaze took them all in. "We've gotten everything we're going to get from Cooper. But Lauren McDougal is in this thing up to her aristocratic neck and she's been lying through her teeth."

He glanced at Mike. "That car we saw being washed at her place...the senator's car. She had to have left the murder scene in it. She arrived with Cooper in the black Honda and left before him. The Honda was in the lot, but the Porsche was gone when state police inventoried the cars in the lot. She left that office after watching her husband be brutally massacred and got in his car and drove away like nothing happened. I want her arrested and brought in here, now."

Mike nodded. "Zach and I will pick her up after we get Cooper back to the jail. Lucas is heading to the office to finalize paperwork for Cooper's transfer."

Gary nodded, then turned back for another look at Cooper and shook his head. "I'm going to the hospital to see Jimmy," he said, suddenly sounding very weary.

Mike glanced at Zach and Lucas, who both looked as surprised as he was by the pronouncement.

"You okay, Dad?" Zach asked, clearly concerned.

Gary turned to look at him. "I'm fine. I just need some fresh air and want to spend some time with Jimmy. Call me when you get Lauren in here and I'll come back."

Thornton didn't wait for a reply; he just turned and walked out the door.

Mike stared after him, worried. He'd never known Thorny to walk away from anything.

"Do you really think he's okay?" Lucas' question reinforced Mike's thought that their boss was acting strangely.

Zach turned to stare after his father, but Gary was out of sight, so Zach turned back to them. "He does a good job of hiding it most times, but I know Dad is really upset over Jimmy. In a way, I think he looks on him like another son. He feels guilty that Jimmy got caught up in the whole thing with Clark and was almost killed in the process. It's been eating away at him, being tied up by this case and not being able to be with Jimmy." Zach shrugged. "On top of that, he's shouldering responsibility for all the medical decisions being made for Jim. And, Dad's got pressure coming at him from all directions to solve the case. That's got to be tough."

Mike knew all of that; he'd just never pieced it together. No wonder Thorny had left.

Now that he thought about it, Mike could use a diversion too. And he knew just the diversion he needed. Jamie.

Mike pulled out his cell phone and called her, glad he'd finally thought to ask for her cell number.

"Hi Mike," she answered cheerily. "What a pleasant surprise."

The weight of the world lifted from Mike's shoulders at the sound of her voice.

"Hi," he replied, unable to stop the smile that curved his lips. "Just checking to see how you're feeling."

"I'm great. Slept like a baby last night, thanks to you."

The memory of her sprawled atop him when he'd awakened flashed through his head, bringing with it an instant reaction in his body. He cursed silently.

"Glad to hear it," he answered, managing to rein in his thoughts. "Don't overdo it today. Remember…you've got a concussion."

"I won't." She paused for a heartbeat. "Are you free for lunch? My treat."

As much as he knew it was wrong to encourage her, he'd like nothing more than to take her up on the offer. Just being with her made him feel years younger. "I wish I could, but I can't. Not today. Too much work."

"Oh."

The regret in that single word twisted Mike's gut.

"I'll tell you what," he said, unable to stop himself. "I'll take you out to dinner tonight to celebrate the end of my case. How's that sound?"

"Wonderful! You've got a date. Maybe we can celebrate two things."

The word *date* gave him pause. But dammit, why not? It was just a meal. Nothing more. He enjoyed her company and they both needed to eat. No big deal. And maybe she'd realize their age difference was too significant for anything permanent to last between them.

He gave himself a mental smack to refocus.

"What do you mean two things?"

"I had a call a few minutes ago. In the wake of what's happened, Bob and Colin have taken stock of their law firm and they want me back. They are even offering me a full partnership."

Mike pulled the phone away from his ear and stared at it for a heartbeat. How could that be? Surely they were busy planning funerals, not reassessing their law firm.

"Are you sure the offer is on the up and up?" he asked, not wanting her hurt or disappointed again.

"I think so. They want me to come in this afternoon. I have an appointment with them at four...so thank you for leaving me keys to your car."

Mike sucked in a breath to hold his tongue. She was a grown woman. The decision was hers to make; not his. And the man who'd given her trouble before...Andrew...was dead, so she no longer had to worry about his unwanted advances.

On the up side, if Jamie accepted the offer she'd stay in Jacob's Valley and he'd get to see her periodically.

Mike winced at that thought. Why did he want to torture himself like that? He and Jamie had no future together. Why did he want to have her around as a constant reminder of what he couldn't have? The thought of her with another man made him half sick in the stomach.

But he also couldn't imagine her leaving town and never seeing her again.

She meant too much to him.

Mike's heart slammed to a stop. She meant too much to him. It was true.

The realization scared the hell out of him.

He'd sworn off getting emotionally attached to women. Abby had cured him of any desire for permanent ties. Funny though, the idea didn't seem so reprehensible when he put Jamie into the role of the *"someone permanent"*. She was definitely a permanent keeper if ever there was one?

But she wasn't his to keep. So get over it.

Man, he needed to see a shrink. His head was so screwed up he was arguing with himself.

Mike smacked his forehead with the palm of his hand to rattle some sense into his brain.

"Well, good luck with the interview. They'll be lucky to get you back, but make sure you get that partnership offer in writing."

Jamie's chuckle wafted through the phone and sent a wave of longing through him. "I will. See you at home later."

As he disconnected the call and returned the phone to the clip on his waist, Mike realized he was alone in the observation room. He glanced through the two way mirror and saw Zach and Lucas getting Scott Cooper ready for transfer back to the jail.

He headed out the door to help them.

Chapter Twenty

Far above him he could vaguely make out dim light and sound…voices. Mustering all his willpower, he swam upward, hunger and thirst driving him toward the beam. He broke the surface and sucking in a breath, his eyes popped open.

"Gimme a loaded pizza and whatever beer you have on tap!"

A colorful string of curses and clattering metal greeted his request. His eyes slowly focused on Gary Thornton, whose gaze flew between him and a tipped over chair.

Righting the chair, Thornton turned back with a look of total shock.

"Jimmy?"

"Hey Thorny," Jim Barrett greeted, his voice sounding hoarse to his ears. But he was glad to see a familiar face. "Sit down. Join me for lunch?"

The big man's chest rose and fell rapidly. Instead of answering, Gary stared at him for a moment with the oddest expression on his face. He looked…afraid?

But that was nonsense. Nothing scared Thorny. Well, almost nothing. Having Kate kidnapped by that lunatic a couple months ago had rattled Thorny more than Jim had ever seen him. But that had been understandable.

Jim shoved away the thought, to concentrate on more important issues. "I'm hungry. How soon is the pizza going to be here?"

Thornton's brow knit and those cobalt eyes of his seemed to question Jim's sanity.

"Do you know where you are?" the familiar deep bass voice asked in all seriousness.

"Sure. Vinny's," Jim answered without thinking. Best pizza in the county. He'd gotten so hungry painting Mike's kitchen, he'd called in his order, cleaned up and made a run into town for some food.

A flicker of doubt worked its way into his subconscious as he catalogued his surroundings. His brow knit in confusion. Okay...so maybe he didn't know where he was. This definitely wasn't Mike's house and there was no pizza or waitress in sight. No smell of wet paint or aroma of Italian food in the air either; just a faint antiseptic odor.

And there was Thorny, too...who continued to eye him warily.

A heartbeat later, his brain kicked into gear. Jim's frown deepened. "Wait a minute. Where am I? Is this a hospital?"

Gary suddenly barked a laugh and the worried look in his eyes vanished, replaced by compassionate concern. "Yes. But let's start with something simple. Do you know who you are?"

Jim didn't care if Gary was his boss or not; they'd been partners for five years so he figured that entitled him to a little insubordination, especially since the question was ludicrous. "Hell yes I know who I am," he quipped, giving Thornton a look intended to telegraph his displeasure. "What kind of a question is that? Do you know who you are?"

He hadn't expected Gary to be riled by the response and the typically unflappable agent wasn't. Thornton chuckled. "Okay...just checking. Do you remember how you got here? What happened?"

Before Jim could even form a reply, the door to the room flew open and a doctor and several nurses rushed into the room. A petite blonde nurse who came up to about Thornton's waist shot a glare at the big man and pointed to the door. "You'll have to step outside," she ordered.

To Jim's astonishment Thorny complied without an argument.

What was going on? Why was he in a hospital? And why were these people all staring at him as if he was some kind of science experiment?

Fifteen minutes passed before some semblance of sanity returned to the room. The medical staff was gone, declaring him on the road to recovery, but his head was still spinning from what the doctor...what was his name? Wells. Yeah. Wells...had told him about his injuries.

Jim guessed he was lucky to be alive. But he still couldn't believe he'd been in a coma for a couple days.

According to Wells, friends had been sitting with him almost constantly since he'd been admitted, talking and reading to him so he'd hear friendly voices and see a familiar face when he awakened. After learning that, Jim understood Thornton's startled reaction.

Jim chuckled to himself remembering the look in Thorny's eyes. Like he'd seen a ghost. But Jim supposed after sitting in dead silence with someone unconscious, to have that person suddenly demanding pizza and beer would be enough to startle even someone with Thorny's nerves of steel.

The door to his room slid open again and Gary poked his head inside. "Are you up for answering some questions?"

Now that he was fully awake and Wells had filled him in on his injuries, Jim's brain had had a chance to click into gear. He recognized the concern in Gary's eyes, concern for him. And while Jim knew the questions Thorny wanted answered were related to a case; he also knew it had been friendship...plain and simple...not a case, which had led Gary to sit quietly, keeping a vigil in his room while he was unconscious.

The nurses had promised they'd rustle up some food for him — unfortunately not the pizza and beer he had his heart set on, but food — so Jim was up for just about anything that didn't require too much moving around.

Still, there was no reason he couldn't have some fun busting Thorny's chops.

"Sure. As long as the questions are more intelligent than asking me if I know who I am."

Gary chuckled and strode over to the chair again. The moment he was seated, his cobalt eyes settled on Jim, studying him with concern. "Do you remember anything about how you were hurt?"

"Now that I'm more awake, I remember everything down to the moment I lost consciousness," Jim answered, already envisioning the nightmare in his mind. "What do you want to know?"

Gary splayed his hands. "How about you start at the beginning. Go at your own pace and when you want to rest, tell me to get lost."

Jim nodded. "That'll be fun."

Gary chuckled again, but his expression sobered quickly and Jim knew it was time to go to work. But first he wanted to know for sure what he was dealing with.

"McDougal is dead, isn't he?" Jim was almost certain the answer was *yes*. He'd seen the senator's injuries, all the blood, the death stare in the old man's eyes.

Gary nodded, but said nothing and Jim recognized the interview technique. Thornton wanted him to give his account without interruption. So he did.

Jim thought a moment. "Clark called while I was cleaning up to go to Vinny's for lunch. He told me to get over to McDougal's office right away, something about a threatening letter. So I pulled on one of my suits and headed off to McDougal's office. I thought it was odd he called instead of you...but then I remembered you and Kate were at a wedding. And Clark told me he'd already cleared with you that he was sending me. So I went."

"When I got to the senator's office the front door was unlocked, so I went inside. It was quiet and except for a young woman at the back of the office, I didn't see or hear anything immediately." He chuckled softly. "I thought the young woman was Kate at first, but quickly realized that couldn't be. And a second later...just outside the senator's door, which was ajar, I caught the smell of blood. I looked inside and saw McDougal slumped against his desk. There was a young man leaning over him with a knife. I pulled my gun as I stepped into the office, identified myself and ordered him to drop the knife. But something slammed into the back of my head."

"That was a golf club," Gary supplied. "We found traces of your hair and blood on it."

Jim tipped his head in acknowledgement. "I didn't see who hit me, but the blow knocked me down and must have stunned me for a moment. Next thing I knew, I felt something slice into my gut and I guess my eyes opened, because I saw the kid was on top of me, slashing away like he was high on something. There was a woman standing behind the office door, watching what he was doing."

Jim shook his head in disbelief. "It was McDougal's wife."

ADRENALINE POURED INTO every cell of Gary's body. Cooper had confirmed Lauren's presence at the scene, but having Jimmy confirm it would put the final nail in the woman's coffin.

"You're sure it was McDougal's wife you saw?"

"Yes. I've seen her on television and in newspaper pictures. It was definitely her. And I remember calling to her to help." With another disbelieving shake of the head, Jim continued. "She ignored me; never even moved."

He paused for a moment to suck in a deep breath. "I honestly don't know how many times the guy stabbed me, but I remember trying to block him with my arms."

Jim glanced at the bandages on his arms and hands and then down at his torso. He shrugged. "Guess I wasn't too effective, but..."

Gary cursed silently when someone rapped on the door. After three days, he was anxious to get Jimmy's account of what had gone down in McDougal's office. An interruption now only delayed the investigation more.

"Come in," Jim called, clearly looking forward to seeing who his visitor was.

The door swung open and all Gary's misgivings flew out the window when he saw his wife standing in the doorway.

With her usual enthusiasm for life, Katie breezed into the room, excited to see Jim awake. After dropping a kiss on Jim's forehead and making a fuss over him for a few moments, she came to him. She greeted him with a tender kiss but then pulled back and smiled up at him.

"I gather you're talking business. So I'll get out of here and let you finish. But don't you dare overtire him," she warned.

Gary chuckled. Katie might be retired, but once a doctor, always a doctor. And her family and friends knew better than to ignore her when she issued medical instructions.

"I won't," he answered dutifully.

Satisfied she'd gotten her message across, she nodded and then turned a stern gaze on Jim. "And you behave. Listen to your doctors and nurses."

"Yes ma'am," Jim replied.

Kate smiled, pleased with his reply. She gave him another motherly kiss and patted his hand. "I'm so glad you're on the mend, Jimmy. You really had us worried for a while."

Jim smiled up at her contritely. "Sorry about that."

She waved away his apology. "Just take care of yourself and I'll pop back again later."

With that, Kate vanished out the door.

For a moment, they both stared after her. But Gary was anxious to get Jim's story before fatigue forced his friend to sleep again.

"So...you tried to defend yourself against the knife attack," Gary prompted. "What happened next?"

Jim closed his eyes as if drawing on the memory. "Two of McDougal's sons suddenly arrived...the sheriff and the mayor...and yanked the kid off me. I remember thinking I was being rescued. But then they started shouting at the kid. They ordered their mother and him to get out of there."

"Both she and the kid had blood on their hands and clothing and I remember wondering if she was the one who'd clobbered me. Anyway, I heard the kid refuse to leave, but Lauren said she'd go. Then she hit me with the golf club again. Just wound up and smashed me on the head again. That's the last thing I remember."

"Can you describe the fellow?"

Gary doubted it was a face Jim would ever forget. Gary had been in a life and death situation himself a couple months ago during a bank robbery and the face of his would-be executioner still haunted him at times.

"Caucasian, mid-to late-twenties, about six foot tall, maybe one eighty, muscular, buzz cut brown hair, green eyes, cleft chin." Jim shrugged slightly. "Nice looking kid. I heard Lauren call him Scott."

For a moment after he finished, Gary merely stared at him admiringly. "You've just sealed this case for us, Jimmy. We've got the killer in custody and he's confessed to what he did. But your solid eye witness testimony will nail him if he recants his confession."

"Who is he?"

"Scott Cooper...a skeleton in Ed McDougal's closet." Gary told him the whole sordid story about Cooper. "You just described him perfectly."

"Damn!"

"Exactly."

When he was sure Jim didn't remember anything else about that day, Gary explained how Mike and Zach had found him in McDougal's office, but soon, he noticed Jim's eyes drifting closed.

Gary stood up and patted him gently on the shoulder. "You forgot to tell me to get lost," he said quietly.

Jim's eyes popped open and he grinned guiltily. "Sorry."

"Get some rest, Jimmy," Gary said, patting him again. "I'll be back later."

As he stepped into the hallway, Gary pulled out his cell phone.

The remarkable clarity of Barrett's recollection of events at the law office was astounding, considering his injuries and surgeries. But Gary had no doubt Jimmy's memory of the events was accurate. Besides the fact he was a trained investigator, too much of his account was supported by other statements and physical evidence collected at the scene.

All the characters involved in the senator's murder and ensuing cover-up were either dead or in custody, except one. Gary intended to rectify that situation immediately.

"If you haven't picked up Lauren McDougal yet, I want an arrest warrant issued for her," he ordered, after updating Mike on Jimmy's account of the murder. "The charges are murder of a U.S. Senator and attempted murder of a federal agent."

"Will do," Mike replied, but there was a hedge in his voice that raised hackles on the back of Gary's neck.

"What's up?" he asked.

"I was just about to call you," Mike offered. "Scott Cooper was shot to death fifteen minutes ago."

Gary cursed aloud. "What? Shot by who?"

"He managed to get hold of a knife and after killing one of the deputies, Cooper used the guy's keys to get out of his cell. Another deputy shot and killed him when Cooper came after him with the knife."

"How did he get a knife?"

"While Zach and I were at her house looking for her, Lauren McDougal was visiting Cooper at the jail. The deputies on duty were young and inexperienced. Out of respect for her position as the senator's wife and Doug's mother, deputies didn't search her. They took her word she didn't have any weapons. But I just looked at their video feed and watched her reach through the bars of Cooper's cell and hand him the switch blade he used to kill the guard."

Gary wasn't sure why the news surprised him. The woman was a cold bitch who'd been stonewalling the investigation from the start. Cooper had placed her at the scene, but he'd glossed over the level of her participation. After talking to Jimmy, Gary knew she'd been present during the senator's murder and had caused Jimmy's head wounds.

"Where was Lucas when all this happened? I thought he was at the jail."

"The paperwork for the transfer had come through from Washington and he'd walked over to the courthouse to get a judge's signature on the release form. He was gone for less than ten minutes and came back to find the carnage."

Gary heaved a weary sigh. "Please tell me we have Lauren in custody."

"I wish I could, but she was gone when the attack occurred," Mike answered. "I've got an APB out on her."

Gary shook his head resignedly. The only saving grace in the whole mess was the amount of money taxpayers would save on trials. Doug, Ed and now Cooper certainly wouldn't be wasting the court's time.

That left only Lauren.

Her trial would be a three-ring circus. With her money and influence she'd pull out all the stops to tip the scales of justice in her favor. But if it was the last thing he did, Gary intended to make her pay for her crimes…especially what she'd done to Jimmy.

"Lucas is still at the jail wrapping up things there, but Zach and I have the photo line-ups for Jim that you requested," Mike continued. "We'll be there shortly."

Gary had texted his team earlier to let them know Jimmy was awake and he'd asked Mike to assemble two photo line-ups, one with Scott Cooper and one with Lauren McDougal. Although Cooper was dead, they still needed Jimmy's identification of Cooper as the man he'd seen stabbing the senator.

"Good Dev. But Jimmy was tired. I left his room so he could rest. So when you get here, I'll be in the cafeteria. Come see me so we can identify loose ends we need to nail down before we close the investigation. We can show Jimmy the line-ups later, when he's rested."

"Sounds like a plan," Mike replied. "See you in ten."

When he disconnected the call, Gary headed to the elevator, letting his mind re-run all he'd learned from Jimmy and Mike. He hadn't been exaggerating when he'd said Jimmy had sealed the case. They'd accumulated a lot of circumstantial evidence and some good solid physical evidence and they had Cooper's taped confession. But murderers had been known to recant confessions and defense attorneys had been known to get them thrown out of court. And nothing trumped an eye witness account, especially one that supported all the other evidence they'd gathered.

Still, it had been disturbing to hear Jimmy relate details of his attack. Gary couldn't imagine what had gone through his head, lying basically helpless while some maniac stabbed him and the sense of betrayal he must have felt when instead of defending him, Lauren McDougal had joined in the attack.

Shaking away the disturbing images, Gary punched the button for the elevator.

Knowing Kate, she was still around somewhere. Instinct told him he'd find her sipping tea in the cafeteria, which is why he'd told Mike to look for him there.

Chapter Twenty-One

The hospital cafeteria was a hubbub of activity with staff and visitors creating a steady stream of dinner time traffic. Kate Thornton sat at a table by the windows, watching all the action wistfully.

For nearly thirty years, hospitals had been her home away from home. Her professional life, working as a trauma surgeon in busy emergency rooms had given her a sense of pride, had helped to define her. But life had thrown her a curve, making her question her fitness as a doctor and surgeon.

A shiver rattled Kate's body as the memory of being kidnapped and buried alive flooded her mind. By the time she'd been rescued, she'd been hovering on the verge of death from internal injuries, dehydration and shock. Fortunately, the physical injuries she'd suffered had healed completely, but the psychological trauma of the horrific nightmare was still alive and well in her subconscious and panic attacks hit her at unsuspecting times, leaving her shaken and on edge.

Perhaps in another career, she would have been able to work around those nightmare moments. But a long time ago Kate had taken the Hippocratic Oath, vowing to do no harm to her patients. When a panic attack had hit her while she was operating on a patient, she'd lost her certainty that she was capable of upholding that oath.

She'd retired before she'd hurt someone or God forbid killed a patient by carelessness.

Giving up a career she loved had been one of the hardest things she'd ever done, but it had been a necessity.

Still, until she'd sat down and begun watching the hospital activity, Kate hadn't realized how much she truly missed being a part of it. She did. More than she ever thought possible.

From the corner of her eye, she caught sight of a familiar figure in the cafeteria doorway.

A smile curved her lips.

Glad for a diversion from her sad thoughts, she settled her gaze on her husband as he filled an insulated cup with ice and what she knew would be a diet cola. His long legged confident stride carried him to the cashier and Kate heard his wonderful deep chuckle in response to something the young woman said.

As Gary approached, she glanced up into his striking cobalt eyes.

"Is this seat taken, pretty lady?" he said in that familiar bass voice she loved so.

"I was saving it for my husband," she teased, taking a sip of her tea.

"Pfft!" He gave her a dismissive wave. "What do you want with an old stuffed shirt like him? I'm much more fun."

Kate nearly choked on her tea at his unexpected repartee. But she was game to play along. She nodded at the seat. "Well, make yourself at home, handsome, and let's hear what you have in mind?"

Molded plastic groaned when he lowered his tall frame into the chair beside her. Mischief alit in his eyes and he turned a sexy grin on her. "My car is out in the parking lot and it's got a nice big back seat. What do you say, beautiful? You want to have some fun?"

A tingling sensation rippled through Kate in anticipation of the sheer pleasure he always brought her when they made love. But the mere idea of Gary in the back seat of any vehicle was ludicrous...hysterical actually. He was so tall he barely fit in the driver's seat of most cars, let alone a back seat. He'd need the flat bed of a large pick-up truck to accomplish the feat he was suggesting.

She tried to contain a laugh, to maintain the charade longer, but her mind, unwilling to let the comical idea go, conjured up tomorrow morning's headline.

Federal Agent And Retired Surgeon Caught Buck Naked In Parking Lot Tryst.

Kate could see it now. A startled photo of the two of them caught in the act. It was too much. She snorted a chuckle that turned to a laugh…a laugh that continued until tears ran down her cheeks.

It didn't help that Gary just sat there grinning at her.

Several gulps of air to catch her breath finally helped Kate regain her composure, but the humor behind the idea wouldn't quit. "Darling, I'm tempted to take you up on that suggestion, just to see how you manage it," she chuckled.

After several moments of shared laughter, they fell into a companionable silence, sipping tea and soda.

Gary finally spoke. "Jimmy looks good, doesn't he?"

Kate smiled. "He looks amazing considering what he's been through."

Another moment of silence ended with Gary shaking his head. "He scared the hell out of me when he woke up."

The admission caught Kate by surprise. Usually nothing rattled her husband. "Why? What happened?" she asked curiously.

"You know that pizza place that was robbed yesterday?"

She nodded. An armed robbery in a small town like Jacob's Valley was big news and had been all over the television.

"Well, I was reading the news article about the hold-up to him," Gary continued. "And he woke up suddenly."

She wasn't surprised to learn Gary had been reading the newspaper to Jim. She'd told him that people in comas can often hear conversations around them. And studies had shown that familiar voices had been known to bring patients out of their coma.

Everyone who knew Jim and knew about his injuries had been taking turns reading and talking to him during visits.

Gary shook his head in disbelief. "His eyes just popped open and he said... *'Give me a loaded pizza and whatever beer you have on tap!'* No warning or anything; just woke up and demanded pizza. He startled me so badly, I almost fell out of my chair," Gary explained with an uneasy chuckle and another shake of his head.

Kate smothered a chuckle, imagining the scene.

"Seriously," Gary continued. "How does someone go from zero to fifty with no warning? He was in a coma for more than two days and all of a sudden demands pizza and a beer."

Kate knew of cases where patients woke up talking, but she'd never experienced it. Even so, it didn't take much imagination to realize what a shock it would be to anyone witnessing it. "I should have warned you it could happen."

Kate chuckled softly suddenly. "I wish I'd been there to capture your reaction with my camera, though." She grinned mischievously and tweaked his cheek. "What a great blackmail photo it would have been."

"Ha, ha," he said, trying to sound annoyed, but she could see he was losing the battle and when a chuckle vibrated through him, she laughed too.

Gary's chuckle slowly faded and he gazed at her adoringly. His hands slid across the table top to capture hers between his warm palms. "Have I told you recently how much I love you?"

Leaning forward he dropped a tender kiss on her lips.

Kate melted a little inside. How could a woman not adore a man who'd make that declaration aloud in the middle of a busy cafeteria? The way he looked at her, he made her feel as if they were the only two people in the world.

"HOW TOUCHING, AGENT Thornton!"

Sarcasm dripped from the taunt hollered from somewhere in the room.

Gary's head jerked up, every instinct instantly on alert. He couldn't be sure whether what happened next took seconds or hours; he suspected the former, but it seemed an eternity. All he knew for certain was that all hell broke loose.

Swinging around, Gary spotted Andrew McDougal's widow slowly advancing on them with a semi-automatic pistol pointed directly at Jamie Kendrick's head.

Screams erupting around them, as people scattered for shelter, seemed to grind the world into slow motion. Instinctively, Gary shifted in front of Kate protectively, but he didn't reach for his gun for fear Lauren would shoot Jamie.

Holding his hands out in a non-threatening gesture, Gary saw the exact moment Lauren shifted tactics.

A deafening shot rang out, echoing through the cafeteria.

Kate screamed. So did Jamie.

And searing pain tore through Gary's right bicep, dropping his arm helplessly to his side. His heart pounded in his ears as blood spurting from the wound quickly soaked his sleeve.

His entire arm was numb. Dead. His hand, too. Completely. He couldn't grip his weapon now if his life depended on it.

Panic tried to gain a foothold in his brain, but he forced it away.

Kate's life was in jeopardy. Jamie's too. If he lost focus, they could be killed. He had to think. To find a way to stop the crazed woman.

"What are you doing?" Kate shouted at Lauren, any fear evident in her voice overshadowed by her outrage, as she grabbed his arm, trying to stem the bleeding.

Shoving away concern for his arm, Gary pushed Kate behind him again as Lauren, now only several yards away, peppered the area around them with gunfire from the extended magazine in her gun.

She was firing so wildly, Gary doubted she'd ever held a firearm before. Regardless, she was no less dangerous than if she'd been an ace markswoman, probably more so because there was no control over her shots.

"Lauren, stop! Think about what you are doing," he called, trying to appeal to whatever grain of sanity the woman still possessed. "Put the gun down and stop this before you do something that can't be undone."

"No! You have to pay for what you've done. You and your agents should have stayed out of it; let my sons handle everything. But you didn't. Nobody humiliates me the way you did. You've destroyed my family," she spat, gazing at him with hate-filled eyes as she continued to spray bullets their way. "My boys...Edward and Douglas...they never hurt anyone. They didn't deserve to die. But you forced them to talk, to turn on Scottie. You cornered him; left him no choice. We didn't go there to kill Andrew. Scott just wanted to make him admit what he'd done. But Andrew dismissed him as if he was garbage and then slapped me for interrupting his day. I couldn't take any more of his abuse. Not after learning he'd hidden a grandchild from me all those years. So, I picked up that letter opener and just started stabbing him. Scott only finished what I started after Andrew punched me again and knocked me down. But you locked Scott away for protecting me and now he's dead too. My grandson...and he's dead. Scott was just a child; he deserved another chance."

Another chance? Not in this lifetime. Scott Cooper had brutally murdered at least six people and tried to kill Jimmy. No court in the country would have considered him a child at age twenty-five.

But had he heard her right? Had Lauren really just admitted that she'd been behind her husband's murder? That she'd actually begun the attack?

Gary had pegged her as an ice cold bitch and Jimmy had placed her in the office when the murder occurred; but nothing, until now had indicated Lauren had been the driving force behind what had gone down at the senator's office.

She was right-handed, based on the hand holding the gun. And Gary's mind flashed for a second back to the bruise he and Mike had seen on her cheek and the gloves she'd worn during her interview. Now those anomalies made sense. She'd been covering injuries sustained during the attack.

Not that it mattered at this point. In the eyes of the law, both she and Cooper were equally guilty. And when this ended, if Gary was still alive, he'd either have her in handcuffs or she'd be dead.

It took every ounce of discipline not to refute her accusation, to tell her she and her family had brought this all on themselves. That if Ed hadn't raped their under-aged housekeeper twenty-five years ago, setting off a lifetime of secrets that had suddenly and violently come back to haunt them, exploding in their faces, none of this would be happening.

Figuring he'd only make a bad situation worse, Gary kept his opinion to himself.

More shots sprayed in his direction and screams of people trying to find escape routes continued to fill the air. But Gary barely heard them.

He was too focused on the abject terror in Jamie's eyes and trying to keep Kate safely behind him.

Pain slammed into him again and only sheer determination kept Gary on his feet as a red stain blossomed on his left thigh. He grabbed at the table to steady himself, but more shots thudded into the table surface, tipping it over and he struggled to keep himself upright, while trying to ignore the blood fountaining down his leg.

Beside them, the window shattered and a rush of warm fresh air poured into the cafeteria from outside.

Lauren's glazed eyes turned to Kate. "Get away from him. I don't want to have to hurt you."

Gary shot a glance back at Kate, hoping she'd take the opportunity and go. More than anything else, he wanted her out of harm's way. The moment he saw her expression, though, he knew that wasn't going to happen.

Katie turned eyes, blazing with rage, on the woman while her vice-like grip on his bicep pinched off the flow of blood. "I am NOT leaving my husband."

Those were the last words Gary wanted to hear, but they didn't surprise him. He knew Kate too well. Still he had to try.

"Katie, go," he pleaded quietly, fumbling to reach with his left hand for the gun holstered on his right hip. Even if he managed to get the gun, though, he doubted he'd be able to get off a shot. Lauren was holding Jamie in front of her as a shield. And although he'd never failed to qualify with it on the shooting range, his left hand was by no means his dominant one. Any shot he attempted would be risky. Jamie could be hit.

Frustrating as it was to admit, he couldn't do anything about Jamie at the moment, but he had to try to get Kate to safety.

"I'll be fine," he told her.

A bold-faced lie. He knew it. And worse yet, he knew Katie knew it. The moment she let go, his arm would bleed uncontrollably.

"No! She'd hit your brachial and femoral arteries. You need surgery...now," Kate countered.

Gary had known as soon as he saw the spurting blood that the bullet had hit an artery, but he hadn't known how badly he was injured. He didn't for second doubt the accuracy of Kate's diagnosis. His arm was dead, but at least he still had feeling in the leg...even if all he felt was pain. And thankfully, he could still stand, but if he didn't stop this fiasco soon; he'd bleed to death.

His heart pounded in his chest, terror invading every cell. He wanted Kate safe, but arguing with her was futile. She was like a mother bear defending a cub when someone she loved was hurt or ill. She'd never leave.

Lauren stared at Kate with a look of disbelief, apparently unable to grasp the concept of loving someone enough to put them above all else. Almost robotically, she pulled the trigger again.

This one found its mark too, unmercifully plowing into Gary's right shoulder.

More pain spiraled through him, but he pushed it away, concentrating on staying upright and in front of Kate. No easy task. He was off balance because of his damn leg and Kate kept moving to keep pressure on his right arm.

Movement behind Lauren caught Gary's attention and he breathed a tentative sigh of relief when he saw Mike and Zach slip furtively into the cafeteria. Both agents had their guns drawn as they shooed people out of their way and quickly moved into position to flank the senator's widow.

Gary wasn't sure which man had the better shot, but he knew for certain that if Mike didn't have a clean shot, Dev would defer to Zach's sharpshooter skills.

Whatever they did, they'd better do it fast though. With the way he was bleeding, he didn't have much time left. He was already lightheaded.

Mike's gaze met his and Dev nodded. A subtle signal, but one Gary knew. They were going to act and he needed to be ready.

"Drop it, Lauren!" Mike's voice rang out over the bedlam.

Steeling himself for what he knew would happen, Gary jerked Kate safely behind him as Mike spoke, breaking her hold on his arm. Blood immediately fountained from his bicep, but fully expecting Lauren to shoot at him again, he captured Kate in his arms, shielding her with his body.

Instead, Lauren's eyes swung to Mike and in that split second, Zach fired, twice. Both shots bore into Lauren's temple, killing her instantly.

More screams erupted from Jamie, terror and confusion etched across her face.

Blinking to focus his rapidly vanishing vision, Gary watched Lauren drop to the floor and saw Mike rush forward to gather Jamie in his arms. Only then did Gary allow his brain to take inventory of his body.

Arm, shoulder, leg.

He was in serious trouble.

His knees turned to gelatin and his legs buckled beneath him.

He felt Kate's arms wrap around his waist, trying to catch him, to ease him down, but his dead weight was too heavy for her.

Boneless, Gary collapsed at her feet.

"Stay with me, darling," Katie pleaded, struggling into position to help him.

Gary's mind floated on the edge of consciousness as Katie clamped off his artery with her hand again. He could hear the fear in her voice and see it in her eyes.

Zach suddenly appeared at his side and grabbed his hand. "Hang in there, Dad," he said, moving slightly to apply pressure to the leg wound.

Mike and Jamie appeared too and scrambled to help any way they could.

"He needs a trauma team!" Kate uttered with a touch of hysteria in her voice that Gary had never heard before.

"Medic!" Zach hollered loud enough for the entire hospital to hear. "Someone get a trauma team in here...now!"

"We need a doctor!" Jamie screamed, near panic herself.

"Help will be here soon, darling," Kate assured him, her voice quivering with fear. "Just stay with me."

She turned to Zach and Mike. "Give me your belts," she demanded urgently.

Staring blankly, Gary watched his son yank the belt from around his waist at the same time Dev unbuckled his own belt and yanked it free. Kate snatched them both.

Confusion and pain clouded Gary's brain, but her intention became clear when she looped Zach's belt around his arm just under his armpit, tightening it into a tourniquet to cut off the flow of blood. And in the blink of an eye, she'd done the same thing to his leg, using Mike's belt.

A gentle hand stroking his hair lifted Gary's eyes from the action and he saw Jamie behind him, caressing his head with terror still ripe in her eyes. His gaze drifted back to Kate.

Motioning Zach to take control of the belt on his leg and Mike to apply pressure to his shoulder wound, Kate continued her determined efforts to clamp off the blood flowing from his arm.

Rationally, Gary knew what she'd done should hurt, but he'd lost all sensation in the arm the moment the bullet had sliced through his bicep and maybe his leg was numb now, too. But even if it hurt, he was too weak to protest.

Men and women in hospital scrubs magically appeared around him and everyone but Kate faded into the crowd. Gary kept his focus on her face.

She was safe; that was the only thing that mattered.

Keeping the belt on his arm cinched tightly, Kate moved slightly to allow other medical personnel to kneel beside him.

"Stay with me sweetheart. You're going to be fine," Kate encouraged again.

Gary gazed up at her hazily, seeing the truth in her eyes. He wasn't going to be fine. He could feel his life draining away.

"Katie…I love yo…" The words died on his lips as darkness swallowed him.

Chapter Twenty-Two

With his arms wrapped around Jamie, Mike watched anxiously as doctors and nurses worked desperately to stabilize Gary enough to move him.

"We're losing him," the man who seemed to be in charge bellowed. "O.R., now. Move!"

The words were the last ones Mike wanted to hear and he saw the stricken look on Kate's face. Then, just as suddenly as everyone had appeared, the medical staff lifted Gary onto a gurney and disappeared at a run out of the cafeteria.

Jamie shuddered a breath against Mike's chest, drawing his attention back to her. He didn't remember the last time he'd been as terrified as he'd been when he'd spotted Lauren using her as a human shield.

Rationally he'd known the only reason Gary had taken three bullets without killing Lauren was because he hadn't wanted to risk accidently hitting Jamie with a shot fired by his left hand. But clear thinking at that moment had been difficult. Mike had wanted Jamie safe.

In truth, though, Mike hadn't trusted himself to make a shot. His heart had been pounding too hard; it still was. He was damn glad Zach had been there to end the chaos and even more relieved Taylor still possessed the steady hands and calm nerves he'd acquired as a Marine sharpshooter.

As police filed into the room and took control of the crime scene, Mike glanced over at Lauren McDougal's limp body. Hair disheveled and blood pooled beneath her, in death the woman didn't look anything like the dignified, well-coifed society matron they'd interviewed.

Was it really only a day ago?

But it was over. Finally over. And thank God, Jamie was safe.

"Is Gary going to be okay?"

Jamie's voice sounding so lost and afraid, twisted Mike's heart. But he couldn't lie to her. Brushing tears from her eyes with the pad of his thumb, Mike shrugged.

"I don't know." And he didn't. As Zach had led Kate out of the cafeteria behind the gurney, he'd turned back, his gaze meeting Mike's. And with a steeled grimace on his face, Zach had shaken his head.

Mike wasn't overly religious, but he knew Thorny's fate was in higher hands than his at this point. "If you know any prayers, he could sure use them."

Further conversation was interrupted when two state police detectives approached and wanted their statements about the shootings. When they finally left, Mike glanced around to make sure he wasn't needed any longer and then turned to Jamie.

"I've got to find Kate and Zach. Maybe I can help in some way." No way was he leaving Jamie alone, though. "Come with me?"

Jamie nodded somberly. "Definitely."

Keeping Jamie sheltered against his side with an arm around her shoulder, Mike headed to the elevators. As they waited for a car to arrive, it dawned on Mike he'd never made sure Jamie was okay. He'd been so focused on Gary and then the detectives' questions.

Turning to face her, he tipped Jamie's chin up, taking a quick mental inventory of the bruises and cuts on the face he'd grown to adore. "Are you okay?"

Jamie pulled in a deep breath and let it out slowly. "Yes. I think so. I owe Gary my life; I know that much. Lauren was like a crazy woman. She was in the parking lot of the law firm when I was leaving and she walked up to me. I started to tell her how sorry I was about Andrew and the next thing I knew she grabbed me around the throat and shoved a gun against my head. I was afraid she'd shoot me, so I drove her here."

"Why here?" Mike had been trying to figure out what had drawn Lauren to the hospital. Had she known Gary would be here?

"In the car she told me she was coming here to kill Jim Barrett and that once he was dead she was going to hunt down all of you and kill you too because of what you'd done to her family."

Mike shook his head. The woman had clearly gone off the deep end to the point where she couldn't see that her own family had brought on all the tragedy themselves.

"Did she know Gary and Kate were here?" he asked, curious how Lauren just happened to end up in the cafeteria.

"No. As she shoved me along the walk toward the doors, she saw them through the window of the cafeteria and went ballistic. She literally dragged me in here and just started shooting at him." Jamie sucked in a deep breath and shivered it away. "I know the only reason he didn't go for his gun was because of me. I could see it in his expression."

She turned to look up at him. "I thought for sure she was going to kill us all. I never saw or heard you and Zach arrive, but I'm so glad you did."

"I'm glad we got here when we did." Mike admitted. He didn't even want to think what might have happened if they'd gotten caught in traffic or stopped to run an errand on their way to the hospital.

A ping announced the arrival of the elevator and when the door whooshed open, they stepped into the empty car. Mike pushed the button for the surgical floor and the doors slid closed, sealing them inside.

"It's getting to be a habit, you know," Jamie said softly.

"What?"

She smiled up at him. "You saving me. You truly are my hero."

Mike wasn't so sure about the hero thing and he definitely wasn't the reason she was alive. Gary keeping Lauren focused on him and Zach's accuracy under incredible pressure. That's what had saved her.

But if Jamie thought he was her hero, who was he to argue? Ever since he'd first seen her a few days ago, he'd been trying to convince himself of all the reasons he was wrong for her. And maybe he wasn't thinking clearly in the wake of what had just gone down.

But he didn't care. He was tired of fighting with himself.

Without analyzing all the reasons he shouldn't, Mike hit the elevator's STOP button. As the car came to an abrupt halt, ignoring Jamie's startled expression, he did what he'd ached to do for days.

He pulled her into his arms and kissed her.

JAMIE'S BREATH CAUGHT in her chest.

She couldn't believe it. Mike was kissing her. And it wasn't some brotherly peck on the cheek. It was the kind of kiss she'd been dreaming about for as long as she could remember.

Last night when she'd asked him to stay with her, she'd never expected him to actually do it and when he'd slid onto the bed with her, she'd nearly died of shock. But snuggling into his arms had felt like heaven. So right.

For the first time since she'd awakened in the hospital and learned what had happened to her, she'd felt safe.

And she'd fallen asleep.

Around four, she'd awakened and at first she'd thought she was dreaming, because Mike was there beside her. But when she'd fallen asleep, he'd been fully clothed and sitting on top of the comforter.

Finding him naked except for a sexy pair of boxers had been surreal.

She had no idea when or why he'd undressed and climbed beneath the covers with her. But once the shock of finding him that way had worn off, she'd realized it was her lifelong dream come true.

Mikey Devlin in her bed.

The fantasy that had played out in her head had been anything but childish, though. Every cell of her body had wanted to wake him up, to show him how much she loved him. How much she'd always loved him.

And she'd almost done it, too. Then she'd looked at him. Really looked at him. And she'd realized he was sound asleep. The poor man had been beyond exhausted and she'd only been thinking about her own pleasure.

She hadn't had the heart to wake him, so she'd contented herself by snuggling against him again. Eventually she'd fallen asleep to dreams of him.

Now, it was as if that dream was coming true…and they were both wide awake. At least she prayed that was the case, because she was in Mike's arms and he was kissing her. Really kissing her.

Unwilling to let the moment pass, she wrapped her arms around his neck, tugged him closer and kissed him back.

Half expecting him to pull away, Jamie moaned in ecstasy when he deepened the kiss. And by the time the need for oxygen drew them apart, they were both flushed.

Mike gasped a breath, staring at her as if he wanted to devour her.

That was just fine with Jamie.

She'd begun to wonder if Mike ever lost his cool, calm composure. And call her silly, but it gave her a warm sense of achievement that she'd been the one to crack his self-control.

As she was patting herself on the back, he took a step away, gave a slight shake of his head and hit the button to get the elevator moving again.

"I'm sorry, Jamie. I shouldn't have done that. It's all wrong. You should find someone your own age. I'm way too old for you."

A tidal wave of anger surged through Jamie.

She loved him. And she damned well wasn't letting him walk away without giving him some food for thought first.

"How dare you!" she stormed, slamming the STOP button again and nearly falling into him when the elevator jerked to a halt. "You're treating me as if I'm still a child. Yes, I fell for you when I was a little girl; I admit that. But in case it's escaped your notice, I'm all grown up now. I'm thirty-three years old, for crying out loud. And if I don't have a problem with our age difference, why should you?"

Mike merely stared at her as if shocked by the vehemence of her anger.

Damn straight she was angry. She was furious.

That kiss had teased her, given her a taste of nirvana and she wanted more. She wanted him. Heart, mind, body and soul.

"The way I see it, there's nothing stopping us from being together except your antiquated sense of chivalry and some trust issues on your part. But I'm not your ex-wife. I'm not going to tire of you or run off with someone else for God only knows what insane reason she did it. I'm me. So get over yourself! The only man I want is you!"

Jamie didn't bother giving him time to argue. She grabbed his arm and pulled him back to her, sealing her mouth to his in a searing kiss.

Heat ignited into passion and Jamie didn't care that the elevator alarm was blaring loud enough to deafen them. As far as she was concerned, whoever was up there could just wait.

She was in heaven.

Gasping a breath, Mike pulled his mouth from hers, but he didn't release her. Instead, he grinned down at her.

"Okay…I give. You win. But I hope you mean what you said, because I want you too. And I have a feeling it's going to take me more than a lifetime to get you out of my system."

Some of the smoothest lines in the world Jamie had ever heard had been uttered by men trying to land her in bed. None of them had ever sounded sweeter or more sincere than Mike's.

"So you're ready to give us a chance?"

He nodded and dropped a soft kiss on her lips. "More than a chance, if you're willing?"

It was Jamie's turn to stare at him in shock. "Do you mean what I think you mean?"

A moment of hesitation flickered in his eyes, but he blinked it away. "I know this is probably the worst timing in the world, but yes…I'm asking you to marry me," he paused as if uncertain what to say next. A half grin tipped his lips. "If I'm moving too fast and you need more time, that's fine. We can take things as slowly as you need. But when I saw Lauren holding that gun to your head I realized how much I love you, Jamie, and the thought of losing you scared me to death. I need you in my life; I want you in my life…if you'll have me."

Jamie snapped out of her shock and laughed elatedly. "Silly, I don't need any time and you're certainly not going to lose me. This is my dream come true and I'm not about to let you think your way out of the proposal. Just tell me you mean it or pinch me so I know I'm not dreaming now."

Chuckling, Mike gathered her into his arms. "I mean every word of it. Crazy as it sounds, you've always held a special place in my heart, even back when we were kids. But from the moment I found you in Andrew's office, I haven't been able to get you out of my head. Then in your hospital room, when I realized who you were…well, I was a goner right then and there. I was a fool to try to deny it; to push you away. And the way I see it, we've wasted a long time getting to this point. I don't want to wait any longer."

Taking her hand in his, he dropped down on one knee. "I love you, Jamie. Will you do me the honor of being my wife? Will you marry me?"

Jamie's heart soared, filling with happiness. For so long she'd dreamt of this moment, but she'd never fully expected it would happen. Now that it had, she nearly couldn't believe it. But one look at the love in Mike's eyes and she knew it was real.

She pulled him back to his feet and wrapping her arms around his neck again, she gazed up at him adoringly. "I love you too, Michael Patrick Devlin. And I can't think of anything in the world I want more than being your wife. Yes...I'll marry you."

Mike kissed her again...thoroughly. And with a groan of regret, he finally let her go. "We'd better get this elevator moving again before they summon the fire department to rescue us."

Jamie laughed aloud and reached forward to push the START button again. When the elevator began to move, she felt Mike's hand slip around hers and she laced her fingers with his.

She wasn't sure how an afternoon that had been so terrifying had suddenly become the happiest day of her life, but it had. And the only thing that would make it perfect was if Mike's friend survived his wounds.

Chapter Twenty-Three

His eyes pried open reluctantly and Gary's hazy gaze slowly took in his surroundings. A flicker of awareness fired in his brain and the beeping he heard above him lifted his gaze to a computer monitor displaying a jagged line bouncing up and down. For a moment he stared at it in a daze, but then movement startled him and his gaze swung to a nearby chair.

Kate! How had he missed her when he'd looked around the room?

He nearly chuckled aloud. He was so drugged up he could barely keep his eyes open and his brain was misfiring more than an old car with dirty spark plugs. That's how he'd missed her.

For several moments he gazed at her silently, drawing comfort from her presence.

They'd known each other since kindergarten, gone all through school together and married while Kate was in medical school. In August they'd celebrated their thirty-second wedding anniversary. He couldn't imagine his life without Katie, didn't want to imagine it. Plain and simple, he adored her.

"Hi sweetheart," Gary croaked around the dryness in his throat.

With surprise in her eyes, Kate's head snapped up from the book she was reading.

"You're awake! How are you feeling, honey?" Smiling, she slipped off the chair and leaned down to drop a soft kiss on his lips.

His tongue felt too thick for his mouth and his throat was sore, very sore. With difficulty, Gary swallowed. "Drier than the Sahara and my throat feels like I swallowed a razor blade," he answered groggily.

"The airway they inserted during surgery irritated your throat, which is why it is sore and your mouth is dry from the anesthesia," Kate explained.

Surgery. Yes. Thankfully, he was too drugged up to feel any pain at the moment, but between the gunshot wounds and surgeons rummaging around inside him to retrieve the slugs and repair the damage, Gary had a feeling there would be plenty of pain to come.

His eyes searched Kate for injuries. "Are you okay? Did she hurt you?"

"I'm fine, thanks to you," she assured him while cradling his head to fluff his pillow. "So is Jamie. And miraculously, no one else in the cafeteria was hurt either."

"Lauren. She's dead, right?"

Nodding, Kate lifted a water glass from his hospital tray. "Just a couple sips," she cautioned holding the straw so he could wrap his mouth around it. "You don't want to get sick."

Heeding Kate's warning, he took two small sips and then dropped his head back on his pillow. "Thank you."

She returned the glass to his tray and pulling the chair close to his bedside, she sat down with a weary smile.

"I'm so sorry Katie," he murmured softly.

"Shh!" She picked up his hand. "There's nothing to be sorry about."

Even drugged into oblivion, he knew that wasn't true, but he was too damn groggy to press the issue. Apparently she read his mind, because she gently patted the hand she held. "We can talk later. You need to rest…"

Gary's brain took her literally and checked out immediately. If she said anything else, it was lost as her voice faded to nothing.

When he opened his eyes again, yellow hues of morning sun were peeking through the window.

"Good morning, sleepyhead." Katie's voice snared his attention and he found her sitting beside his bed in the chair where she'd been when he fell asleep. Knowing her, she'd been there all night.

"Good morning," he uttered with more gravel in his voice than he usually had in the morning. "Did I fall asleep on you last night?"

She nodded with an understanding smile. "Right in the middle of my reassuring you that you needed rest. For once you listened to me."

He chuckled. But then glancing down at the highway of tubes and wires attached to him, he mentally shook his head. He must have had a guardian angel watching over him in that cafeteria.

He vaguely recalled the surgeon talking to him in the recovery room, after his surgery, but he'd been so drugged, he hadn't really registered the full scope of what had happened. Now, though, there was no denying the severity of his injuries and the ramifications they held for him.

The wounds to his leg and shoulder were considered minor, in relation to the one to his right arm. His doctor had used the word devastating to describe that injury.

Gary still couldn't feel the arm. He knew it was there, though, because he could see his hand and fingers...all five of them...peeking out from a cast immobilizing his arm from shoulder to wrist. But no matter what he tried, he couldn't get a response from his fingers. Nothing would move.

When that shot, which had actually been two bullets, hit him, he'd known the injury was bad. Now he knew just how bad. Massive damage; a shattered humerus and both the brachial artery and brachial plexus severed.

The broken bone accounted for the cast on his arm. And doctors had transplanted arteries in both his arm and leg to replace the ones damaged by bullets. They'd assured him circulation in his hand and foot was good, which apparently meant the new arteries were working properly.

But the brachial plexus...that one was a problem. The major network of nerves controlling his arm had been severed, damaged beyond repair. But doctors had been so busy keeping him alive during surgery, they'd only repaired the damage necessary to stop his bleeding and insert a plate and screws to repair the broken bone. The nerve center had been deemed secondary to his survival, so he was faced with a paralyzed arm...at least for a few months until he was sufficiently recovered and strong enough to undergo the hours of complex surgery required by a nerve transplant.

His doctor had been brutally honest, too. Apparently nerve transplants were tricky business and there was no guarantee a graft would work or that he'd ever regain full use of his arm and hand. Gary had heard the pessimism in his doctor's voice, had seen the concern in Kate's eyes and if he said he hadn't been shaken by the news, he'd be a damn liar. Sure he'd been rattled...scared even. He still was.

But considering his injuries, at least he was still breathing and he hadn't lost his arm. He wasn't ready to concede defeat. And if the doctors thought there was any chance at all that a nerve transplant might work, he was game to try it. Anything beat not being able to move his dominant arm...or even feel it.

But for now, he was too damn weak and frankly his mind was still swimming from everything that had happened to think about more surgery months down the road...let alone worry about it.

Gary hauled in a deep breath.

What a wild few days it had been. Andrew, Ed and Doug and two officers all dead at the hands of Scott Cooper and Lauren McDougal. But thankfully, both of them were dead too and couldn't hurt anyone else. And it was only a matter of time before lady justice caught up with the other characters Gary and his team had encountered during their investigation.

If it hadn't happened yet, Joseph Kanell would soon be arrested for penning a threatening letter to a United States senator, but since there'd been no evidence he'd ever attempted to act on any of those threats, he'd most likely be fined and released.

Gary suspected others wouldn't be so lucky. Once the Internal Revenue Service began investigating all the women who'd been receiving hush money payments from Andrew McDougal, he had a feeling they'd all find themselves the subject of federal audits for failing to claim the income.

Maybe the job had hardened him to the plights of these people, but Gary had trouble feeling sorry for any of them. They all had no one but themselves to thank for their troubles.

As the old adage claimed...*crime doesn't pay*.

Gary was just glad the case was closed. Now maybe life would return to some semblance of normal again. Well, as normal as it could be not being able to use his dominant arm and hand.

He glanced over at Kate and saw tears burning in her eyes.

Gary's gut twisted with guilt.

He knew exactly what had her upset. Him.

"I'm so sorry, Katie."

Kate drew in a shaky breath. "I don't know how much more of this I can take, Gary. I was terrified I was going to lose you this time. I almost did."

Yup. He'd guessed that right. She was upset over the shooting, over his injuries, over the entire fiasco. Just one more in a long string of them that had befallen them all too often recently.

Gary could see the torment in her eyes, the tears she was fighting desperately to contain. He wanted nothing more than to hold her, to comfort her, but between intravenous tubes snaking from his arms, bed rails designed to prevent him from falling and an alarm that went off if he shifted weight off the mattress or someone sat down beside him, he couldn't hold her.

With one arm immobilized in a cast he couldn't even give her a decent hug. Instead, he laced his fingers with hers. "I know you're upset sweetheart and you have every right to be. But before you tell me what's on your mind, please hear me out."

She gave a silent nod.

He lifted her hand to his mouth and pressed a tender kiss on it. "Katie, I've been doing a lot of thinking recently…even before yesterday…and I've had enough…you've had enough…more than enough. And if you're okay with it, I'm going to hang up my badge and retire."

Relief! For just an instant before Kate had managed to mask it, he'd seen it in her eyes. And with that instant reaction, Gary knew he'd said the right thing. But it hadn't been a snap decision. He'd been thinking about it for a long time.

For nearly a year and a half now, his career had been putting Kate through an emotional wringer, almost constantly and endangering her life more times than he cared to remember. And when she'd retired last month, he'd seriously considered retiring at the same time, but Zach, Jimmy and Mike had argued against it. Kate had abstained, leaving the decision to him. Like an idiot, he'd let the guys talk him out of it; foolishly convincing himself that Kate supported the decision.

But deep down he'd been questioning his decision ever since.

Now he was back in the hospital again recovering from bullet wounds. And he knew damn well if Katie hadn't been by his side when he'd been shot, he would have bled to death. But again, she'd been smack dab in the middle of the danger.

He and his job had put her through that emotional hell.

Law enforcement was hard on marriages. Many agents and cops Gary knew were on their second or third wife; some had traded in their marriages in favor of booze. But Katie had stuck with him and she'd put up with more than any wife should ever have had to endure, in the name of her husband's career.

Maybe that was because she loved him unconditionally. Maybe it was because they'd been in love with each other since they were kids. And maybe it was because they were soul mates.

Gary couldn't speak for Kate's reasons. But one thing he knew for certain. After thirty-two years of marriage he loved her more now than the day they'd married. And he'd do anything for her.

The tentative smile tugging at Kate's lips told him she was struggling to believe what she'd heard him say. He smiled to help her along.

"You think you can handle having me around 24-7?" he asked, softly caressing her cheek.

Kate gazed at him lovingly. "There's no one I'd rather be with. But, darling, are you sure this is what you want? You love your job."

"I love you more. And this is what I want for us."

Kate gave him the heart-stopping smile that was his alone. When she leaned down to kiss him, he threw caution to the wind and pulled her into a one-armed embrace. The sound of the bed alarm caused them both to chuckle, but they ignored it, neither willing to end the kiss.

"Good grief, they're at it again!"

Zach's teasing voice achieved what the bed alarm hadn't. They drew back from the kiss and in unison turned to see their son and daughter-in-law, along with a nurse, standing in the doorway grinning at them.

As the nurse reset the alarm and gently reminded him of his injuries, Mike and Jamie walked into the room.

If he hadn't already been lying down, Gary would have fallen over at the sight of them holding hands. He couldn't hold back a smile. He'd known from the start Dev hadn't stood a chance of resisting Jamie Kendrick. Some things were just too obvious to miss. And Mike deserved to find happiness again. Gary was happy for him.

But before he could say anything, Lucas appeared in the doorway, pushing Jimmy into the room in a wheelchair. The grocery bag on Barrett's lap piqued Gary's curiosity.

"It's about time you wake up." Barrett grinned at him and pulled two bottles of champagne from the bag. "We're here to celebrate."

At the look of horror on the nurse's face, Lucas chimed in. "It's strictly non-alcoholic. You're welcome to join us, if you'd like."

A smile broke out on the young woman's face. "Thank you, but I'll pass and I'll leave you to your party. But please...keep the noise down and only stay a few minutes, then move the celebration to the waiting room and let my patient rest."

She eyed Gary. "Only one sip for you." When Gary nodded, her gaze shifted to Jim. "Only one for you, too. Then I want you back in your room and in your bed. No arguments."

"Yes ma'am," Jim answered, giving her one of his killer smiles that tended to make women melt. It seemed to have no effect on her as she studied the group, apparently trying to decide if she'd made a mistake allowing them to stay for even a minute.

"I'll make sure they all listen," Kate added, drawing a chuckle from the group, but Nurse Jessica, according to her name tag, didn't look convinced.

"My wife is a retired trauma surgeon," Gary explained. "And trust me, no one in this room will disobey her orders. We all know better."

Amid another round of chuckles were unanimous nods of agreement.

Kate gave her a nod of assurance and satisfied she had an ally in the room, Nurse Jessica walked out the door.

"What's the occasion," Gary asked once she left.

"We're celebrating Mike and Jamie's engagement, the conclusion of another case and the fact you're too ornery to die," Jim announced.

Lucas tapped Barrett on the shoulder. "That's the pot calling the kettle black. We could say the same thing about you. In fact, we did."

Smiling, Gary listened as Shaw's friendly jab set off a round of good natured kidding between his agents. While the chatter continued, Lucas popped the cork on one of the bottles and Cassie pulled a pack of paper cups from the bag. Within moments they all had a drink in their hand.

Zach draped his arm around Cassie's shoulder and held up his cup. "To all of us!"

Smiling, Mike winked at Jamie. "I'll second that."

"Cheers," Jim and Lucas echoed in unison.

Although the sweet liquid didn't sound at all appetizing, Gary took a sip for the toast and then set his cup aside to savor the moment with his family and friends. He wasn't sure what he'd done to deserve them all, but he was thankful for each of them.

A moment later, Kate set down her cup and slipping her hand into his, together they watched their extended family celebrate life.

Made in the USA
Middletown, DE
08 August 2023

36346757R00156